WILKIE COLLINS

THE YELLOW MASK
& OTHER STORIES

D0280117

ALAN SUTTON
1987

Alan Sutton Publishing Limited
Brunswick Road · Gloucester

First published 1855

Copyright © in this edition 1987
Alan Sutton Publishing Limited

British Library Cataloguing in Publication Data

Collins, Wilkie
   The yellow mask & other stories.
   I. Title
   823′.8[F]   PR4492

   ISBN 0-86299-324-5

Cover picture: detail from The Happy Marriage VI,
The Dance *by William Hogarth.*
Photograph: Bridgeman Art Library.

Typesetting and origination by
Alan Sutton Publishing Limited.
Photoset Bembo 9/10
Printed in Great Britain
by The Guernsey Press Company Limited,
Guernsey, Channel Islands.

CONTENTS

BIOGRAPHICAL NOTE

William Wilkie Collins was born on 8 January 1824, in New Cavendish Street, London, the elder son of William Collins, a fashionable and successful painter of the early nineteenth century, who counted among his friends Wordsworth and Coleridge. William Collins was a religious man, and in his strict observances may have been a repressive influence on his son, who appears to have inherited his mother's, Harriet Geddes, attractive and friendly personality. Wilkie was named after his godfather, Sir David Wilkie, R.A., a bachelor and close friend of the family.

Little is known of Wilkie's early life. His brother, Charles, was born in 1828, and the family lived comfortably, first in Hampstead, then in Bayswater, where Wilkie attended Maida Hill Academy. The following year the whole family left for Italy, where they spent two years, visiting the major art collections and learning Italian. On their return, Wilkie attended a private boarding school in Highbury, where his story-telling talent was recognized and exploited by a senior prefect who demanded, with the threat of physical violence, to be entertained. 'Thus', wrote Collins, 'I learnt to be amusing on a short notice and have derived benefit from those early lessons.'

When he left school in 1840, he showed no inclination to enter the Church, as his father wished, and chose, without enthusiasm, the world of commerce, accepting a post with Antrobus & Co., tea importers. He was totally unsuited to the regularity of business life, preferring to escape to the vibrant atmosphere of Paris. He started to write articles and short stories, which were accepted for publicaation, albeit anonymously, and in 1846 his father agreed that he should leave commerce and take up law, which would, in theory, provide him with a regular income. He studied at Lincoln's Inn Fields, and was finally called to the bar, but his legal knowledge was to be applied creatively in his novels, rather than practically in the law courts.

In his early twenties Collins also painted as well as writing. He had many friends who were artists, and he supported the new Pre-Raphaelite movement. In 1848 he had a picture exhibited in the Royal Academy. In the same year his first book was published: the memoirs of his father, who had died the previous year. These were diligently researched and provided a training ground for the emerging writer, developing his thorough methodical approach to compilation and exercising his descriptive ability. His first novel, *Antonina*, was published by Bentley two years later. Although of no great literary merit, it was written in the then popular mode of historical romance, and so enjoyed instant success. The following year Bentley published *Rambles beyond Railways*, an account of a holiday in Cornwall, which reflected Collins' life-long love of wild and remote places.

It was in the same year, 1851, that Wilkie Collins first met Charles Dickens, an introduction effected by their mutual friend, the artist, Augustus Egg. The meeting was significant for both, leading to a close friendship and working partnership from which both benefitted. Dickens had found a friend of more stable temperament than himself, affable and tolerant, responsive to his restless demanding nature. From Collins he acquired the skill of economic and taut plotting, as evidenced in *A Tale of Two Cities*, (which may be interestingly compared with Collins' story of the French Revolution, *Sister Rose*, 1855) and in his later novels. Collins was welcomed by the Dickens family, and spent many holidays with them in England and France. He was encouraged and guided in his writing by Dickens, and he must have been stimulated by the latter's enthusiasm and vitality. The two authors worked together on Dickens' magazines, *Household Words*, and *All the Year Round*. Collins was employed as an editor, and many of his works appeared first in these publications, while both writers collaborated on several short stories.

A Terribly Strange Bed was the first short story to appear in *Household Words*, in 1852, Collins' first work in the macabre genre, followed the next year by *Gabriel's Marriage*, a story of a Breton fishing community. In the interim, Dickens had turned down *Mad Monkton*, a study of inherited insanity, as unsuitable subject matter, and this was later published by *Fraser's Magazine* in 1855. These two, along with *Sister Rose*, *The yellow Mask*, and *A Stolen Letter*, were originally published in *Household Words*, and reprinted in *After Dark*, 1855, for which anthology Collins wrote the successfully economic and melodramatic *Lady of Glenwith Grange* (an inspiration for Miss Havisham?). *A Rogue's Life*, Collins' venture into the picaresque, was serialised in 1856. This was followed in 1857 by *The Dead Secret*, a full length novel, which in its complexity suggests the author's technical potential. *The Biter Bit*, 1858, is believed to be the first humorous detective story, and develops Collins' use of the epistolary form. His two greatest novels, *A Woman in White*, 1860, a masterpiece of suspence and melodrama, and *The Moonstone*, 1868, the original detective story, as well as the less well known *No Name*, 1862, an unconventional study of illegitimacy first appeared in *All the Year Round*, in serial form.

Another interest shared by Collins and Dickens was a love of the theatre. *the Frozen Deep*, 1857, written by Collins and starring Dickens was inspired by an interest in the Arctic exploration of the time. It was followed by a series of minor productions, the stage version of *No Thoroughfare*, (with combined authorship), enjoying a record run of two hundred nights in 1867.

Anyone meeting Collins in those days would have seen:

A neat figure of a cheerful plumpness, very small feet and hands, a full brown beard, a high and rounded forehead, a small note not naturally intended to support a pair of large spectacles behind which his eyes shone with humour and friendship.

R.C. Lehmann, *Memories of Half a Century*

but how many would have glimpsed, as did the young artist, Rudolf Lehmann, the strange far-off look in his eyes, which gave the impression of investing "almost everything with an air of mystery and romance"? It was suggestive of a depth of personality not accessible to many, but demonstrated by the author's expressed unconventional views of the class and social *mores* of the day; which were further borne out by what is known of his personal life. During the 1860s, Collins met and fell in love with Caroline Graves, who had a daughter by a previous marriage. He never married her, but lived with mother and daughter for most of the remainder of his life. In 1868, Caroline mysteriously married another, and Collins entered into a relationship with Martha Judd, by whom he had three children. However by the early 1870s, he was once more living with caroline, who was still known as Mrs Graves. It has been suggested that Martha Judd may have been employed originally by Collins as an amanuensis. Over the years Collins' health had been deteriorating. He was a victim of gout, which attacked his whole body, including his eyes. He suffered a particularly severe attack in 1868, when his mother died, and he was working on *The Moonstone*. A dedicated woman, capable of disregarding his suffering and attending only to his words was employed, who has never been named.

In 1870 Charles Dickens died. During the previous ten years Collins had produced his best work: the three novels serialised in *All the Year Round*; *Armadale*, 1866, in the *Cornhill Magazine*, and *Man and Wife*, 1870, in *Cassell's Magazine*. But with Dickens' death, something in Collins seemed to die too, although his popularity remained undiminished. His novels, produced regularly until his death, were widely read – his was some of the first fiction to appear in cheap editions – but they lacked the sparkle and technical virtuosity of his earlier work. In the 1970s he enjoyed some success with the stage versions of his novels, which were produced both in London and the provinces. Not only was Collins' work popular in England; his novels and plays were translated and produced in most European countries, including Russia, and were widely available in America. In 1873 Collins was invited to give readings in the eastern United States and Canada. Although his reading lacked the vitality of Dickens, the Americans were charmed by him.

Of course, it was not only Dickens' death which adversely affected Collins work. His gout was becoming persistent, and he relied increasingly on laudenum to relieve the pain. However, he never lost his mental clarity, as was clearly shown in the detailed notes he left for his last novel, *Blind Love*, 1890; completed at his request, posthumously, by Walter Besant. During his later years, his social life was restricted by poor health, but he did not become a recluse as has been suggested. His maintained close friendships with Charles Reade, Holman Hunt, the Beard and the Lehmann families, and theatrical people, including Ada Cavendish and Mary Anderson. In 1889, after being involved in a cab accident, Collins' health rapidly declined, and he died while suffering from bronchitis on 23 September. He was buried at Kensal Green Cemetery.

SHEILA MICHELL

THE PROFESSOR'S STORY
OF THE YELLOW MASK

PROLOGUE

On the last occasion when I made a lengthened stay in London, my wife and I were surprised and amused one morning by the receipt of the following note, addressed to me in a small, crabbed, foreign-looking handwriting:-

'Professor Tizzi presents amiable compliments to Mr Kerby, the artist, and is desirous of having his portrait done, to be engraved from, and placed at the beginning of the voluminous work on The Vital Principle, or Invisible Essence of Life, which the Professor is now preparing for the press – and posterity.

'The Professor will give five pounds; and will look upon his face with satisfaction, as an object perpetuated for public contemplation at a reasonable rate, if Mr Kerby will accept the sum just mentioned.

'In regard to the Professor's ability to pay five pounds, as well as to offer them, if Mr Kerby should from ignorance entertain injurious doubts, he is requested to apply to the Professor's honourable friend, Mr Lanfray, of Rockleigh Place.'

But for the reference at the end of this strange note, I should certainly have considered it as a mere trap set to make a fool of me by some mischievous friend. As it was, I rather doubted the propriety of taking any serious notice of Professor Tizzi's offer; and I might probably have ended by putting the letter in the fire without further thought about it, but for the arrival by the next post of a note from Mr Lanfray, which solved all my doubts, and sent me away at once to make the acquaintance of the learned discoverer of the Essence of Life.

'Do not be surprised' (Mr Lanfray wrote) 'if you get a strange note from a very eccentric Italian, one Professor Tizzi, formerly of the University of Padua. I have known him for some years. Scientific inquiry is his monomania, and vanity his ruling passion. He has written a book on the principle of life, which nobody but himself will ever read; but which he is determined to publish, with his own portrait for frontispiece. If it is worth your while to accept the little he can offer you, take it by all means, for he is a character worth knowing. He was exiled, I should tell you, years ago, for some absurd political reason, and has lived in England ever since. All the money he inherits from his father, who was a mail-contractor in the north of Italy, goes in books and experiments, but I think I can answer for his solvency, at any rate, for the large sum of five pounds. If you are not very much occupied just now, go and see him. He is sure to amuse you.'

Professor Tizzi lived in the northern suburb of London. On approaching his house, I found it, so far as outward appearance went, excessively dirty and neglected, but in no other respect different from the 'Villas' in its neighbourhood. The front garden door, after I had rung twice, was opened by a yellow-faced, suspicious old foreigner, dressed in worn-out clothes, and completely and consistently dirty all over from top to toe. On mentioning my name and business, this old man led me across a weedy neglected garden, and admitted me into the house. At the first step into the passage I was surrounded by books. Closely packed in plain wooden shelves, they ran all along the wall on either side to the back of the house; and when I looked up at the carpetless staircase, I saw nothing but books again, running all the way up the wall, as far as my eye could reach. 'Here is the Artist Painter!' cried the old servant, throwing open one of the parlour doors, before I had half done looking at the books, and signing impatiently to me to walk into the room.

Books again! all round the walls, and all over the floor – among them a plain deal table, with leaves of manuscript piled high on every part of it – among the leaves a head of long elfish white hair covered with a black skullcap, and bent down over a book – above the head a sallow withered hand shaking itself at me as a sign that I must not venture to speak just at that moment – on the tops of the book-cases glass vases full of spirits of some kind, with horrible objects floating in the liquid – dirt on the window- panes, cobwebs hanging from the ceiling , dust springing up in clouds under my intruding feet – these were the things I observed on first entering the study of Professor Tizzi.

After I had waited for a minute or so, the shaking hand stopped, descended with a smack on the nearest pile of manuscript, seized the book that the head had been bending over, and flung it contemptuously to the other end of the room. 'I've refuted *you*, at any rate!' said Professor Tizzi, looking with extreme complacency at the cloud of dust raised by the fall of the rejected volume.

He turned next to me. What a grand face it was! What a broad white forehead – what fiercely brilliant black eyes – what perfect regularity and refinement in the other features; with the long, venerable hair, framing them in, as it were, on either side! Poor as I was, I felt that I could have painted his portrait for nothing. Titian, Vandyke, Velasquez – any of the three would have paid him to sit to them!

'Accept my humblest excuses, sir,' said the old man, speaking English with a singularly pure accent for a foreigner. 'That absurd book plunged me so deep down in the quagmires of sophistry and error, Mr Kerby, that I really could not get to the surface at once when you came into the room. So you are willing to draw my likeness for such a small sum as five pounds?' he continued, rising, and showing me that he wore a long black velvet gown, instead of the paltry and senseless costume of modern times.

I informed him that five pounds was as much as I generally got for a drawing.

'It seems little,' said the Professor; 'but if you want fame, I can make it up to you in that way. There is my great work' (he pointed to the piles of manuscript), 'the portrait of my mind and the mirror of my learning: put a likeness of my face on the first page, and posterity will then be thoroughly acquainted with me, outside and in. Your portrait will be engraved, Mr Kerby, and your name shall be inscribed under the print. You shall be associated, sir, in that way with a work which will form an epoch in the history of human science. The Vital Principle, – or, in other words, the essence of that mysterious Something which we call Life, and which extends down from Man to the feeblest insect and the smallest plant – has been an unguessed riddle from the beginning of the world to the present time. I, alone, have found the answer; and here it is!' He fixed his dazzling eyes on me in triumph, and smacked the piles of manuscript fiercely with both his sallow hands.

I saw that he was waiting for me to say something; so I asked if his great work had not cost a vast expenditure of time and pains.

'I am seventy, sir,' said the Professor; 'and I began preparing myself for that book at twenty. After mature consideration, I have written it in English (having three other foreign languages at my fingers' ends), as a substantial proof of my gratitude to the nation that has given me an asylum. Perhaps you think the work looks rather long in its manuscript state? It will occupy twelve volumes, sir, and it is not half long enough, even then, for the subject. I take two volumes (and no man could do it in less) to examine the theories of all the philosophers in the world, ancient and modern, on the Vital Principle. I take two more (and little enough) to scatter every one of the theories, seriatim, to the winds. I take two more (at the risk, for brevity's sake, of doing things by halves) to explain the exact stuff, or vital compound, of which the first man and woman in the world were made – calling them Adam and Eve, out of deference to popular prejudices. I take two more – but you are standing all this time, Mr Kerby; and I am talking instead of sitting for my portrait. Pray take any books you want, anywhere off the floor, and make a seat of any height you please. Furniture would only be in my way here, so I don't trouble myself with anything of the kind.'

I obediently followed the Professor's directions, and had just heaped up a pile of grimy quartos when the old servant entered the room with a shabby little tray in his hand. In the middle of the tray I saw a crust of bread and a bit of garlic, encircled by a glass of water, a knife, salt, pepper, a bottle of vinegar, and a flask of oil.

'With your permission, I am going to breakfast,' said Professor Tizzi, as the tray was set down before him on the part of his great work relating to the vital compound of Adam and Eve. As he spoke, he took up the piece of bread, and rubbed the crusty part of it with the bit of garlic, till it looked as polished as a new dining-table. That done, he turned the bread, crumb uppermost, and saturated it with oil, added a few drops of vinegar, sprinkled with pepper and salt, and, with a gleam of something very like greediness in his bright eyes, took up the knife to cut himself a first mouthful of the horrible mess that he had just concocted. 'The best of breakfasts,' said the Professor, seeing me look amazed. 'Not a cannibal meal of chicken-life in embryo (vulgarly called an Egg); not a dog's gorge of a dead animal's flesh, blood, and bones, warmed with fire (popularly known as a Chop); not a breakfast sir, that lions, tigers, Carribbees, and Coster-mongers could all partake of alike; but an innocent, nutritive, simple, vegetable meal; a philosopher's refection; a breakfast that a prizefighter would turn from in disgust, and that a Plato would share with relish.'

I have no doubt that he was right, and that I was prejudiced; but as I saw the first oily, vinegary, garlicky morsel slide noiselessly into his mouth, I began to feel rather sick. My hands were dirty with moving the books, and I asked if I could wash them before beginning to work at the likeness, as a good excuse for getting out of the room, while Professor Tizzi was unctuously disposing of his simple vegetable meal.

The philosopher looked a little astonished at my request, as if the washing of hands at irregular times and seasons offered a comparatively new subject of contemplation to him; but he rang a hand-bell on his table immediately, and told the old servant to take me up into his bedroom.

The interior of the parlour had astonished me; but a sight of the bedroom was a new sensation – not of the most agreeable kind. The couch on which the philosopher sought repose after his labours was a truckle-bed that would not have fetched half-a-crown at a sale. On one side of it dangled from the ceiling a complete male skeleton, looking like all that was left of a man who might have hung himself about a century ago, and who had never been disturbed since the moment of his suicide. On the other side of the bed stood a long press, in which I observed hideous coloured preparations of the muscular system, and bottles with curious, twining, thread-like substances inside them, which might have been remark-able worms or dissections of nerves, scattered amicably side by side with the Professor's hairbrush (three parts worn out), with remnants of his beard on bits of shaving paper, with a broken shoe-horn, and with a travelling looking-glass of the sort usually sold at sixpence a-piece. Repetitions of the litter of books in the parlour lay all about over the floor; coloured anatomical prints were nailed anyhow against the walls; rolled-up towels were scattered here, there, and everywhere, in the wildest confusion, as if the room had been bombarded with them; and last, but by no means least remarkable among the extraordinary objects in the bed-chamber, the stuffed figure of a large unshaven poodle-dog, stood on an old card-table, keeping perpetual watch over a pair of the philosopher's black breeches twisted round his forepaws.

I had started, on entering the room, at the skeleton, and I started once more at the dog. The old servant noticed me each time with a sardonic grin. 'Don't be afraid,' he said; 'one is as dead as the other.' With these words he left me to wash my hands.

Finding little more than a pint of water at my disposal, and failing altogether to discover where the soap was kept, I was not long in performing my ablutions. Before leaving the room, I looked again at the stuffed poodle. On the board to which he was fixed, I saw painted in faded letters the word 'Scarammuccia,' evidently the comic Italian name to which he had answered in his lifetime. There was no other inscription; but I made up my mind that the dog must have been the Professor's pet, and that he kept the animal stuffed in his bed-room as a remembrance of past times. 'Who would have suspected so great a philosopher of having so much heart!' thought I, leaving the bed- room to go down stairs again.

The Professor had done his breakfast, and was anxious to begin the sitting; so I took out my chalks and paper, and set to work at once – I seated on one pile of books and he on another.

'Fine anatomical preparations in my room, are there not, Mr Kerby?' said the old gentleman. 'Did you notice a very interesting and perfect arrangement of the intestinal ganglia? They form the subject of an important chapter in my great work.'

'I am afraid you will think me very ignorant,' I replied. 'But I really do not know the intestinal ganglia when I see them. The object I noticed with most curiosity in your room was something more on a level with my own small capacity.'

'And what was that?' asked the Professor.

'The figure of the stuffed poodle. I suppose he was a favourite of yours?'

'Of mine? No, no: – a young woman's favourite, sir, before I was born; and a very remarkable dog, too. The vital principle in that poodle, Mr Kerby, must have been singularly intensified. He lived to a fabulous old age, and he was clever enough to play an important part of his own, in what you English call a Romance of Real Life! If I could only have dissected that poodle, I would have put him into my book – he should have headed my chapter on the Vital Principle of Beasts.'

'Here is a story in prospect,' thought I, 'if I can only keep his attention up to the subject.'

'He should have figured in my great work, sir,' the Professor went on. 'Scarammuccia should have taken his place among the examples that prove my new theory; but unfortunately he died before I was born. His mistress gave him, stuffed, as you see up stairs, to my father to take care of for her, and he has descended as an heir-loom to me. Talking of dogs, Mr Kerby, I have ascertained, beyond the possibility of doubt, that the brachial plexus in people who die of hydrophobia – but stop! I had better show you how it is – the preparation is up stairs under my wash-hand stand.'

He left his seat as he spoke. In another minute he would have sent the servant to fetch the 'preparation,' and I should have lost the story. At the risk of his taking offence, I begged him not to move just then, unless he wished me to spoil his likeness. This alarmed, but fortunately did not irritate him. He returned to his seat, and I resumed the subject of the stuffed poodle, asking him boldly to tell me the story with which the dog was connected. The demand seemed to impress him with no very favourable opinion of my intellectual tastes; but he complied with it, and related, not without many a wearisome digression to the subject of his great work, the narrative which I propose calling by the name of 'The Yellow Mask.' After the slight specimens that I have given of his character and style of conversation, it will be almost unnecessary for me to premise that I tell this story in my own language, and according to my own plan in the disposition of the incidents – adding nothing, of course, to the facts, but keeping them within the limits which my disposable space prescribes to me.

I may perhaps be allowed to add in this place, that I have not yet seen or heard of my portrait in an engraved state. Professor Tizzi is still alive; but I look in vain through the publishers' lists for an announcement of his learned work on the Vital Principle. Possibly, he may be adding a volume or two to the twelve already completed, by way of increasing the debt which a deeply obliged posterity is, sooner or later, sure of owing to him.

PART FIRST

CHAPTER ONE

About a century ago, there lived in the ancient city of Pisa a famous Italian milliner, who, by way of vindicating to all customers her familiarity with Paris fashions, adopted a French title, and called herself the Demoiselle Grifoni. She was a wizen little woman, with a mischievous face, a quick tongue, a nimble foot, a talent for business, and an uncertain disposition. Rumour hinted that she was immensely rich; and scandal suggested that she would do anything for money.

The one undeniable good quality which raised Demoiselle Grifoni above all her rivals in the trade was her inexhaustible fortitude. She was never known to yield an inch under any pressure of adverse circumstances. Thus the memorable occasion of her life on which she was threatened with ruin was also the occasion on which she most triumphantly asserted the energy and decision of her character. At the height of the demoiselle's prosperity, her skilled forewoman and cutter-out basely married and started in business as a rival. Such a calamity as this would have ruined an ordinary milliner; but the invincible Grifoni rose superior to it almost without an effort, and proved incontestably that it was impossible for hostile Fortune to catch her at the end of her resources. While the minor milliners were prophesying that she would shut up shop, she was quietly carrying on a private correspondence with an agent in Paris. Nobody knew what these letters were about until a few weeks had elapsed, and then circulars were received by all the ladies in Pisa, announcing that the best French forewoman who could be got for money was engaged to superintend the great Grifoni establishment. This master-stroke decided the victory. All the demoiselle's customers declined giving orders elsewhere until the forewoman from Paris had exhibited to the natives of Pisa the latest fashions from the metropolis of the world of dress.

The Frenchwoman arrived punctual to the appointed day, – glib and curt, smiling and flippant, tight of face and supple of figure. Her name was Mademoiselle Virginie, and her family had inhumanly deserted her. She was set to work the moment she was inside the doors of the Grifoni establishment. A room was devoted to her own private use; magnificent materials in velvet, silk, and satin, with due accompaniment of muslins, laces, and ribbons, were placed at her disposal; she was told to spare no expense, and to produce, in the shortest possible time, the finest and newest specimen-dresses for exhibition in the show-room. Mademoiselle Virginie undertook to do everything required of her, produced her portfolios of patterns and her book of coloured designs, and asked for one assistant who could speak French enough to interpret her orders to the Italian girls in the work-room.

'I have the very person you want,' cried Demoiselle Grifoni. 'A workwoman we call Brigida here – the idlest slut in Pisa, but as sharp as a needle – has been in France, and speaks the language like a native. I'll send her to you directly.'

Mademoiselle Virginie was not left long alone with her patterns and silks. A tall woman, with bold black eyes, a reckless manner, and a step as firm as a man's, stalked into the room with the gait of a tragedy-queen crossing the stage. The instant her eyes fell on the French forewoman, she stopped, threw up her hands in astonishment, and exclaimed, 'Finette!'

'Teresa!' cried the Frenchwoman, casting her scissors on the table, and advancing a few steps.

'Hush! call me Brigida.'

'Hush! call me Virginie.'

These two exclamations were uttered at the same moment, and then the two women scrutinized each other in silence. The swarthy cheeks of the Italian turned to a dull yellow, and the voice of the Frenchwoman trembled a little when she spoke again.

'How, in the name of Heaven, have you dropped down in the world as low as this?' she asked. 'I thought you were provided for when —'

'Silence!' interrupted Brigida. 'You see I was not provided for. I have had my misfortunes; and you are the last woman alive who ought to refer to them.'

'Do you think I have not had my misfortunes, too, since we met?' (Brigida's face brightened maliciously at those words.) 'You have had your revenge,' continued Mademoiselle Virginie coldly, turning away to the table and taking up the scissors again.

Brigida followed her, threw one arm roughly round her neck, and kissed her on the cheek. 'Let us be friends again,' she said. The Frenchwoman laughed. 'Tell me how I have had my revenge,' pursued the other, tightening her grasp. Mademoiselle Virginie signed to Brigida to stoop, and whispered rapidly in her ear. The Italian listened eagerly, with fierce suspicious eyes fixed on the door. When the whispering ceased, she loosened her hold; and, with a sigh of relief, pushed back her heavy black hair from her temples. 'Now we are friends,' she said, and sat down indolently in a chair placed by the work-table.

'Friends,' repeated Mademoiselle Virginie, with another laugh. 'And now for business,' she continued,' getting a row of pins ready for use by putting them between her teeth. 'I am here, I believe, for the purpose of ruining the late forewoman, who has set up in opposition to us? Good! I *will* ruin her. Spread out the yellow brocaded silk, my dear, and pin that pattern on at your end, while I pin at mine. And what are your plans, Brigida? (Mind you don't forget that Finette is dead, and that Virginie has risen from her ashes.) You can't possibly intend to stop here all your life? (Leave an inch outside the paper, all round.) You must have projects? What are they?'

'Look at my figure,' said Brigida, placing herself in an attitude in the middle of the room.

'Ah!' rejoined the other, 'it's not what is was. There's too much of it. You want diet, walking, and a French staymaker,' muttered Mademoiselle Virginie through her chevaux-de-frise of pins.

'Did the goddess Minerva walk, and employ a French staymaker? I thought she rode upon clouds, and lived at a period before waists were invented.'

'What do you mean?'

'This – that my present project is to try if I can't make my fortune by sitting as a model for Minerva in the studio of the best sculptor in Pisa.'

'And who is he? (Unwind me a yard or two of that black lace.)'

'The master sculptor, Luca Lomi, – an old family, once noble, but down in the world now. The master is obliged to make statues to get a living for his daughter and himself.'

'More of the lace – double it over the bosom of the dress. And how is sitting to this needy sculptor to make your fortune?'

'Wait a minute. There are other sculptors besides him in the studio. There is, first, his brother, the priest – Father Rocco, who passes all his spare time with the master. He is a good sculptor in his way – has cast statues and made a font for his church – a holy man, who devotes all his work in the studio to the cause of piety.'

'Ah, bah! we should think him a droll priest in France. (More pins.) You don't expect *him* to put money in your pocket surely?'

'Wait, I say again. There is a third sculptor in the studio – actually a nobleman! His name is Fabio d'Ascoli. He is rich, young, handsome, an only child, and little better than a fool. Fancy his working at sculpture, as if he had his bread to get by it – and thinking that an amusement! Imagine a man belonging to one of the best families in Pisa mad enough to want to make a reputation as an artist! – Wait! wait! the best is to come. His father and mother are dead – he has no near relations in the world to exercise authority over him – he is a bachelor, and his fortune is all at his own disposal; going a-begging, my friend; absolutely going a-begging for want of a clever woman to hold out her hand and take it from him.'

'Yes, yes – now I understand. The goddess Minerva is a clever woman, and she will hold out her hand and take his fortune from him with the utmost docility.'

'The first thing is to get him to offer it. I must tell you that I am not going to sit to him, but to his master, Luca Lomi, who is doing the statue of Minerva. The face is modelled from his daughter; and now he wants somebody to sit for the bust and arms. Maddalena Lomi and I are as nearly as possible the same height, I hear – the difference between us being that I have a good figure and she has a bad one. I have offered to sit, through a friend who is employed in the studio. If the master accepts, I am sure of an introduction to our rich young gentleman; and then leave it to my good looks, my various accomplishments, and my ready tongue, to do the rest.'

'Stop! I won't have the lace doubled, on second thoughts. I'll have it single, and running all round the dress in curves – so. Well, and who is this friend of yours employed in the studio? A fourth sculptor?'

'No! no! the strangest, simplest little creature —

Just then a faint tap was audible at the door of the room.

Brigida laid her finger on her lips, and called impatiently to the person outside to come in.

The door opened gently, and a young girl, poorly but very neatly dressed, entered the room. She was rather thin, and under the average height; but her head and figure were in perfect proportion. Her hair was of that gorgeous auburn colour, her eyes of that deep violet blue, which the portraits of Giorgione and Titian have made famous as the type of Venetian beauty. Her features possessed the definiteness and regularity, the 'good modelling' (to use an artist's term), which is the rarest of all womanly charms, in Italy as elsewhere. The one serious defect of her face was its paleness. Her cheeks, wanting nothing in form, wanted everything in colour. That look of health, which is the essential crowning-point of beauty, was the one attraction which her face did not possess.

She came into the room with a sad and weary expression in her eyes, which changed, however, the moment she observed the magnificently dressed French forewoman, into a look of astonishment, and almost of awe. Her manner became shy and embarrassed; and after an instant of hesitation, she turned back silently to the door.

"Stop, stop, Nanina,' said Brigida, in Italian. 'Don't be afraid of that lady. She is our new forewoman; and she has it in her power to do all sorts of kind things for you. Look up, and tell us what you want. You were sixteen last birth-day, Nanina, and you behave like a baby of two years old!'

'I only came to know if there was any work for me to-day,' said the girl, in a very sweet voice, that trembled a little as she tried to face the fashionable French forewoman again.

'No work, child, that is easy enough for *you* to do,' said Brigida. 'Are you going to the studio today?'

Some of the colour that Nanina's cheeks wanted began to steal over them as she answered 'Yes.'

'Don't forget my message, darling. And if Master Luca Lomi asks where I live, answer that you are ready to deliver a letter to me; but that you are forbidden to enter into any particulars at first, about who I am, or where I live.'

'Why am I forbidden?' inquired Nanina, innocently.

'Don't ask questions, baby! Do as you are told. Bring me back a nice note or message to-morrow from the studio, and I will intercede with this lady to get you some work. You are a foolish child to want it, when you might make more money here and at Florence, by sitting to painters and sculptors: though what they can see to paint or model in you I never could understand.'

'I like working at home better than going abroad to sit,' said Nanina, looking very much abashed as she faltered out the answer, and escaping from the room with a terrified farewell obeisance, which was an eccentric compound of a start, a bow, and a curtsy.

'That awkward child would be pretty,' said Mademoiselle Virgine, making rapid progress with the cutting out of her dress, 'if she knew how to give herself a complexion, and had a presentable gown on her back. Who is she?'

'The friend who is to get me into Master Luca Lomi's studio,' replied Brigida, laughing. 'Rather a curious ally for me to take up with, isn't she?'

'Where did you meet with her?'

'Here, to be sure, she hangs about this place for any plain work she can get to do; and takes it home to the oddest little room in a street near the Campo Santo. I had the curiosity to follow her one day, and knocked at her door soon after she had gone in, as if I was a visitor. She answered my knock in a great flurry and fright, as you may imagine. I made myself agreeable, affected immense interest in her affairs, and so got into her room. Such a place! A mere corner of it curtained off to make a bed-room. One chair, one stool, one saucepan on the fire. Before the hearth, the most grotesquely hideous, unshaven poodle-dog you ever saw; and on the stool a fair little girl plaiting dinner-mats. Such was the household – furniture and all included. 'Where is your father?' I asked. 'He ran away and left us, years ago,' answers my awkward little friend who has just left the room, speaking in that simple way of hers, with all the composure in the world. 'And your mother?' – 'Dead.' – She went up to the little mat-plaiting girl, as she gave that answer, and began playing with her long flaxen hair. 'Your sister, I suppose,' said I. 'What is her name?' – 'They call me La Biondella,' says the child, looking up from her mat (La Biondella, Virginie, means The Fair). – 'And why do you let that great, shaggy, ill-looking brute lie before your fireplace?' I asked. – 'O!' cried the little mat-plaiter, 'that is our dear old dog, Scarammuccia. He takes care of the house when Nanina is not at home. He dances on his hind legs, and jumps through a hoop, and tumbles down dead when I cry Bang! Scarammuccia followed us home one night, years ago, and he has lived with us ever since. He goes out every day by himself, we can't tell where, and generally returns licking his chops, which makes us afraid that he is a thief; but nobody finds him out, because he is the cleverest dog that ever lived!' The child ran on in this way about the great beast by the fireplace, till I was obliged to stop her; while that simpleton Nanina stood by, laughing and encouraging her. I asked them a few more questions, which produced some strange answers. They did not seem to know of any relations of theirs in the world. The neighbours in the house had helped them, after their father ran away, until they were old enough to help themselves; and they did not seem to think there was anything in the least wretched or pitiable in their way of living. The last thing I heard when I left that day, was La Biondella crying 'Bang!' – then a bark, a thump on the floor, and a scream of laughter. If it was not for their dog I should go and see them oftener. But the ill-conditioned beast has taken a dislike to me, and growls and shows his teeth whenever I come near him.'

'The girl looked sickly when she came in here. Is she always like that?'

'No. She has altered within the last month. I suspect our interesting young nobleman has produced an impression. The oftener the girl has sat to him lately, the paler and more out of spirits she has become.'

'O! she has sat to him, has she?'

'She is sitting to him now. He is doing a bust of some Pagan nymph or other, and prevailed on Nanina to let him copy from her head and face. According to her own account the little fool was frightened at first, and gave him all the trouble in the world before she would consent.'

'And now she has consented, don't you think it likely she may turn out rather a dangerous rival? Men are such fools, and take such fancies into their heads —'

'Ridiculous! A thread-paper of a girl like that, who has no manner, no talk, no intelligence; who has nothing to recommend her but an awkward babyish-prettiness! – Dangerous to me? No! no! If there is danger at all, I have to dread it from the sculptor's daughter. I don't mind confessing that I am anxious to see Maddalena Lomi. But as for Nanina, she will simply be of use to me. All I know already about the studio and the artists in it, I know through her. She will deliver my message, and procure me my introduction; and when we have got so far, I shall give her an old gown and a shake of the hand; and then, good bye for our little Innocent!'

'Well, well, for your sake I hope you are the wiser of the two in this matter. For my part, I always distrust innocence. Wait one moment and I shall have the body and sleeves of this dress ready for the needlewomen. There, ring the bell, and order them up; for I have directions to give, and you must interpret for me.'

While Brigida went to the bell, the energetic Frenchwoman began planning out the skirt of the new dress. She laughed as she measured off yard after yard of the silk.

'What are you laughing about?' asked Brigida, opening the door and ringing a hand-bell in the passage.

'I can't help fancying, dear, in spite of her innocent face and her artless ways, that your young friend is a hypocrite.'

'And I am quite certain, love, that she is only a simpleton.'

CHAPTER II

The studio of the Master-Sculptor, Luca Lomi, was composed of two large rooms, unequally divided by a wooden partition, with an arched doorway cut in the middle of it.

While the milliners of the Grifoni establishment were industriously shaping dresses, the sculptors in Luca Lomi's workshop were, in their way, quite as hard at work shaping marble and clay. In the smaller of the two rooms the young nobleman (only addressed in the studio by his Christian name of Fabio) was busily engaged on his bust, with Nanina sitting before him as a model. His was not one of those traditional Italian faces from which subtlety and suspicion are always supposed to look out darkly on the world at large. Both countenance and expression proclaimed his character frankly and freely to all who saw him. Quick intelligence looked brightly from his eyes; and easy good-humour laughed out pleasantly in the rather quaint curve of his lips. For the rest, his face expressed the defects as well as the merits of his character, showing that he wanted resolution and perseverance just as plainly as it showed also that he possessed amiability and intelligence.

At the end of the large room, nearest to the street door, Luca Lomi was standing by his life-size statue of Minerva, and was issuing directions, from time to time, to some of his workmen, who were roughly chiselling the drapery of another figure. At the opposite side of the room, nearest to the partition, his brother, Father Rocco, was taking a cast from a statuette of the Madonna; while Maddalena Lomi, the sculptor's daughter, released from sitting for Minerva's face, walked about the two rooms, and watched what was going on in them.

There was a strong family likeness of a certain kind between father, brother, and daughter. All three were tall, handsome, dark-haired, and dark-eyed; nevertheless, they

19

differed in expression, strikingly as they resembled one another in feature. Maddalena Lomi's face betrayed strong passions, but not an ungenerous nature. Her father, with the same indications of a violent temper, had some sinister lines about his mouth and forehead which suggested anything rather than an open disposition. Father Rocco's countenance, on the other hand, looked like the personification of absolute calmness and invincible moderation; and his manner, which, in a very firm way, was singularly quiet and deliberate, assisted in carrying out the impression produced by his face. The daughter seemed as if she could fly into a passion at a moment's notice, and forgive also at a moment's notice. The father, appearing to be just as irritable, had something in his face which said, as plainly as if in words, 'Anger me, and I never pardon.' The priest looked as if he need never be called on either to ask forgiveness or to grant it, for the double reason that he could irritate nobody else, and that nobody else could irritate him.

'Rocco,' said Luca, looking at the face of his Minerva, which was now finished; 'this statue of mine will make a sensation.'

'I am glad to hear it,' rejoined the priest drily.

'It is a new thing in art,' continued Luca enthusiastically. 'Other sculptors, with a classical subject like mine, limit themselves to the ideal classical face, and never think of aiming at individual character. Now I do precisely the reverse of that. I get my handsome daughter, Maddalena, to sit for Minerva, and I make an exact likeness of her. I may lose in ideal beauty, but I gain in individual character. People may accuse me of disregarding established rules – but my answer is, that I make my own rules. My daughter looks like a Minerva, and there she is exactly as she looks.'

'It is certainly a wonderful likeness,' said Father Rocco, approaching the statue.

'It is the girl herself,' cried the other. 'Exactly her expression, and exactly her features. Measure Maddalena, and measure Minerva, and, from forehead to chin, you won't find a hair's breadth of difference between them.' 'But how about the bust and arms of the figure, now the face is done?' asked the priest, returning, as he spoke, to his own work.

'I may have the very model I want for them tomorrow. Little Nanina has just given me the strangest message. What do you think of a mysterious lady-admirer who offers to sit for the bust and arms of my Minerva?'

'Are you going to accept the offer?' inquired the priest.

'I am going to receive her to-morrow; and if I really find that she is the same height as Maddalena, and has a bust and arms worth modelling, of course I shall accept her offer; for she will be the very sitter I have been looking after for weeks past. Who can she be? That's the mystery I want to find out. Which do you say, Rocco – an enthusiast or an adventuress?'

'I do not presume to say, for I have no means of knowing.'

'Ah! there you are with your moderation again. Now, I do presume to assert, that she must be either one or the other – or she would not have forbidden Nanina to say anything about her, in answer to all my first natural inquiries. Where is Maddalena? I thought she was here a minute ago.'

'She is in Fabio's room,' answered Father Rocco, softly. 'Shall I call her?'

'No, no!' returned Luca. He stopped, looked round at the workmen, who were chipping away mechanically at their bit of drapery; then advanced close to the priest, with a cunning smile, and continued in a whisper: 'If Maddalena can only get from Fabio's room here to Fabio's palace over the way, on the Arno – come, come, Rocco! don't shake your head. If I brought her up to your church-door one of these days, as Fabio d'Ascoli's betrothed, you would be glad enough to take the rest of the business off my hands, and make her Fabio d'Ascoli's wife. You are a very holy man, Rocco, but you know the difference between the clink of the moneybag and the clink of the chisel, for all that!'

'I am sorry to find, Luca,' returned the priest coldly, 'that you allow yourself to talk of the most delicate subjects in the coarsest way. This is one of the minor sins of the tongue which is growing on you. When we are alone in the studio I will endeavour to lead you into speaking of the young man in the room there, and of your daughter, in terms more becoming to you, to me, and to them. Until that time, allow me to go on with my work.'

Luca shrugged his shoulders and went back to his statue.

Father Rocco, who had been engaged during the last ten minutes in mixing wet plaster to the right consistency for taking a cast, suspended his occupation, and, crossing the room to a corner next to the partition, removed from it a cheval-glass which stood there. He lifted it away gently, while his brother's back was turned, carried it close to the table at which he had been at work, and then resumed his employment of mixing the plaster. Having at last prepared the composition for use, he laid it over the exposed half of the statuette with a neatness and dexterity which showed him to be a practised hand at cast-taking. Just as he had covered the necessary extent of surface, Luca turned round from his statue.

'How are you getting on with the cast?' he asked. 'Do you want any help?'

'None, brother, I thank you,' answered the priest. 'Pray do not disturb either yourself or your workmen on my account.'

Luca turned again to the statue: and, at the same moment, Father Rocco softly moved the cheval-glass towards the open doorway between the two rooms, placing it at such an angle as to make it reflect the figures of the persons in the smaller studio. He did this with significant quickness and precision. It was evidently not the first time he had used the glass for purposes of secret observation.

Mechanically stirring the wet plaster round and round for the second casting, the priest looked into the glass, and saw, as in a picture, all that was going forward in the inner room. Maddalena Lomi was standing behind the young nobleman, watching the progress he made with his bust. Occasionally she took the modelling-tool out of his hand, and showed him, with her sweetest smile, that she too, as a sculptor's daughter, understood something of the sculptor's art; and, now and then, in the pauses of the conversation, when her interest was especially intense in Fabio's work, she suffered her hand to drop absently on his shoulder, or stooped forward so close to him that her hair mingled for a moment with his. Moving the glass and inch or two, so as to bring Nanina well under his eye, Father Rocco found that he could trace each repetition of these little acts of familiarity by the immediate effect which they produced on the girl's face and manner. Whenever Maddalena so much as touched the young nobleman – no matter whether she did so by premeditation, or really by accident – Nanina's features contracted, her pale cheeks grew paler, she fidgeted on her chair, and her fingers nervously twisted and untwisted the loose ends of the ribbon fastened round her waist.

'Jealous,' thought Father Rocco; 'I suspected it weeks ago.'

He turned away, and gave his whole attention for a few minutes to the mixing of the plaster. When he looked back again at the glass, he was just in time to witness a little accident which suddenly changed the relative positions of the three persons in the inner room.

He saw Maddalena take up a modelling-tool which lay on a table near her, and begin to help Fabio in altering the arrangement of the hair on his bust. The young man watched what she was doing earnestly enough for a few moments; then his attention wandered away to Nanina. She looked at him reproachfully, and he answered by a sign which brought a smile to her face directly. Maddalena surprised her at the instant of the change; and, following the direction of her eyes, easily discovered at whom the smile was directed. She darted a glance of contempt at Nanina, threw down the modelling-tool, and turned indignantly to the young sculptor, who was affecting to be hard at work again.

'Signor Fabio,' she said, 'the next time you forget what is due to your rank and yourself, warn me of it, if you please, beforehand, and I will take care to leave the room.' While speaking the last words she passed through the doorway. Father Rocco, bending abstractedly over his plaster mixture, heard her continue to herself in a whisper, as she went by him: 'If I have any influence at all with my father, that impudent beggar-girl shall be forbidden the studio.'

'Jealousy on the other side,' thought the priest. 'Something must be done at once, or this will end badly.'

He looked again at the glass, and saw Fabio, after an instant of hesitation, beckon to Nanina to approach him. She left her seat, advanced half-way to his, then stopped. He stepped forward to meet her, and, taking her by the hand, whispered earnestly in her ear. When he had done, before dropping her hand, he touched her cheek with his lips, and then helped her on with the little white mantilla which covered her head and shoulders out of doors. The girl trembled violently, and drew the linen close to her face as Fabio walked into the larger studio, and, addressing Father Rocco, said:

'I am afraid I am more idle, or more stupid, than ever to-day. I can't get on with the bust at all to my satisfaction, so I have cut short the sitting, and given Nanina a half-holiday.'

At the first sound of his voice, Maddalena, who was speaking to her father, stopped; and, with another look of scorn at Nanina standing trembling in the doorway, left the room. Luca Lomi called Fabio to him as she went away, and Father Rocco turning to the statuette, looked to see how the plaster was hardening on it. Seeing them thus engaged, Nanina attempted to escape from the studio without being noticed; but the priest stopped her just as she was hurrying by him.

'My child,' said he, in his gentle quiet way, 'are you going home?'

Nanina's heart beat too fast for her to reply in words – she could only answer by bowing her head.

'Take this for your little sister,' pursued Father Rocco, putting a few silver coins in her hand; 'I have got some customers for those mats she plaits so nicely. You need not bring them to my rooms – I will come and see you this evening, when I am going my rounds among my parishioners, and will take the mats away with me. You are a good girl, Nanina – you have always been a good girl – and as long as I am alive, my child, you shall never want an friend and an adviser.'

Nanina's eyes filled with tears. She drew the mantilla closer than ever round her face as she tried to thank the priest. Father Rocco nodded to her kindly, and laid his hand lightly on her head for a moment, then turned round again to his cast.

'Don't forget my message to the lady who is to sit to me to-morrow,' said Luca to Nanina, as she passed him on her way out of the studio.

After she had gone, Fabio returned to the priest, who was still busy over his cast.

'I hope you will get on better with the bust to-morrow,' said Father Rocco, politely; 'I am sure you cannot complain of your model.'

'Complain of her!' cried the young man, warmly; 'she has the most beautiful head I ever saw. If I were twenty times the sculptor that I am, I should despair of being able to do her justice.'

He walked into the inner room to look at his bust again – lingered before it for a little while – and then turned to retrace his steps to the larger studio. Between him and the doorway stood three chairs. As he went by them, he absently touched the backs of the first two, and passed the third; but just as he was entering the larger room, stopped, as if struck by a sudden recollection, returned hastily, and touched the third chair. Raising his eyes, as he approached the large studio again after doing this, he met the eyes of the priest fixed on his in unconcealed astonishment.

'Signor Fabio!' exclaimed Father Rocco, with a sarcastic smile; 'who would ever have imagined that you were superstitious?'

'My nurse was,' returned the young man, reddening, and laughing rather uneasily. 'She taught me some bad habits that I have not got over yet.' With those words he nodded, and hastily went out.

'Superstitious!' said Father Rocco softly to himself. He smiled again, reflected for a moment, and then, going to the window, looked into the street. The way to the left led to Fabio's palace, and the way to the right to the Campo Santo, in the neighbourhood of which Nanina lived. The priest was just in time to see the young sculptor take the way to the right.

After another half-hour had elapsed, the two work-men quitted the studio to go to dinner, and Luca and his brother were left alone.

'We may return now,' said Father Rocco, 'to that conversation which was suspended between us earlier in the day.'

'I have nothing more to say,' rejoined Luca, sulkily.

Then you can listen to me, brother, with the greater attention,' pursued the priest. 'I objected to the coarseness of your tone in talking of our young pupil and your daughter – I object still more strongly to your insinuation that my desire to see them married (provided always that they are sincerely attached to each other) springs from a mercenary motive.'

'You are trying to snare me, Rocco, in a mesh of fine phrases; but I am not to be caught. I know what my own motive is for hoping that Maddalena may get an offer of marriage from this wealthy young gentleman – she will have his money, and we shall all profit by it. That is coarse and mercenary, if you please; but it is the true reason why I want to see Maddalena married to Fabio. You want to see it, too – and for what reason, I should like to know, if not for mine?'

'Of what use would wealthy relations be to me? What are people with money – what is money itself – to a man who follows my calling?'

'Money is something to everybody.'

'Is it? When have you found that I have taken any account of it? Give me money enough to buy my daily bread and to pay for my lodging and my coarse cassock – and though I may want much for the poor, for myself I want no more. When have you found me mercenary? Do I not help you in this studio for love of you and of the art without exacting so much as journeyman's wages? Have I ever asked you for more than a few crowns to give away on feast-days among my parishioners? Money! money for a man who may be summoned to Rome to-morrow, who may be told to go at half an hour's notice on a foreign mission that may take him to the ends of the earth, and who would be ready to go the moment when he was called on! Money to a man who has no wife, no children, no interests outside the sacred circle of the church! Brother! do you see the dust and dirt and shapeless marble-chips lying around your statue there? Cover that floor instead with gold – and, though the litter may have changed in colour and form, in my eyes it would be litter still.'

'A very noble sentiment, I dare say, Rocco, but I can't echo it. Granting that you care nothing for money, will you explain to me why you are so anxious that Maddalena should marry Fabio? She has had offers from poorer men – you knew of them – but you have never taken the least interest in her accepting or rejecting a proposal before.'

'I hinted the reason to you, months ago, when Fabio first entered the studio.'

'It was rather a vague hint, brother – can't you be plainer to-day?'

'I think I can. In the first place, let me begin by assuring you, that I have no objection to the young man himself. He may be a little capricious and undecided, but he has no incorrigible faults that I have discovered.'

'That is rather a cool way of praising him, Rocco.'

'I should speak of him warmly enough if he were not the representative of an intolerable corruption, and a monstrous wrong. Whenever I think of him I think of an injury which his present existence perpetuates, and if I do speak of him coldly it is only for that reason.'

Luca looked away quickly from his brother, and began kicking absently at the marble chips which were scattered over the floor around him.

'I now remember,' he said, 'what that hint of yours pointed at. I know what you mean.'

'Then you know,' answered the priest, 'that while part of the wealth which Fabio d'Ascoli possesses is honestly and incontestably his own; part, also, has been inherited by him from the spoilers and robbers of the church —'

'Blame his ancestors for that; don't blame him.'

'I blame him as long as the spoil is not restored.'

'How do you know that it was spoil, after all?'

'I have examined more carefully than most men the records of the Civil Wars in Italy; and I know that the ancestors of Fabio d'Ascoli wrung from the church, in her hour of weakness, property which they dared to claim as their right. I know of titles to lands signed away, in those stormy times, under the influence of fear, or through false representations of which the law takes no account – I call the money thus obtained, spoil – and I say that it ought to be restored, and shall be restored to the church from which it was taken.'

'And what does Fabio answer to that, brother?'

'I have not spoken to him on the subject.'

'Why not?'

'Because, I have, as yet, no influence over him. When he is married, his wife will have influence over him; and she shall speak.'

'Maddalena, I suppose? How do you know that she will speak?'

'Have I not educated her? Does she not understand what her duties are towards the church, in whose bosom she has been reared?'

Luca hesitated uneasily, and walked away a step or two before he spoke again.

'Does this spoil, as you call it, amount to a large sum of money?' he asked, in an anxious whisper.

'I may answer that question, Luca, at some future time,' said the priest. 'For the present, let it be enough that you are acquainted with all I undertook to inform you of when we began our conversation. You now know that if I am anxious for this marriage to take place, it is from motives entirely unconnected with self-interest. If all the property which Fabio's ancestors wrongfully obtained from the church, were restored to the church to-morrow, not one paulo of it would go into my pocket. I am a poor priest now, and to the end of my days shall remain so. You soldiers of the world, brother, fight for your pay – I am a soldier of the church, and I fight for my cause.'

Saying these words, he returned abruptly to the statuette; and refused to speak, or leave his employment again, until he had taken the mould off, and had carefully put away the various fragments of which it consisted. This done, he drew a writing-desk from the drawer of his working-table, and taking out a slip of paper, wrote these lines:

'Come down to the studio to-morrow. Fabio will be with us, but Nanina will return no more.'

Without signing what he had written, he sealed it up, and directed it to – 'Donna Maddalena.' Then took his hat, and handed the note to his brother.

'Oblige me by giving that to my niece,' he said.

'Tell me, Rocco,' said Luca, turning the note round and round perplexedly between his finger and thumb. 'Do you think Maddalena will be lucky enough to get married to Fabio?'

'Still coarse in your expressions, brother!'

'Never mind my expressions. Is it likely?'

'Yes, Luca, I think it is likely.'

With those words he waved his hand pleasantly to his brother, and went out.

CHAPTER III

From the studio, Father Rocco went straight to his own rooms, hard by the church to which he was attached. Opening a cabinet in his study, he took from one of its drawers a handful of small silver money – consulted for a minute or so a slate on which several names and addresses were written – provided himself with a portable inkhorn and some strips of paper, and again went out.

He directed his steps to the poorest part of the neighbourhood; and entering some very wretched houses, was greeted by the inhabitants with great respect and affection. The women, especially, kissed his hands with more reverence than they would have shown to the highest crowned head in Europe. In return, he talked to them as easily and unconstrainedly as if they were his equals; sat down cheerfully on dirty bed-sides and rickety benches; and distributed his little gifts of money with the air of a man who was paying debts rather than bestowing charity. Where he encountered cases of illness, he pulled out his inkhorn and slips of paper, and wrote simple prescriptions to be made up from the medicine-chest of a neighbouring convent, which served the same merciful purpose then that is answered by dispensaries in our days. When he had exhausted his money and had got through his visits, he was escorted out of the poor quarter by a perfect train of enthusiastic followers. The women kissed his hand again, and the men uncovered as he turned, and, with a friendly sign, bade them farewell.

As soon as he was alone again, he walked towards the Campo Santo; and passing the house in which Nanina lived, sauntered up and down the street thoughtfully, for some minutes: when he at length ascended the steep staircase that led to the room occupied by the sisters, he found the door ajar. Pushing it open gently, he saw La Biondella, sitting with her pretty fair profile turned towards him, eating her evening meal of bread and grapes. At the opposite end of the room, Scarammuccia was perched up on his hind quarters in a corner, with his mouth wide open to catch the morsel of bread which he evidently expected the child to throw to him. What the elder sister was doing the priest had not time to see; for the dog barked the moment he presented himself, and Nanina hastened to the door to ascertain who the intruder might be. All that he could observe was that she was too confused, on catching sight of him, to be able to utter a word. La Biondella was the first to speak.

'Thank you, Father Rocco,' said the child, jumping up, with her bread in one hand and her grapes in the other: 'Thank you for giving me so much money for my dinner-mats. There they are tied up together in one little parcel, in the corner. Nanina said she was ashamed to think of your carrying them; and I said I knew where you lived, and I should like to ask you to let me take them home.'

'Do you think you can carry them all the way, my dear?' asked the priest.

'Look, Father Rocco, see if I can't carry them!' cried La Biondella, cramming her bread into one of the pockets of her little apron, holding her bunch of grapes by the stalk in her mouth, and hoisting the packet of dinner-mats on her head in a moment. 'See, I am strong enough to carry double,' said the child, looking up proudly into the priest's face.

'Can you trust her to take them home for me?' asked Father Rocco, turning to Nanina. 'I want to speak to you alone; and her absence will give me the opportunity. Can you trust her out by herself?'

'Yes, Father Rocco, she often goes out alone.' Nanina gave this answer in low, trembling tones, and looked down confusedly on the ground.

'Go then, my dear,' said Father Rocco, patting the child on the shoulder. 'And come back here to your sister, as soon as you have left the mats.'

La Biondella went out directly in great triumph, with Scarammuccia walking by her side, and keeping his muzzle suspiciously close to the pocket in which she had put her bread. Father Rocco closed the door after them; and then, taking the one chair which the room possessed, motioned to

Nanina to sit by him on the stool.

'Do you believe that I am your friend, my child; and that I have always meant well towards you?' he began.

'The best and kindest of friends,' answered Nanina.

'Then you will hear what I have to say patiently; and you will believe that I am speaking for your good, even if my words should distress you?' (Nanina turned away her head.) 'Now, tell me; should I be wrong, to begin with, if I said that my brother's pupil, the young nobleman whom we call "Signor Fabio," had been here to see you to-day?' (Nanina started up affrightedly from the stool.) 'Sit down again, my child; I am not going to blame you. I am only going to tell you what you must do for the future.'

He took her hand; it was cold, and it trembled violently in his.

'I will not ask what he has been saying to you,' continued the priest; 'for it might distress you to answer; and I have, moreover, had means of knowing that your youth and beauty have made a strong impression on him. I will pass over, then, all reference to the words he may be speaking to you; and I will come at once to what I have now to say, in my turn. Nanina, my child, arm yourself with all your courage, and promise me, before we part to-night, that you will see Signor Fabio no more.'

Nanina turned round suddenly, and fixed her eyes on him, with an expression of terrified incredulity. 'No more?'

'You are very young, and very innocent,' said Father Rocco; 'but surely you must have thought, before now, of the difference between Signor Fabio and you. Surely you must have often remembered that you are low down among the ranks of the poor, and that he is high up among the rich and the nobly-born?'

Nanina's hands dropped on the priest's knees. She bent her head down on them, and began to weep bitterly.

'Surely you must have thought of that?' reiterated Father Rocco.

'O, I have often, often thought of it!' murmured the girl. 'I have mourned over it, and cried about it in secret for many nights past. He said I looked pale, and ill, and out of spirits to-day; and I told him it was with thinking of that!'

'And what did he say in return?'

There was no answer. Father Rocco looked down. Nanina raised her head directly from his knees, and tried to turn it away again. He took her hand and stopped her.

'Come!' he said; 'speak frankly to me. Say what you ought to say to your father and your friend. What was his answer, my child, when you reminded him of the difference between you?'

'He said I was born to be a lady,' faltered the girl, still struggling to turn her face away, 'and that I might make myself one if I would learn and be patient. He said that if he had all the noble ladies in Pisa to choose from on one side, and only little Nanina on the other, he would hold out his hand to me, and tell them, 'This shall be my wife.' He said Love knew no difference of rank; and that if he was a nobleman and rich, it was all the more reason why he should please himself. He was so kind, that I thought my heart would burst while he was speaking; and my little sister liked him so, that she got upon his knee and kissed him. Even our dog, who growls at other strangers, stole to his side and licked his hand. O, Father Rocco! Father Rocco!' The tears burst out afresh, and the lovely head dropped once more, wearily, on the priest's knee.

Father Rocco smiled to himself, and waited to speak again till she was calmer.

'Supposing,' he resumed, after some minutes of silence, 'supposing Signor Fabio really meant all he said to you —'

Nanina started up, and confronted the priest boldly for the first time since he had entered the room.

'Supposing' she exclaimed, her cheeks beginning to redden, and her dark blue eyes flashing suddenly through her tears. 'Supposing! Father Rocco, Fabio would never deceive me and I would die here at your feet, rather than doubt the least word he said to me!'

The priest signed to her quietly to return to the stool. 'I never suspected the child had so much spirit in her,' he thought to himself.

'I would die,' repeated Nanina, in a voice that began to falter now. 'I would die rather than doubt him.'

'I will not ask you to doubt him,' said Father Rocco, gently; 'and I will believe in him myself as firmly as you do. Let us suppose, my child, that you have learnt patiently all the many things of which you are now ignorant, and which it is necessary for a lady to know. Let us suppose that Signor Fabio has really violated all the laws that govern people in his high station, and has taken you to him publicly as his wife. You would be happy then, Nanina; but would he? He has no father or mother to control him, it is true; but he has friends – many friends and intimates in his own rank – proud, heartless people, who know nothing of your worth and goodness; who, hearing of your low birth, would look on you, and on your husband too, my child, with contempt. He has not your patience and fortitude. Think how bitter it would be for him to bear that contempt – to see you shunned by proud women, and carelessly pitied or patronized by insolent men. Yet all this, and more, he would have to endure, or else to quit the world he has lived in from his boyhood – the world he was born to live in. You love him, I know —'

Nanina's tears burst out afresh 'O, how dearly! – how dearly!' she murmured.

'Yes, you love him dearly,' continued the priest; 'but would all your love compensate him for everything else that he must lose? It might, at first; but there would come a time when the world would assert its influence over him again; when he would feel a want which you could not supply – a weariness which you could not solace. Think of his life, then, and of yours. Think of the first day when the first secret doubt whether he had done rightly in marrying you would steal into his mind. We are not masters of all our impulses. The lightest spirits have their moments of irresistible depression; the bravest hearts are not always superior to doubt. My child, my child, the world is strong, the pride of rank is rooted deep, and the human will is frail at best! Be warned! For your own sake and for Fabio's, be warned in time'

Nanina stretched out her hands towards the priest in despair.

'O, Father Rocco! Father Rocco!' she cried; 'why did you not tell me this before?'

'Because, my child, I only knew of the necessity for telling you, to-day. But it is not too late, it is never too late, to do a good action. You love Fabio, Nanina? Will you prove that love by making a great sacrifice for his good?'

'I would die for his good!'

'Will you nobly cure him of a passion which will be his ruin, if not yours, by leaving Pisa tomorrow?'

'Leave Pisa!' exclaimed Nanina. Her face grew deadly pale: she rose and moved back a step or two from the priest.

Listen to me,' pursued Father Rocco, 'I have heard your complain that you could not get regular employment at needlework. You shall have that employment, if you will go with me – you and your little sister too, of course – to Florence to-morrow.'

'I promised Fabio to go to the studio,' began Nanina, affrightedly. 'I promised to go at ten o'clock. How can I —

She stopped suddenly, as if her breath were failing her.

'I myself will take you and your sister to Florence,' said Father Rocco, without noticing the interruption. 'I will place you under the care of a lady who will be as kind as a mother to you both. I will answer for your getting such work to do as will enable you to keep yourself honestly and independently; and I will undertake, if you do not like your life at Florence, to bring you back to Pisa after a lapse of three months only. Three months, Nanina. It is not a long exile.'

'Fabio! Fabio!' cried the girl, sinking again on the seat, and hiding her face.

'It is for his good,' said Father Rocco, calmly; 'for Fabio's good, remember.'

'What would he think of me if I went away? O, if I had but learnt to write. If I could only write Fabio a letter!'

'Am I not to be depended on to explain to him all that he ought to know?'

'How can I go away from him? O, Father Rocco, how can you ask me to go away from him?'

'I will ask you to do nothing hastily. I will leave you till to-morrow morning to decide. At nine o'clock I shall be in the street; and I will not even so much as enter this house, unless I know beforehand that you have resolved to follow my advise. Give me a sign from your window. If I see you wave your white mantilla out of it, I shall know that you have taken the noble resolution to save Fabio and to save yourself. I will say no more, my child; for, unless I am grievously mistaken in you, I have already said enough.'

He went out, leaving her still weeping bitterly.

Not far from the house, he met La Biondella and the dog on their way back. The little girl stopped to report to him the safe delivery of her dinner-mats; but he passed on quickly with a nod and a smile. His interview with Nanina had left some influence behind it which unfitted him just then for the occupation of talking to a child.

Nearly half-an hour before nine o'clock on the following morning, Father Rocco set forth for the street in which Nanina lived. On his way thither he overtook a dog walking lazily a few paced a-head in the road-way; and saw, at the same time, an elegantly dressed lady advancing towards him. The dog stopped suspiciously as she approached, and growled and showed his teeth when she passed him. The lady, on her side, uttered an exclamation of disgust; but did not seem to be either astonished or frightened by the animal's threatening attitude. Father Rocco looked after her with some curiosity, as she walked by him. She was a handsome woman, and he admired her courage. 'I know that growling brute well enough,' he said to himself, 'but who can the lady be?'

The dog was Scarammuccia, returning from one of his marauding expeditions. The lady was Brigida, on her way to Luca Lomi's studio.

Some minutes before nine o'clock, the priest took his post in the street, opposite Nanina's window. It was open; but neither she nor her little sister appeared at it. He looked up anxiously as the church-clocks struck the hour; but there was no sign for a minute or so after they were all silent. 'Is she hesitating still?' said Father Rocco to himself.

Just as the words passed his lips, the white mantilla waved out of the window.

PART SECOND

CHAPTER I

Even the masterstoke of replacing the treacherous Italian forewoman by a French dressmaker, engaged direct from Paris, did not at first avail to eleviate the great Grifoni establishment above the reach of minor calamities. Mademoiselle Virginie had not occupied her new situation at Pisa quite a week, before she fell ill. All sorts of reports were circulated as to the cause of this illness; and the Demoiselle Grifoni even went so far as to suggest that the health of the new forewoman had fallen a sacrifice to some nefarious practices of the chemical sort, on the part of her rival in the trade. But, however the misfortune had been produced, it was a fact that Mademoiselle Virginie was certainly very ill, and another fact, that the doctor insisted on her being sent to the Baths of Lucca as soon as she could be moved from her bed.

Fortunately for the Demoiselle Griffoni, the Frenchwoman had succeeded in producing three specimens of her art before her health broke down. They compromised the evening dress of yellow brocaded silk, to which she had devoted herself on the morning when she first assumed her duties at Pisa; a black cloak and hood of an entirely new shape; and an irresistibly fascinating dressing-gown, said to have been first brought into fashion by the princesses of the blood-royal of France. These articles of costume, on being exhibited in the show-room, electrified the ladies of Pisa; and orders from all sides flowed in immediately on the Grifoni establishment. They were, of course, easily executed by the inferior workwomen, from the specimen-designs of the French dressmaker. So that the illness of Mademoiselle Virginie, though it might cause her mistress some temporary inconvenience, was, after all, productive of no absolute loss.

Two months at the Baths of Lucca restored the new

forewoman to health. She returned to Pisa, and resumed her place in the private work-room. Once re-established there, she discovered that an important change had taken place during her absence. Her friend and assistant, Brigida, had resigned her situation. All inquiries made of the Demoiselle Grifoni only elicited one answer: the missing workwoman had abruptly left her place at five minutes' warning, and had departed without confiding to any one what she thought of doing, or whether she intended to turn her steps.

Months elapsed. The new year came; but no explanatory letter arrived from Brigida. The spring season passed off, with all its accompaniments of dress-making and dress-buying; but still there was no news of her. The first anniversary of Mademoiselle Virginie's engagement with the Demoiselle Grifoni came round; and then, at last, a note arrived, stating that Brigida had returned to Pisa, and that, if the French forewoman would send an answer, mentioning where her private lodgings were, she would visit her old friend that evening after business-hours. The information was gladly enough given; and punctually to the appointed time, Brigida arrived in Mademoiselle Virginie's little sitting-room.

Advancing with her usual indolent stateliness of gait, the Italian asked after her friend's health as coolly, and sat down in the nearest chair as carelessly, as if they had not been separated for more than a few days. Mademoiselle Virginie laughed in her loveliest manner, and raised her mobile French eye-brows in sprightly astonishment.

'Well, Brigida!' she exclaimed, 'they certainly did you no injustice when they nicknamed you "Care-for-Nothing," in old Grifoni's work-room. Where have you been? Why have you never written to me?'

'I had nothing particular to write about; and besides, I always intended to come back to Pisa and see you,' answered Brigida, leaning back luxuriously in her chair.

'But where have you been for nearly a whole year past? In Italy?

'No; at Paris. You know I can sing? – not very well; but I have a voice, and most French-women (excuse the impertinence) have none. I met with a friend, a got introduced to a manager; and I have been singing at the theatre – not the great parts, only

only the second. Your amiable countrywomen could not screech me down on the stage, but they intrigued against me successfully behind the scenes. In short, I quarrelled with our principal lady, quarrelled with the manager, quarrelled with my friend; and here I am back at Pisa, with a little money saved in my pocket, and no great notion what I am to do next.'

'Back at Pisa! Why did you leave it?'

Brigida's eyes began to lose their indolent expression. She sat up suddenly in her chair, and set one of her hands heavily on a little table by her side.

'Why?' she repeated, 'Because when I find the game going against me, I prefer giving it up at once to waiting to be beaten.'

'Ah! you refer to that last year's project of yours for making your fortune among the sculptors. I should like to hear how it was you failed with the wealthy young amateur. Remember that I fell ill before you had any news to give me. Your absence when I returned from Luca, and, almost immediately afterwards, the marriage of your intended conquest to the sculptor's daughter, proved to me, of course, that you must have failed. But I never heard how. I know nothing at this moment but the bare fact that Maddalena Lomi won the prize.'

'Tell me first, do she and her husband live together happily?'

'There are no stories of their disagreeing. She has dresses, horses, carriages, a negro page, the smallest lap-dog in Italy – in short, all the luxuries that a woman can want; and a child, by-the-by, into the bargain.'

'A child!'

Yes; a child, born little more than a week ago.'

'Not a boy, I hope?'

'No; a girl.'

'I am glad of that. Those rich people always want the first born to be an heir. They will both be disappointed. I am glad of that!'

'Mercy on us, Brigida, how fierce you look!'

'Do I? It's likely enough. I hate Fabio d'Ascoli and Maddalena Lomi – singly as man and woman, doubly as man and wife. Stop! I'll tell you what you want to know directly. Only answer me another question or two first. Have you heard anything about her health?'

'How should I hear? Dressmakers can't inquire at the doors of the nobility.'

'True. Now one last question: That little simpleton, Nanina?'

'I have never seen or heard anything of her. She can't be at Pisa, or she would have called at our place for work.'

'Ah! I need not have asked about her if I had thought a moment beforehand. Father Rocco would be sure to keep her out of Fabio's sight for his niece's sake.'

'What, he really loved that 'thread-paper of a girl,' as you called her?'

'Better than fifty such wives as he has got now! I was in the studio the morning he was told of her departure from Pisa. A letter was privately given to him, telling him that the girl had left the place out of a feeling of honour, and had hidden herself beyond the possibility of discovery to prevent him from compromising himself with all his friends by marrying her. Naturally enough he would not believe that this was her own doing; and, naturally enough also, when Father Rocco was sent for, and was not to be found, he suspected the priest of being at the bottom of the business. I never saw a man in such a fury of despair and rage before. He swore that he would have all Italy searched for the girl, that he would be the death of the priest, and that he would never enter Luca Lomi's studio again —'

'And, as to this last particular, of course being a man, he failed to keep his word?'

'Of course. At that first visit of mine to the studio I discovered two things. The first, as I said, that Fabio was really in love with the girl – the second, that Maddalena Lomi was really in love with him. You may suppose I looked at her attentively while the disturbance was going on, and while no-body's notice was directed on me. All women are vain, I know, but vanity never blinded my eyes. I saw directly that I had but one superiority over her ——my figure. She was my height, but not well made. She had hair as dark and as glossy as mine; eyes as bright and as black as mine; and the rest of her face better than mine. My nose is coarse, my lips are too thick, and my upper lip overhangs my under too far. She had none of those personal faults; and, as for capacity, she managed the young fool in his passion, as well as I could have managed him in her place.'

'How?'

'She stood silent, with downcast eyes and a distressed look, all the time he was raving up and down the studio. She must have hated the girl, and been rejoicing at her disappearance; but she never showed it. "You would be an awkward rival," (I thought to myself) "even to a handsomer woman than I am". However, I determined not to despair too soon, and made up my mind to follow my plan just as if the accident of the girl's disappearance had never occurred. I smoothed down the master sculptor easily enough – flattering him about his reputation, assuring him that the works of Luca Lomi had been the objects of my adoration since childhood, telling him that I had heard of his difficulty in finding a model to complete his Minerva from, and offering myself (if he thought me worthy) for the honour – laying great stress on that word – for the honour of sitting to him. I don't know whether he was altogether deceived by what I told him; but he was sharp enough to see that I really could be of use, and he accepted my offer with a profusion of compliments. We parted, having arranged that I was to give him a first sitting in a week's time.'

'Why put it off so long?'

'To allow our young gentleman time to cool down and return to the studio, to be sure. What was the use of my being there while he was away?'

'Yes, yes – I forgot. And how long was it before he came back?'

'I had allowed him more time than enough. When I had given my first sitting, I saw him in the studio, and heard it was his second visit there since the day of the girl's disappearance. Those very violent men are always changeable and irresolute.'

'Had he made no attempt, then, to discover Nanina?'

'Oh, yes! He had searched for her himself, and had set others searching for her, but to no purpose. Four days of perpetual disappointment had been enough to bring him to his senses. Luca Lomi had written him a peace-making letter, asking what harm he or his daughter had done, even supposing Father Rocco was to blame. Maddalena Lomi had met him in the street, and had looked resignedly away from him, as if she expected him to pass her. In short, they had awakened his sense of justice and his good nature (you see I can impartially give him his due), and they had got him back. He was silent and sentimental enough at first, and shockingly sulky and savage with the priest —'

'I wonder Father Rocco ventured within his reach.'

'Father Rocco is not a man to be daunted or defeated by anybody, I can tell you. The same day on which Fabio came back to the studio, he returned to it. Beyond boldly declaring that he thought Nanina had done quite right, and had acted like a good and virtuous girl, he would say nothing about her or her disappearance. It was quite useless to ask him questions – he denied that any one had a right to put them. Threatening, entreating, flattering – all modes of appeal were thrown away on him. Ah, my dear! depend upon it, the cleverest and politest man in Pisa, the most dangerous to an enemy and the most delightful to a friend, is Father Rocco. The rest of them, when I began to play my cards a little too openly, behaved with brutal rudeness to me. Father Rocco, from first to last, treated me like a lady. Sincere or not, I don't care – he treated me like a lady when the others treated me like —'

'There! there! don't get hot about it now. Tell me instead how you made your first approaches to the young gentleman whom you talk of so contemptuously as Fabio.'

'As it turned out, in the worst possible way. First, of course, I made sure of interesting him in me by telling him that I had known Nanina. So far it was all well enough. My next object was to persuade him that she could never have gone away if she had truly loved him alone; and that he must have had some fortunate rival in her own rank of life, to whom she had sacrificed him, after gratifying her vanity for a time by bringing a young nobleman to her feet. I had, as you will easily imagine, difficulty enough in making him take this view of Nanina's flight. His pride and his love for the girl were both concerned in refusing to admit the truth of my suggestion. At last I succeeded. I brought him to that state of ruffled vanity and fretful self-assertion in which it is easiest to work on a man's feelings – in which a man's own wounded pride makes the best pitfalls to catch him in. I brought him, I say, to that state, and then – *she* stepped in, and profited by what I had done. Is it wonderful now that I rejoice in her disappointments; that I should be glad to hear any ill thing of her that any one could tell me?'

'But how did she first get the advantage of you?'

'If I had found out, she would never have succeeded where I failed. All I know is, that she had more opportunities of seeing him than I, and that she used them cunningly enough even to deceive me. While I thought I was gaining ground with Fabio, I was actually losing it. My first suspicions were excited by a change in Luca Lomi's conduct towards me. He grew cold, neglectful – at last absolutely rude. I was resolved not to see this; but accident soon obliged me to open my eyes. One morning I heard Fabio and Maddalena talking of me when they imagined I had left the studio. I can't repeat their words, especially hers. The blood flies into my head, and the cold catches me at the heart, when I only think of them. It will be enough if I tell you that he laughed at me, and that she —'

'Hush! not so loud. There are other people lodging in the house. Never mind about telling me what you heard; it only irritates you to no purpose. I can guess that they had discovered —'

'Through her, remember – all through her!'

'Yes, yes, I understand. They had discovered a great deal more than you ever intended them to know, and all through her.'

'But for the priest, Virginie, I should have been openly insulted and driven from their doors. He had insisted on their behaving with decent civility towards me. They said he was afraid of me, and laughed at the notion of his trying to make them afraid too. That was the last thing I heard. The fury I was in, and the necessity of keeping it down, almost suffocated me. I turned round, to leave the place for ever, when who should I see, standing close behind me, but Father Rocco. He must have discovered in my face that I knew all; but he took no notice of it. He only asked, in his usual quiet, polite way, if I was looking for anything I had lost, and if he could help me. I managed to thank him, and to get to the door. He opened it for me respectfully, and bowed – he treated me like a lady to the last! It was evening when I left the studio in that way. The next morning I threw up my situation, and turned my back on Pisa. Now you know everything.'

'Did you hear of the marriage? or did you only assume from what you knew that it would take place?'

'I heard of it about six months ago. A man came to sing in the chorus of our theatre, who had been employed some time before at the grand concert given on the occasion of the marriage. But let us drop the subject now. I am in a fever already with talking of it. You are in a bad situation here, my dear – I declare your room is almost stifling.'

'Shall I open the other window?'

'No: let us go out and get a breath of air by the river-side. Come! take your hood and fan – it is getting dark – nobody will see us, and we can come back here, if you like, in half an hour.'

Mademoiselle Virginie acceded to her friend's wish rather reluctantly. They walked towards the river. The sun was down, and the sudden night of Italy was gathering fast. Although Brigida did not say another word on the subject of Fabio or his wife, she led the way to the bank of the Arno, on which the young nobleman's palace stood.

Just as they got near the great door of entrance, a sedan-chair, approaching in the opposite direction, was set down before it; and a footman, after a moment's conference with a lady inside the chair, advanced to the porter's lodge in the court-yard. Leaving her friend to go on, Brigida slipped in after the servant by the open wicket, and concealed herself in the shadow cast by the great closed gates.

'The Marchesa Melani to inquire how the Countess d'Ascoli and the infant are this evening,' said the footman.

'My mistress has not changed at all for the better since the morning,' answered the porter. 'The child is doing quite well.'

The footman went back to the sedan-chair; then returned to the porter's lodge.

'The Marchesa desires me to ask if fresh medical advice has been sent for?' he said.

'Another doctor has arrived from Florence to-day,' replied the porter.

Mademoiselle Virginie, missing her friend suddenly, turned back towards the place to look after her, and was rather surprised to see Brigida slip out of the wicket-gate. There were two oil-lamps burning on the pillars outside the door-way, and their light glancing on the Italian's face, as she passed under them, showed that she was smiling.

CHAPTER II

While the Marchesa Melani was making inquiries at the gate of
the place, Fabio was sitting alone in the apartment which his
wife usually occupied when she was in health. It was her
favourite room, and had been prettily decorated, by her own
desire, with hangings in yellow satin, and furniture of the
same colour. Fabio was now waiting in it to hear the report of
the doctors after their evening visit.

Although Maddalena Lomi had not been his first love, and
although he had married her under circumstances which are
generally and rightly considered to afford few chances of
lasting happiness in wedded life, still they had lived together
through the one year of their union tranquilly, if not fondly.
She had moulded herself wisely to his peculiar humours, had
made the most of his easy disposition, and, when her quick
temper had got the better of her, had seldom hesitated in her
cooler moments to acknowledge that she had been wrong. She
had been extravagant, it is true, and had irritated him by fits of
unreasonable jealousy; but these were faults not to be thought
of now. He could only remember that she was the mother of
his child, and that she lay ill but two rooms away from him –
dangerously ill, as the doctors had unwillingly confessed on
that very day.

The darkness was closing upon him, and he took up the
hand-bell to ring for lights. When the servant entered there
was genuine sorrow in his face, genuine anxiety in his voice,
as he inquired for news from the sick-room. The man only
answered that his mistress was still asleep; and then withdrew,
after first leaving a sealed letter on the table by his master's
side. Fabio summoned him back into the room, and asked
when the letter had arrived. He replied that it had been
delivered at the place two days' since, and that he had
observed it lying unopened on a desk in his master's study.

Left alone again, Fabio remembered that the letter had

44

arrived at the time when the first dangerous symptoms of his wife's illness had declared themselves, and that he had thrown it aside after observing the address to be in a handwriting unknown to him. In his present state of suspense, any occupation was better than sitting idle. So he took up the letter with a sigh, broke the seal, and turned inquiringly to the name signed at the end.

It was 'NANINA.'

He started, and changed colour, 'A letter from her,' he whispered to himself. 'Why does it come at such a time as this?'

His face grew paler, and the letter trembled in his fingers. Those superstitious feelings which he had ascribed to the nursery influences of his childhood, when Father Rocco charged him with them in the studio, seemed to be overcoming him now. He hesitated and listened anxiously in the direction of his wife's room before reading the letter. Was its arrival ominous of good or evil! That was the thought in his heart as he drew the lamp near to him and looked at the first lines.

'Am I wrong in writing to you?' (the letter began abruptly.) 'If I am, you have but to throw this little leaf of paper into the fire, and to think no more of it, after it is burnt up and gone. I can never reproach you for treating my letter in that way; for we are never likely to meet again.

'Why did I go away? – Only to save you from the consequences of marrying a poor girl who was not fit to become your wife. It almost broke my heart to leave you; for I had nothing to keep up my courage but the remembrance that I was going away for your sake. I had to think of that, morning and night – to think of it always, or I am afraid I should have faltered in my resolution, and have gone back to Pisa, I longed so much at first to see you once more – only to tell you that Nanina was not heartless and ungrateful, and that you might pity her and think kindly of her, though you might love her no longer.

'Only to tell you that! If I had been a lady I might have told it to you in a letter; but I had never learnt to write, and I could not prevail on myself to get others to take the pen for me. All I could do was to learn secretly how to write with my own hand. It was long, long work; but the uppermost thought in my heart was always the thought of justifying myself to you, and that made me patient and persevering. I learnt, at last, to write so as not to be ashamed of myself, or to make you ashamed of me. I began a letter – my first letter to you – but I heard of your marriage before it was done, and then I had to tear the paper up, and put the pen down again.

'I had no right to come between you and your wife even with so little a thing as a letter – I had no right to do anything but hope and pray for your happiness. Are you happy? I am sure you ought to be; for how can your wife help loving you?'

'It is very hard for me to explain why I have ventured on writing now, and yet I can't think that I am doing wrong. I heard a few days ago (for I have a friend at Pisa who keeps me informed, by my own desire, of all the pleasant changes in your life) – I heard of your child being born; and I thought myself, after that, justified at last in writing to you. No letter from me, at such a time as this, can rob your child's mother of so much as a thought of yours that is due to her. Thus, at least, it seems to me. I wish so well to your child, that I cannot surely be doing wrong in writing these lines.'

'I have said already what I wanted to say – what I have been longing to say for a whole year past. I have told you why I left Pisa; and have perhaps persuaded you that I have gone through some suffering, and borne some heartaches for your sake. Have I more to write? Only a word or two to tell you that I am earning my bread, as I always wished to earn it, quietly at home – at least, at what I must call home now. I am living with reputable people, and I want for nothing. La Biondella has grown very much, she would hardly be obliged to get on your knee to kiss you now; and she can plait her dinner-mats faster and more neatly than ever. Our old dog is with us, and has learnt two new tricks; but you can't be expected to remember him, although you were the only stranger I ever saw him take kindly to at first.'

'It is time I finished. If you have read this letter through to the end, I am sure you will excuse me, if I have written badly. There is no date to it, because I feel that it is safest and best for both of us, that you should know nothing of where I am living. I bless you and pray for you, and bid you affectionately farewell. If You can think of me as a sister, think of me sometimes still.'

Fabio sighed bitterly while he read the letter. 'Why,' he whispered to himself, 'why does it come at such a time as this, when I cannot, dare not think of her?' As he slowly folded the letter up, the tears came into his eyes, and he half raised the paper to his lips. At the same moment, some one knocked at the door of the room. He started, and felt himself changing colour guiltily, as one of his servants entered.

'My mistress is awake,' the man said, with a very grave face, and a very constrained manner; 'and the gentlemen in attendance desire me to say—'

He was interrupted, before he could give his message, by one of the medical men, who had followed him into the room.

'I wish I had better news to communicate,' began the doctor gently.

'She is worse, then?' said Fabio, sinking back into the chair from which he had risen the moment before.

'She has awakened weaker instead of stronger after her sleep,' returned the doctor, evasively. 'I never like to give up all hope, till the very last, but—'

'It is cruel not to be candid with him,' interposed another voice – the voice of the doctor from Florence, who had just entered the room. 'Strengthen yourself to bear the worst,' he continued addressing himself to Fabio. 'She is dying. Can you compose yourself enough to go to her bedside!'

Pale and speechless, Fabio rose from his chair, and made a sign in the affirmative. He trembled so, that the doctor who had first spoken was obliged to lead him out of the room.

'Your mistress has some near relations in Pisa, has she not?' said the doctor from Florence, appealing to the servant who waited near him.

'Her father, sir, Signor Luca Lomi; and her uncle, Father Rocco,' answered the man. 'They were here all through the day, until my mistress fell asleep.'

'Do you know where to find them now?'

'Signor Luca told me he should be at his studio; and Father Rocco said, I might find him at his lodgings.'

'Send for them both directly. Stay! who is your mistress's

confessor? He ought to be summoned with loss of time.'

'My mistress's confessor is Father Rocco, sir.'

'Very well – send, or go yourself, at once. Even minutes may be of importance, now.' Saying this, the doctor turned away, and sat down to wait for any last demands on his services, in the chair which Fabio had just left.

CHAPTER III

Before the servant could get to the priest's lodgings a visitor had applied there for admission, and had been immediately received by Father Rocco himself. This favoured guest was a little man, very sprucely and neatly dressed, and oppressively polite in his manner. He bowed when he first sat down, he bowed when he answered the usual inquiries about his health, and he bowed for the third time, when Father Rocco asked what had brought him from Florence.

'Rather an awkward business,' replied the little man, recovering himself uneasily after his third bow.

'The dressmaker, named Nanina, whom you placed under my wife's protection, about a year ago —'

'What of her?' inquired the priest eagerly.

'I regret to say she has left us, with her child-sister, and their very disagreeable dog, that growls at everybody.'

'When did they go?'

'Only yesterday. I came here at once to tell you, as you were so very particular in recommending us to take care of her. It is not our fault that she has gone. My wife was kindness itself to her, and I always treated her like a duchess. I bought dinner-mats of her sister; I even put up with the thieving and growling of the disagreeable dog —'

'Where have they gone to? Have you found out that?'

'I have found out, by application at the passport office, that they have not left Florence – but what particular part of the city they have removed to, I have not yet had time to discover.'

'And pray why did they leave you, in the first place? Nanina is not a girl to do anything without a reason. She must have had some cause for going away. What was it?'

The little man hesitated, and made a fourth bow.

'You remember your private instructions to my wife and myself, when you first brought Nanina to our house?' he said,

49

looking away rather uneasily while he spoke.

'Yes; you were to watch her, but to take care that she did not suspect you. It was just possible, at that time, that she might try to get back to Pisa without my knowing it; and everything depended on her remaining at Florence. I think, now, that I did wrong to distrust her; but it was of the last importance to provide against all possibilities, and to abstain from putting too much faith in my own good opinion of the girl. For these reasons, I certainly did instruct you to watch her privately. So far, you are quite right; and I have nothing to complain of. Go on.'

'You remember,' resumed the little man, 'that the first consequence of our following your instructions was a discovery (which we immediately communicated to you) that she was secretly learning to write?'

'Yes; and I also remember sending you word not to show that you knew what she was doing; but to wait and see if she turned her knowledge of writing to account, and took or sent any letters to the post. You informed me in your regular monthly report, that she never did anything of the kind.'

'Never, until three days ago: and then she was traced from her room in my house to the post-office with a letter, which she dropped into the box.'

'And the address of which you discovered before she took it from your house?'

'Unfortunately I did not,' answered the little man, reddening and looking askance at the priest, as if he expected to receive a severe reprimand.

But Father Rocco said nothing. He was thinking. Who could she have written to? If to Fabio, why should she have waited for months and months, after she had learnt how to use her pen, before sending him a letter? If not to Fabio, to what other person could she have written?

'I regret not discovering the address – regret it most deeply,' said the little man, with a low bow of apology.

'It is too late for regret,' said Father Rocco, coldly. 'Tell me how she came to leave your house; I have not heard that yet. Be as brief as you can. I expect to be called every moment to the bedside of a near and dear relation, who is suffering from severe illness. You shall have all my attention; but you must ask it for as short a time as possible.'

'I will be briefness itself. In the first place, you must know that I have – or rather had – an idle, unscrupulous rascal of an apprentice in my business.'

The priest pursed up his mouth contemptuously.

'In the second place, this same good-for-nothing fellow had the impertinence to fall in love with Nanina.'

Father Rocco started, and listened eagerly.

'But I must do the girl justice to say that she never gave him the slightest encouragement; and that, whenever he ventured to speak to her, she always quietly but very decidedly repelled him.'

'A good girl!' said Father Rocco. 'I always said she was a good girl. It was a mistake on my part ever to have distrusted her.'

'Among the other offences,' continued the little man, 'of which I now find my scoundrel of an apprentice to have been guilty, was the enormity of picking the lock of my desk, and prying into my private papers.'

'You ought not to have had any. Private papers should always be burnt papers.'

'They shall be for the future; I will take good care of that.'

'Were any of my letters to you about Nanina among these private papers?'

'Unfortunately, there were. Pray, pray, excuse my want of caution this time. It shall never happen again.'

'Go on. Such imprudence as yours can never be excused; it can only be provided against for the future. I suppose the apprentice showed my letters to the girl?'

'I infer as much; though why he should do so —'

'Simpleton! Did you not say that he was in love with her (as you term it), and that he got no encouragement?'

'Yes: I said that – and I know it to be true.'

'Well! Was it not his interest, being unable to make any impression on the girl's fancy, to establish some claim to her gratitude; and try if he could not win her that way? By showing her my letters, he would make her indebted to him for knowing that she was watched in your house. But this is not the matter in question now. You say you infer that she had seen my letters. On what grounds?'

'On the strength of this bit of paper,' answered the little man, ruefully producing a note from his pocket. 'She must have had your letters shown to her soon after putting her own letter into the post. For, on the evening of the same day, when I went up into her room, I found that she and her sister and the disagreeable dog had all gone, and observed this note laid on the table.'

Father Rocco took the note, and read these lines:–

'I have just discovered that I have been watched and suspected ever since my stay under your roof. It is impossible that I can remain another night in the house of a spy. I go with my sister. We owe you nothing, and we are free to live honestly where we please. If you see Father Rocco, tell him that I can forgive his distrust of me, but that I can never forget it. I, who had full faith in him, had a right to expect that he should have full faith in me. It was always an encouragement to me to think of him as a father and a friend. I have lost that encouragement for ever – and it was the last I had left to me!

'NANINA.'

The priest rose from his seat as he handed the note back, and the visitor immediately followed his example.

'We must remedy this misfortune as we best may,' he said with a sigh. 'Are you ready to go back to Florence to-morrow?'

The little man bowed again.

'Find out where she is, and ascertain if she wants for anything, and if she is living in a safe place. Say nothing about me, and make no attempt to induce her to return to your house. Simply let me know what you discover. The poor child has a spirit that no ordinary people would suspect in her. She must be soothed and treated tenderly, and we shall manage her yet. No mistakes, mind, this time! Do just what I tell you, and do no more. Have you anything else to say to me?'

The little man shook his head and shrugged his shoulders.

'Good-night, then,' said the priest.

'Good-night,' said the little man, slipping through the door that was held open for him with the politest alacrity.

'This is vexatious,' said Father Rocco, taking a turn or two in the study after his visitor had gone. 'It was bad to have done the child an injustice – it is worse to have been found out. There is nothing for it now but to wait till I know where she is. I like her, and I like that note she left behind her. It is bravely, delicately, and honestly written – a good girl – a very good girl indeed!'

He walked to the window, breathed the fresh air for a few moments, and quietly dismissed the subject from his mind. When he returned to his table, he had no thoughts for any one but his sick niece.

'It seems strange,' he said, 'that I have had no message about her yet. Perhaps Luca has heard something. It may be well if I go to the studio at once to find out.'

He took up his hat and went to the door. Just as he opened it, Fabio's servant confronted him on the threshold.

'I am sent to summon you to the palace,' said the man. 'The doctors have given up all hope.'

Father Rocco turned deadly pale, and drew back a step. 'Have you told my brother of this?' he asked.

'I was just on my way to the studio,' answered the servant.

'I will go there instead of you, and break the bad news to him,' said the priest.

They descended the stairs in silence. Just as they were about to separate at the street door, Farther Rocco stopped the servant.

'How is the child?' he asked, with such sudden eagerness and impatience that the man looked quite startled as he answered that the child was perfectly well.

'There is some consolation in that,' said Father Rocco, walking away, and speaking partly to the servant, partly to himself. 'My caution has misled me,' he continued, pausing thoughtfully when he was left alone in the roadway. 'I should have risked using the mother's influence sooner to procure the righteous restitution. All hope of compassing it now rests on the life of the child. Infant as she is, her father's ill-gotten wealth may yet be gathered back to the church by her hands.'

He proceeded rapidly on his way to the studio, until he reached the river-side and drew close to the bridge which it was necessary to cross in order to get to his brother's house.

Here he stopped abruptly, as if struck by a sudden idea. The moon had just risen, and her light, streaming across the river, fell full upon his face as he stood by the parapet wall that led up to the bridge. He was so lost in thought that he did not hear the conversation of two ladies who were advancing along the pathway close behind him. As they brushed by him, the taller of the two turned round and looked back at his face.

'Father Rocco!' exclaimed the lady, stopping.

'Donna Brigida!' cried the priest, looking surprised at first, but recovering himself directly, and bowing with his usual quiet politeness. 'Pardon me if I thank you for honouring me by renewing our acquaintance, and then pass on to my brother's studio. A heavy affliction is likely to befall us, and I go to prepare him for it.'

You refer to the dangerous illness of your niece?' said Brigida. 'I heard of it this evening. Let us hope that your fears are exaggerated, and that we may yet meet under less distressing circumstances. I have no present intention of leaving Pisa for some time, and I shall always be glad to thank Father Rocco for the politeness and consideration which he showed to me, under delicate circumstances, a year ago.'

With these words she curtseyed deferentially, and moved away to rejoin her friend. The priest observed that Mademoiselle Virginie lingered rather near, as if anxious to catch a few words of the conversation between Brigida and himself. Seeing this, he, in his turn, listened as the two women slowly walked away together, and heard the Italian say to her companion —

'Virginie, I will lay you the price of a new dress that Fabio d'Ascoli marries again.'

Father Rocco started when she said those words as if he had trodden on fire.

'My thought!' he whispered nervously to himself. 'My thought at the moment when she spoke to me! Marry again? Another wife, over whom I should have no influence! Other children, whose education would not be confided to me! What would become, then, of the restitution that I have hoped for, wrought for, prayed for?'

He stopped, and looked fixedly at the sky above him. The bridge was deserted. His black figure rose up erect, motionless, and spectral, with the white still light falling solemnly all around it. Standing so for some minutes, his first movement was to drop his hand angrily on the parapet of the bridge. He then turned round slowly in the direction by which the two women had walked away.

'Donna Brigida,' he said, 'I will lay you the price of fifty new dresses that Fabio d'Ascoli never marries again!'

He set his face once more towards the studio, and walked on without stopping until he arrived at the master-sculptor's door.

'Marries again?' he thought to himself as he rang the bell: 'Donna Brigida, was your first failure not enough for you? Are you going to try a second time?'

Luca Lomi himself opened the door. He drew Father Rocco hurriedly into the studio, towards a single lamp burning on a stand near the partition between the two rooms.

'Have you heard any thing of our poor child?' he asked. 'Tell me the truth! – tell me the truth at once!'

'Hush! compose yourself, I have heard,' said Father Rocco, in low, mournful tones.

Luca tightened his hold on the priest's arm, and looked into his face with breathless, speechless eagerness.

'Compose yourself,' repeated Father Rocco. 'Compose yourself to hear the worst. My poor Luca, the doctors have given up all hope.'

Luca dropped his brother's arm with a groan of despair. 'Oh, Maddalena! my child – my only child!'

Reiterating these words again and again, he leaned his head against the partition and burst into tears. Sordid and coarse as his nature was, he really loved his daughter. All the heart he had was in his statues and in her.

After the first burst of his grief was exhausted, he was recalled to himself by a sensation as if some change had taken place in the lighting of the studio. He looked up directly, and dimly discerned the priest standing far down at the end of the room nearest the door, with the lamp in his hand, eagerly looking at something.

'Rocco!' he exclaimed – 'Rocco, why have you taken the lamp away? What are you doing there?'

There was no movement and no answer. Luca advanced a step or two, and called again – 'Rocco, what are you doing there?'

The priest heard this time, and came suddenly towards his brother with the lamp in his hand – so suddenly that Luca started.

'What is it?' he asked, in astonishment. 'Gracious God, Rocco, how pale you are!'

Still the priest never said a word. He put the lamp down on the nearest table. Luca observed that his hand shook. He had never seen his brother violently agitated before. When Rocco had announced, but a few minutes ago, that Maddalena's life was despaired of, it was in a voice which, though sorrowful, was perfectly calm. What was the meaning of this sudden panic – this strange, silent terror?'

The priest observed that his brother was looking at him earnestly. 'Come!' he said in a faint whisper – 'come to her bedside; we have no time to lose. Get your hat, and leave it to me to put out the lamp.'

He hurriedly extinguished the light while he spoke. They went down the studio side by side towards the door. The moonlight streamed through the window full on the place where the priest had been standing alone with the lamp in his hand. As they passed it, Luca felt his brother tremble, and saw him turn away his head.

*   *   *   *

Two hours later, Fabio d'Ascoli and his wife were separated in this world for ever; and the servants of the palace were anticipating in whispers the order of their mistress's funeral-procession at the burial-ground of the Campo Santo.

PART THIRD

CHAPTER I

About eight months after the Countess d'Ascoli had been laid in her grave in the Campo Santo, two reports were circulated through the gay world of Pisa, which excited curiosity and awakened expectation everywhere.

The first report announced that a grand masked ball was to be given at the Melani Palace, to celebrate the day on which the heir of the house attained his majority. All the friends of the family were delighted at the prospect of this festival; for the old Marquis Melani had the reputation of being one of the most hospitable, and, at the same time, one of the most eccentric men in Pisa. Every one expected, therefore, that he would secure for the entertainment of his guests, if he really gave the ball, the most whimsical novelties in the way of masks, dances, and amusements generally, that had ever been seen.

The second report was, that the rich widower, Fabio d'Ascoli, was on the point of returning to Pisa, after having improved his health and spirits by travelling in foreign countries; and that he might be expected to appear again in society, for the first time since the death of his wife, at the masked ball which was to be given in the Melani Palace. This announcement excited special interest among the young ladies of Pisa. Fabio had only reached his thirtieth year; and it was universally agreed that his return to society in his native city could indicate nothing more certainly than his desire to find a second mother for his infant child. All the single ladies would now have been ready to bet, as confidently as Brigida had offered to bet eight months before, that Fabio d'Ascoli would marry again.

For once in a way, report turned out to be true, in both the cases just mentioned. Invitations were actually issued from the

Melani Palace, and Fabio returned from abroad to his home on
the Arno.

In settling all the arrangements connected with his masked
ball, the Marquis Melani showed that he was determined not
only to deserve, but to increase, his reputation for oddity. He
invented the most extravagant disguises, to be worn by some
of his more intimate friends; he arranged grotesque dances, to
be performed at stated periods of the evening by professional
buffoons, hired from Florence. He composed a toy-
symphony, which included solos on every noisy plaything at
that time manufactured for children's use. And, not content
with thus avoiding the beaten track in preparing the entertain-
ments at the ball, he determined also to show decided
originality, even in selecting the attendants who were to wait
on the company. Other people in his rank of life were
accustomed to employ their own and hired footmen for this
purpose; the marquis resolved that his attendants should be
composed of young women only; that two of his rooms
should be fitted up as Arcadian bowers; and that all the
prettiest girls in Pisa should be placed in them to preside over
the refreshments, dressed, in accordance with the mock-
classical taste of the period, as shepherdesses of the time of
Virgil.

The only defect of this brilliantly new idea was the
difficulty of executing it. The marquis had expressly ordered
that not fewer than thirty shepherdesses were to be engaged,
fifteen for each bower. It would have been easy to find double
this number in Pisa, if beauty had been the only quality
required in the attendant damsels. But it was also absolutely
necessary, for the security of the marquis's gold and silver
plate, that the shepherdesses should possess, besides good
looks, the very homely recommendation of a fair character.
This last qualification proved, it is sad to say, to be the one
small merit which the majority of the ladies willing to accept
engagements at the palace did not possess. Day after day
passed on; and the marquis's steward found more and more
difficulty in obtaining the appointed number of trustworthy
beauties. At last, his resources failed him altogether; and he
appeared in his master's presence about a week before the
night of the ball, to make the humiliating acknowledgement,

that he was entirely at his wits' end. The total number of fair shepherdesses with fair characters, whom he had been able to engage, amounted to twenty-three.

'Nonsense!' cried the marquis, irritably, as soon as the steward had made his confession. 'I told you to get thirty girls, and thirty I mean to have. What's the use of shaking your head, when all their dresses are ordered? Thirty tunics, thirty wreaths, thirty pairs of sandals and silk stockings, thirty crooks, you scoundrel – and you have the impudence to offer me only twenty-three hands to hold them. Not a word! I won't hear a word! Get me my thirty girls, or lose your place.' The marquis roared out this last terrible sentence at the top of his voice, and pointed peremptorily to the door.

The steward knew his master too well to remonstrate. He took his hat and cane, and went out. It was useless to look through the ranks of rejected volunteers again; there was not the slightest hope in that quarter. The only chance left was to call on all his friends in Pisa who had daughters out at service, and to try what he could accomplish, by bribery and per-suasion, that way.

After a whole day occupied in solicitations, promises, and patient smoothing down of innumerable difficulties, the result of his efforts in the new direction was an accession of six more shepherdesses. This brought him on bravely from twenty-three to twenty-nine, and left him, at last, with only one anxiety – where was he now to find shepherdess number thirty?

He mentally asked himself that important question, as he entered a shady by-street in the neighbourhood of the Campo Santo, on his way back to the Melani Palace. Sauntering slowly along in the middle of the road, and fanning himself with his handkerchief after the oppressive exertions of the day, he passed a young girl who was standing at the street-door of one of the houses, apparently waiting for somebody to join her before she entered the building.

'Body of Bacchus!' exclaimed the steward (using one of those old Pagan ejaculations which survive in Italy even to the present day); 'There stands the prettiest girl I have seen yet. If she would only be shepherdess number thirty, I should go home to supper with my mind at ease. I'll ask her, at any rate.

Nothing can be lost by asking, and everything may be gained. 'Stop, my dear,' he continued, seeing the girl turn to go into the house, as he approached her. 'Don't be afraid of me. I am steward to the Marquis Melani, and well known in Pisa as an eminently respectable man. I have something to say to you which may be greatly for your benefit. Don't look surprised; I am coming to the point at once. Do you want to earn a little money? – honestly, of course. You don't look as if you were very rich child.'

'I am very poor, and very much in want of some honest work to do,' answered the girl, sadly.

'Then we shall suit each other to a nicety; for I have work of the pleasantest kind to give you, and plenty of money to pay for it. But before we say anything more about that, suppose you tell me first something about yourself – who you are, and so forth. You know who I am already.'

'I am only a poor work-girl, and my name is Nanina. I have nothing more, sir, to say about myself than that.'

'Do you belong to Pisa?'

'Yes, sir – at least, I did. But I have been away for some time. I was a year at Florence, employed in needlework.'

'All by yourself?'

'No, sir, with my little sister. I was waiting for her when you came up.'

'Have you never done anything else but needlework? – never been out at service?'

'Yes, sir. For the last eight months I have had a situation to wait on a lady at Florence, and my sister (who is turned eleven, sir, and can make herself very useful) was allowed to help in the nursery.'

'How came you to leave this situation?'

'The lady and her family were going to Rome, sir. They would have taken me with them, but they could not take my sister. We are alone in the world, and we never have been parted from each other and never shall be – so I was obliged to leave the situation.'

'And here you are back at Pisa – with nothing to do, I suppose?'

'Nothing yet, sir. We only came back yesterday.'

'Only yesterday! You are a lucky girl, let me tell you, to

have met with me. I suppose you have somebody in the town who can speak to your character?'

'The landlady of this house can, sir.'

'And who is she, pray?'

'Marta Angrisani, sir.'

'What! the well-known sick-nurse? You could not possibly have a better recommendation, child. I remember her being employed at the Melani Palace at the time of the marquis's last attack of gout; but I never knew that she kept a lodging-house.'

'She and her daughter, sir, have owned this house longer than I can recollect. My sister and I have lived in it since I was quite a little child, and I had hoped we might be able to live here again. But the top room we used to have is taken, and the room to let lower down is far more, I am afraid, than we can afford.'

'How much is it?'

Nanina mentioned the weekly rent of the room in fear and trembling. The steward burst out laughing

'Suppose I offered you money enough to be able to take that room for a whole year at once?' he said.

Nanina looked at him in speechless amazement.

'Suppose I offered you that?' continued the steward. 'And suppose I only asked you in return to put on a fine dress and serve refreshments in a beautiful room to the company at the Marquis Melani's grand ball? What should you say to that?'

Nanina said nothing. She drew back a step or two, and looked more bewildered than before.

'You must have heard of the ball,' said the steward pompously. 'The poorest people in Pisa have heard of it. It is the talk of the whole city.'

Still Nanina made no answer. To have replied truthfully, she must have confessed that 'talk of the whole city' had now no interest for her. The last news from Pisa that had appealed to her sympathies was the news of the Countess d'Ascoli's death, and of Fabio's departure to travel in foreign countries. Since then, she had heard nothing more of him. She was as ignorant of his return to his native city as of all the reports connected with the marquis's ball. Something in her own heart – some feeling which she had neither the desire nor the capacity to analyse – had brought her back to Pisa and to the old home which now connected itself with her tenderest recollections. Believing that Fabio was still absent, she felt that no ill motive could now be attributed to her return; and she had not been able to resist the temptation of revisiting the scene that had been associated with the first great happiness as well as with the first great sorrow of her life. Among all the poor people of Pisa, she was perhaps the very last whose curiosity could be awakened, or whose attentions could be attracted by the rumour of gaieties at the Melani Palace.

But she could not confess all this; she could only listen with great humility and no small surprise, while the steward, in compassion for her ignorance, and with the hope of tempting her into accepting his offered engagement, described the arrangements of the approaching festival, and dwelt fondly on the magnificence of the Arcadian bowers, and the beauty of the shepherdesses' tunics. As soon as he had done, Nanina ventured on the confession that she should feel rather nervous in a grand dress that did not belong to her, and that she doubted very much her own capability of waiting properly on the great people at the ball. The steward, however, would hear of no objections, and called peremptorily for Marta Angrisani to make the necessary statement as to Nanina's character. While the formality was being complied with to the steward's perfect satisfaction, La Biondella came in, unaccompanied on this occasion by the usual companion of all her walks, the learned poodle Scarammuccia.

'This is Nanina's sister, sir,' said the good-natured sick-nurse, taking the first opportunity of introducing La Biondella to the great marquis's great man. 'A very good, industrious little girl; and very clever at plaiting dinner-mats, in case his excellency should ever want any. What have you done with the dog, my dear?'

'I couldn't get him past the pork-butcher's, three streets off,' replied La Biondella. 'He would sit down and look at the sausages. I am more than half afraid he means to steal some of them?'

'A very pretty child,' said the steward, patting La Biondella on the cheek. 'We ought to have her at the ball. If his excellency should want a Cupid, or a youthful nymph, or anything small and light in that way, I shall come back and let you know. In the meantime Nanina, consider yourself Shepherdess number Thirty, and come to the housekeeper's room at the palace to try on your dress to-morrow. Nonsense! don't talk to me about being afraid and awkward. All you're wanted to do is to look pretty; and your glass must have told you you could do that long ago. Remember the rent of the room, my dear, and don't stand in your light and your sister's. Does the little girl like sweetmeats? Of course she does! Well, I promise you a whole box of sugar-plums to take home for her, if you will come and wait at the ball.'

'Oh, go to the ball, Nanina, go to the ball!' cried La Biondella, clapping her hands.

'Of course she will go to the ball,' said the nurse. 'She would be mad to throw away such an excellent chance.'

Nanina looked perplexed. She hesitated a little, then drew Marta Angrisani away into a corner, and whispered this question to her:-

'Do you think there will be any priests at the palace where the marquis lives?'

'Heavens, child, what a thing to ask!' returned the nurse. 'Priests at a masked ball! You might as well expect to find Turks performing high mass in the cathedral. But supposing you did meet with priests at the palace, what then?'

'Nothing,' said Nanina, constrainedly. She turned pale, and walked away as she spoke. Her great dread in returning to Pisa, was the dread of meeting with Father Rocco again. She had never forgotten her first discovery at Florence of his distrust of her. The bare thought of seeing him any more, after her faith in him had been shaken for ever, made her feel faint and sick at heart.

'To-morrow, in the housekeeper's room,' said the steward, putting on his hat, 'you will find your new dress all ready for you.'

Nanina curtsyed, and ventured on no more objections. The prospect of securing a home for a whole year to come among people whom she knew, reconciled her – influenced as she was also by Marta Angrisani's advice, and by her sister's anxiety for the promised present – to brave the trial of appearing at the ball.

'What a comfort to have it all settled at last,' said the steward, as soon as he was out again in the street. 'We shall see what the marquis says now. If he doesn't apologize for calling me a scoundrel the moment he sets eyes on Number Thirty, he is the most ungrateful nobleman that ever existed.'

Arriving in front of the palace, the steward found workmen engaged in planning the external decorations and illuminations for the night of the ball. A little crowd had already assembled to see the ladders raised, and the scaffoldings put up. He observed among them, standing near the outskirts of the throng, a lady who attracted his attention (he was an ardent admirer of the fair sex) by the beauty and symmetry of her figure. While he lingered for a moment to look at her, a shaggy poodle dog (licking his chops, as if he had just had something to eat) trotted by, stopped suddenly close to the lady, sniffed suspiciously for an instant, and then began to growl at her without the slightest apparent provocation. The steward advancing politely with his stick to drive the dog away, saw the lady start, and heard her exclaim to herself amazedly:-

'You here, you beast! Can Nanina have come back to Pisa?'

This last exclamation gave the steward, as a gallant man, an excuse for speaking to the elegant stranger.

'Excuse me, madam, he said, 'but I heard you mention the name of Nanina. May I ask whether you mean a pretty little work-girl who lives near the Campo Santo?'

'The same,' said the lady, looking very much surprised and interested immediately.

'It may be a gratification to you, madam, to know that she has just returned to Pisa,' continued the steward, politely; 'and, moreover, that she is in a fair way to rise in the world. I have just engaged her to wait at the marquis's grand ball, and I need hardly say, under those circumstances, that if she plays her cards properly, her fortune is made.'

The lady bowed, looked at her informant very intently and thoughtfully for a moment, then suddenly walked away without uttering a word.

'A curious woman,' thought the steward, entering the palace. 'I must ask Number Thirty about her to-morrow.'

CHAPTER II

The death of Maddalena d'Ascoli produced a complete change in the lives of her father and her uncle. After the first shock of the bereavement was over, Luca Lomi declared that it would be impossible for him to work in his studio again – for some time to come at least – after the death of the beloved daughter, with whom every corner of it was now so sadly and closely associated. He accordingly accepted an engagement to assist in restoring several newly discovered works of ancient sculpture at Naples, and set forth for that city, leaving the care of his work-rooms at Pisa entirely to his brother.

On the master-sculptor's departure, Father Rocco caused the statues and busts to be carefully enveloped in linen cloths, locked the studio doors, and, to the astonishment of all who knew of his former industry and dexterity as a sculptor, never approached the place again. His clerical duties he performed with the same assiduity as ever; but he went out less than had been his custom hitherto, to the houses of his friends. His most regular visits were to the Ascoli Palace, to inquire at the porter's lodge after the health of Maddalena's child, who was always reported to be thriving admirably under the care of the best nurses that could be found in Pisa. As for any communications with his polite little friend from Florence, they had ceased months ago. The information – speedily conveyed to him – that Nanina was in the service of one of the most respectable ladies in the city, seemed to relieve any anxieties which he might otherwise have felt on her account. He made no attempt to justify himself to her; and only required that his over-courteous little visitor of former days should let him know whenever the girl might happen to leave her new situation.

The admirers of Father Rocco, seeing the alteration in his life, and the increased quietness of his manner, said, that as he was growing older he was getting more and more above the things of this world. His enemies (for even Father Rocco had them) did not scruple to assert that the change in him was decidedly for the worse, and that he belonged to the order of men who are most to be distrusted when they become most subdued. The priest himself paid no attention either to his eulogists or his depreciators. Nothing disturbed the regularity and discipline of his daily habits; and vigilant Scandal, though she sought often to surprise him, sought always in vain.

Such was Father Rocco's life from the period of his niece's death to Fabio's return to Pisa.

As a matter of course, the priest was one of the first to call at the palace and welcome the young nobleman back. What passed between them at this interview never was precisely known; but it was surmised readily enough that some misunderstanding had taken place, for Father Rocco did not repeat his visit. He made no complaints of Fabio, but simply stated that he had said something, intended for the young man's good, which had not been received in a right spirit; and that he thought it desirable to avoid the painful chance of any further collision by not presenting himself at the palace again for some little time. People were rather amazed at this. They would have been still more surprised if the subject of the masked ball had not just then occupied all their attention, and prevented their noticing it, by another strange event in connexion with the priest. Father Rocco, some weeks after the cessation of his intercourse with Fabio, returned one morning to his old way of life as a sculptor, and opened the long-closed doors of his brother's studio.

Luca Lomi's former workmen, discovering this, applied to him immediately for employment; but were informed that their services would not be needed. Visitors called at the studio, but were always sent away again by the disappointing announcement that there was nothing new to show them. So the days passed on until Nanina left her situation and returned to Pisa. This circumstance was duly reported to Father Rocco by his correspondent at Florence; but, whether he was too much occupied among the statues, or whether it was one result of his cautious resolution never to expose himself unnecessarily to so much as the breath of detraction, he made no attempt to see Nanina, or even to justify himself towards her by writing her a letter. All his mornings continued to be spent alone in the studio, and all his afternoons to be occupied by his clerical duties, until the day before the masked ball at the Melani Palace.

Early on that day, he covered over the statues, and locked the doors of the work-rooms once more; then returned to his own lodgings, and did not go out again. One or two of his friends who wanted to see him were informed that he was not well enough to be able to receive them. If they had penetrated into his little study, and had seen him, they would have been easily satisfied that this was no mere excuse. They would have noticed that his face was startlingly pale, and that the ordinary composure of his manner was singularly disturbed.

Towards evening this restlessness increased; and his old housekeeper, on pressing him to take some nourishment, was astonished to hear him answer her sharply and irritably for the first time since she had been in his service. A little later her surprise was increased by his sending her with a note to the Ascoli Palace, and by the quick return of an answer, brought ceremoniously by one of Fabio's servants. 'It is long since he has had any communication with that quarter. Are they going to be friends again?' thought the housekeeper as she took the answer up stairs to her master.

'I feel better to-night,' he said as he read it: 'Well enough indeed to venture out. If any one inquires for me, tell them that I am gone to the Ascoli Palace.' Saying this, he walked to the door – then returned, and trying the lock of his cabinet, satisfied himself that it was properly secured – then went out.

He found Fabio in one of the large drawing-rooms of the palace, walking irritably backwards and forwards, with several little notes crumpled together in his hands, and a plain black domino dress for the masquerade of the ensuing night spread out on one of the tables.

'I was just going to write to you,' said the young man, abruptly, 'when I received your letter. You offer me a renewal of our friendship, and I accept the offer. I have no doubt those references of yours, when we last met, to the subject of second marriages, were well meant, but they irritated me; and, speaking under that irritation, I said words that I had better not have spoken. If I pained you I am sorry for it. Wait!

pardon me for one moment. I have not quite done yet. It seems that you are by no means the only person in Pisa to whom the question of my possibly marrying again appears to have presented itself. Ever since it was known that I intended to renew my intercourse with society at the ball to-morrow night, I have been persecuted by anonymous letters – infamous letters, written from some motive which it is impossible for me to understand. I want your advice on the best means of discovering the writers; and I have also a very important question to ask you. But read one of the letters first yourself: any one will do as a sample of the rest.'

Fixing his eyes searchingly on the priest, he handed him one of the notes. Still a little paler than usual, Father Rocco sat down by the nearest lamp, and shading his eyes read these lines:-

'Count Fabio:– It is the common talk of Pisa that you are likely, as a young man left with a motherless child, to marry again. Your having accepted an invitation to the Melani Palace gives a colour of truth to this report. Widowers who are true to the departed do not go among all the handsomest single women in a city at a masked ball. Reconsider your determination and remain at home. I know you, and I knew your wife, and I say to you solemnly, avoid temptation, for you must never marry again. Neglect my advice and you will repent it to the end of your life. I have reasons for what I say – serious, fatal reasons, which I cannot divulge. If you would let your wife lie easy in her grave, if you would avoid a terrible warning, go not to the masked ball!'

'I ask you, and I ask any man, if that is not infamous?' exclaimed Fabio, passionately, as the priest handed him back the letter. 'An attempt to work on my fears through the memory of my poor dead wife! An insolent assumption that I want to marry, when I myself have not even so much as thought of the subject at all! What is the secret object of this letter, and of the rest here that resemble it! Whose interest is it to keep me away from the ball? What is the meaning of such a phrase as – 'if you would let your wife lie easy in her grave?' Have you no advice to give me? – No plan to propose for discovering the vile hand that traced these lines? – Speak to me! – Why, in Heaven's name don't you speak?'

The priest leant his head on his hand, and, turning his face from the light as if it dazzled his eyes, replied in his lowest and quietest tones:

'I cannot speak till I have had time to think. The mystery of that letter is not to be solved in a moment. There are things in it that are enough to perplex and amaze any man'

'What things?'

'It is impossible for me to go into details – at least, at the present moment.'

You speak with a strange air of secrecy. Have you nothing definite to say? – No advice to give me?'

'I should advise you not to go to the ball.'

'You would! Why?'

'If I gave you my reasons, I am afraid I should only be irritating you to no purpose.'

'Father Rocco! Neither your words nor your manner satisfy me. You speak in riddles; and you sit there in the dark with your face hidden from me —'

The priest instantly started up and turned his face to the light.

'I recommend you to control your temper, and to treat me with common courtesy,' he said, in his quietest, firmest tones, looking at Fabio steadily while he spoke.

'We will not prolong this interview,' said the young man, calming himself by an evident effort. 'I have one question to ask you, and then no more to say.'

The priest bowed his head, in token that he was ready to listen. He still stood up, calm, pale, and firm, in the full light of the lamp.

'It is just possible,' continued Fabio, 'that these letters may refer to some incautious words which my late wife might have spoken. I ask you, as her spiritual director, and as a near relation who enjoyed her confidence, if you ever heard her express a wish, in the event of my surviving her, that I should abstain from marrying again?'

'Did she never express such a wish to you?'

'Never. But why do you evade my question by asking me another?'

'It is impossible for me to reply to your question.'

'For what reason?'

'Because it is impossible for me to give answers which must refer, whether they are affirmative or negative, to what I have heard in confession.'

'We have spoken enough,' said Fabio, turning angrily from the priest. 'I expected you to help me in clearing up these mysteries, and you do your best to thicken them. What your motives are, what your conduct means, it is impossible for me to know; but I say to you, what I would say in far other terms, if they were here, to the villains who have written these letters – no menaces, no mysteries, no conspiracies, will prevent me from being at the ball to-morrow. I can listen to persuasion, but I scorn threats. There lies my dress for the masquerade: no power on earth shall prevent me from wearing it to-morrow night!' He pointed, as he spoke, to the black domino and half-mask lying on the table.

'No power on *earth!*' repeated Father Rocco, with a smile, and an emphasis on the last word. 'Superstitious still, Count Fabio! Do you suspect the powers of the other world of interfering with mortals at masquerades?'

Fabio started, and, turning from the table, fixed his eyes intently on the priest's face.

'You suggested just now that we had better not prolong this interview,' said Father Rocco, still smiling. 'I think you were right: if we part at once, we may still part friends. You have had my advice not to go to the ball, and you decline following it. I have nothing more to say. Good night!'

Before Fabio could utter the angry rejoinder that rose to his lips, the door of the room had opened and closed again, and the priest was gone.

CHAPTER III

The next night, at the time of assembling specified in the invitations to the masked ball, Fabio was still lingering in his palace, and still allowing the black domino to lie untouched and unheeded on his dressing-table. This delay was not produced by any change in his resolution to go to the Melani Palace. His determination to be present at the ball remained unshaken; and yet, at the last moment, he lingered and lingered on, without knowing why. Some strange influence seemed to be keeping him within the walls of his lonely home. It was as if the great, empty, silent palace had almost recovered on that night the charm which it had lost when its mistress died.

He left his own apartment and went to the bedroom where his infant child lay asleep in her little crib. He sat watching her, and thinking quietly and tenderly of many past events in his life for a long time, then returned to his room. A sudden sense of loneliness came upon him after his visit to the child's bedside; but he did not attempt to raise his spirits even then by going to the ball. He descended instead to his study, lit his reading-lamp, and then opening a bureau, took from one of the drawers in it the letter which Nanina had written to him. This was not the first time that a sudden sense of his solitude had connected itself inexplicably with the remembrance of the work-girl's letter.

He read it through slowly, and when he had done, kept it open in his hand. 'I have youth, titles, wealth,' he thought to himself sadly; 'everything that is sought after in this world. And yet if I try to think of any human being who really and truly loves me, I can remember but one – the poor, faithful girl who wrote these lines!'

Old recollections of the first day when he met with Nanina, of the first sitting she had given him in Luca Lomi's studio, of the first visit to the neat little room in the by-street, began to

71

rise more and more vividly in his mind. Entirely absorbed by
them, he sat absently drawing with pen and ink, on some
sheets of letter-paper lying under his hand, lines and circles,
and fragments of decorations, and vague remembrances of old
ideas for statues, until the sudden sinking of the flame of his
lamp awoke his attention abruptly to present things.

He looked at his watch. It was close on midnight,

This discovery at last aroused him to the necessity of
immediate departure. In a few minutes he had put on his
domino mask, and was on his way to the ball.

Before he reached the Melani Palace the first part of the
entertainment had come to an end. The 'Toy-Symphony' had
been played, the grotesque dance performed, amid universal
laughter; and now the guests were for the most part fortifying
themselves in the Arcadian bowers for new dances, in which
all persons present were expected to take part. The Marquis
Melani had, with characteristic oddity, divided his two
classical refreshment-rooms into what he termed the Light and
Heavy Departments. Fruit, pastry, sweetmeats, salads, and
harmless drinks were included under the first head, and all the
stimulating liquors and solid eatables under the last. The thirty
shepherdess had been, according to the marquis's order,
equally divided at the outset of the evening between the two
rooms. But as the company began to crowd more and more
resolutely in the direction of the Heavy Department, ten of the
shepherdesses attached to the Light Department were told off
to assist in attending on the hungary and thirsty majority of
guests who were not to be appeased by pastry and lemonade.
Among the five girls who were left behind in the room for the
light refreshments, was Nanina. The steward soon discovered
that the novelty of her situation made her really nervous, and
he wisely concluded that if he trusted her where the crowd
was greatest and the noise loudest, she would not only be
utterly useless, but also very much in the way of her more
confident and experienced companions.

When Fabio arrived at the palace, the jovial uproar in the
Heavy Department was at its height, and several gentlemen,
fired by the classical costumes of the shepherdesses, were
beginning to speak Latin to them with a thick utterance and a
valorous contempt for all restrictions of gender, number, and

case. As soon as he could escape from the congratulations on his return to his friends, which poured on him from all sides, Fabio withdrew to seek some quieter room. The heat, noise, and confusion, had so bewildered him, after the tranquil life he had been leading for many months past, that it was quite a relief to stroll through the half-deserted dancing-rooms, to the opposite extremity of the great suite of apartments, and there to find himself in a second arcadian bower, which seemed peaceful enough to deserve its name.

A few guests were in this room when he first entered it; but the distant sound of some first notes of dance-music drew them all away. After a careless look at the quaint decorations about him, he sat down alone on a divan near the door, and beginning already to feel the heat and discomfort of his mask, took it off. He had not removed it more than a moment, before he heard a faint cry in the direction of a long refreshment table, behind which the five waiting-girls were standing. He started up directly, and could hardly believe his senses, when he found himself standing face to face with Nanina.

Her cheeks had turned perfectly colourless. Her astonishment at seeing the young nobleman appeared to have some sensation of terror mingled with it. The waiting-women who happened to stand by her side instinctively stretched out an arm to support her, observing that she caught at the edge of the table as Fabio hurried round to get behind it and speak to her. When he drew near, her head drooped on her breast, and she said, faintly, 'I never knew you were at Pisa: I never thought you would be here. Oh, I am true to what I said in my letter, though I seem so false to it!'

'I want to speak to you about the letter – to tell you how carefully I have kept it, how often I have read it,' said Fabio.

She turned away her head, and tried hard to repress the tears that would force their way into her eyes. 'We should never have met,' she said, 'never, never have met again!'

Before Fabio could reply, the waiting-woman by Nanina's side interposed.

'For heaven's sake, don't, stop speaking to her here!' she exclaimed impatiently. 'If the steward or one of the upper servants was to come in, you would get her into dreadful trouble. Wait till to-morrow, and find some fitter place than this.'

Fabio felt the justice of the reproof immediately. He tore a leaf out of his pocket-book, and wrote on it: "I must tell you how I honour and thank you for that letter. To-morrow – ten o'clock – the wicket-gate at the back of the Ascoli gardens. Believe in my truth and honour, Nanina, for I believe implicitly in yours." Having written these lines, he took from among his bunch of watch seals a little key, wrapped it up in the note, and pressed it into her hand. In spite of himself his fingers lingered round hers, and he was on the point of speaking to her again, when he saw the waiting-woman's hand, which was just raised to motion him away, suddenly drop. Her colour changed at the same moment, and she looked fixedly across the table.

He turned round immediately, and saw a masked woman standing alone in the room, dressed entirely in yellow, from head to foot. She had a yellow hood, a yellow half-mask with deep fringe hanging down over her mouth, and a yellow domino, cut at the sleeves and edges into long flame-shaped points, which waved backwards and forwards tremulously in the light air wafted through the doorway. The woman's black eyes seemed to gleam with an evil brightness through the sight-holes of the mask; and the tawny fringe hanging before her mouth fluttered slowly with every breath she drew. Without a work or a gesture she stood before the table, and her gleaming black eyes fixed steadily on Fabio, the instant he confronted her. A sudden chill struck through him, as he observed that the yellow of the stranger's domino and the mask was of precisely the same shade as the yellow of the hangings and furniture which his wife had chosen after their marriage for the decoration of her favourite sitting-room.

'The Yellow Mask!' whispered the waiting girls nervously, crowding together behind the table. 'The Yellow Mask again!'

'Make her speak!'

'Ask her to have something!'

'This gentlemen will ask her. Speak to her, sir. Do speak to her! She glides about in that fearful yellow dress like a ghost.'

Fabio looked round mechanically at the girl who was whispering to him. He saw at the same time that Nanina still kept her head turned away, and that she had her handkerchief at her eyes. She was evidently struggling yet with the agitation produced by their unexpected meeting, and was, most probably for that reason, the only person in the room not conscious of the presence of the Yellow Mask.

'Speak to her, sir. Do speak to her!' whispered two of the waiting-girls together.

Fabio turned again towards the table. The black eyes were still gleaming at him from behind the tawny yellow of the mask. He nodded to the girls who had just spoken, cast one farewell look at Nanina, and moved down the room to get round to the side of the table at which the Yellow Mask was standing. Step by step as he moved, the bright eyes followed him. Steadily and more steadily their evil light seemed to shine through and through him, as he turned the corner of the table, and approached the still, spectral figure.

He came close up to the woman, but she never moved; her eyes never wavered for an instant. He stopped and tried to speak; but the chill struck through him again. An overpowering dread, an unutterable loathing seized him; all sense of outer things – the whispering of the waiting-girls behind the table, the gentle cadence of the dance-music, the distant hum of joyous talk – suddenly left him. He turned away shuddering, and quitted the room.

Following the sound of the music, and desiring before all things now to join the crowd wherever it was largest, he was stopped in one of the smaller apartments by a gentleman who had just risen from the card-table, and who held out his hand with the cordiality of an old friend.

'Welcome back to the world, Count Fabio!' he began gaily, then suddenly checked himself. 'Why, you look pale, and your hand feels cold. Not ill, I hope?'

'No, no. I have been rather startled – I can't say why – by a very strangely dressed woman, who fairly stared me out of countenance.'

'You don't mean the Yellow Mask?'

'Yes I do. Have you seen her?'

'Everybody has seen her; but nobody can make her unmask, or get her to speak. Our host has not the slightest notion who she is; and our hostess is horribly frightened at her. For my part, I think she has given us quite enough of her mystery and her grim dress; and if my name, instead of being nothing but plain Andrea d'Arbino, was Marquis Melani, I would say to her, 'Madam, we are here to laugh and amuse ourselves; suppose you open your lips, and charm us by appearing in a prettier dress!'

During this conversation they had sat down together, with their backs towards the door, by the side of one of the card-tables. While d'Arbino was speaking, Fabio suddenly felt himself shuddering again, and became conscious of a sound of low breathing behind him.

He turned round instantly, and there, standing between them, and peering down at them, was the Yellow Mask!

Fabio started up, and his friend followed his example. Again the gleaming black eyes rested steadily on the young nobleman's face, and again their look chilled him to the heart.

'Yellow Lady, do you know my friend?' exclaimed d'Arbino, with mock solemnity.

There was no answer. The fatal eyes never moved from Fabio's face.

'Yellow Lady,' continued the other, 'listen to the music. Will you dance with me?'

The eyes looked away, and the figure glided slowly from the room.

'My dear count,' said d'Arbino, 'that woman seems to have quite an effect on you. I declare she has left you paler than ever. Come into the supper-room with me, and have some wine; you really look as if you wanted it.

They went at once to the large refreshment-room. Nearly all the guests had by this time begun to dance again. They had the whole apartment, therefore, almost entirely to themselves.

Among the decorations of the room, which were not strictly in accordance with genuine Arcadian simplicity, was a large looking-glass, placed over a well-furnished sideboard. D'Arbino led Fabio in this direction, exchanging greetings as he advanced with a gentleman who stood near the glass looking into it, and carelessly fanning himself with his mask.

'My dear friend!' cried d'Arbino, 'you are the very man to lead us straight to the best bottle of wine in the palace. Count

Fabio, let me present to you my intimate and good friend the Cavaliere Finello, with whose family I know you are well acquainted. Finello, the count is a little out of spirits, and I have prescribed a good dose of wine. I see a whole row of bottles at your side, and I leave it to you to apply the remedy. Glasses there! three glasses, my lovely shepherdess with the black eyes – the three largest you have got.

The glasses were brought; the Cavaliere Finello chose a particular bottle, and filled them. All three gentlemen turned round to the sideboard to use it as a table, and thus necessarily faced the looking-glass.

'Now, let us drink the toast of toasts,' said d'Arbino. 'Finello, Count Fabio – the ladies of Pisa!'

Fabio raised the wine to his lips, and was on the point of drinking it, when he saw reflected in the glass the figure of the Yellow Mask. The glittering eyes were again fixed on him, and the yellow-hooded head bowed slowly, as if in acknowledgement of the toast he was about to drink. For the third time the strange chill seized him, and he sat down his glass of wine untasted.

'What is the matter?' asked d'Arbino.

'Have you any dislike, count, to that particular wine?' inquired the Cavaliere.

'The Yellow Mask!' whispered Fabio. 'The Yellow Mask again!'

They all three turned round directly towards the door. But it was too late – the figure had disappeared.

'Does any one know who this Yellow Mask is' asked Finello. 'One may guess by the walk that the figure is a woman's. Perhaps it may be the strange colour she has chosen for her dress, or perhaps her stealthy way of moving from room to room; but there is certainly something mysterious and startling about her.'

'Startling enough, as the count would tell you,' said d'Arbino. 'The Yellow Mask has been responsible for his loss of spirits and change of complexion, and now she has prevented him even from drinking his wine.'

'I can't account for it,' said Fabio, looking round him uneasily; 'but this is the third room into which she has followed me – the third time she has seemed to fix her eyes on me alone. I suppose my nerves are hardly in a fit state yet for masked balls and adventures; the sight of her seems to chill me. Who can she be?'

'If she followed me a fourth time,' said Finello, 'I should insist on her unmasking.'

'And suppose she refused?' asked his friend.

'Then I should take her mask off for her.'

'It is impossible to do that with a woman,' said Fabio. 'I prefer trying to lose her in the crowd. Excuse me, gentlemen, if I leave you to finish the wine, and then to meet me, if you like, in the great ball-room.'

He retired as he spoke, put on his mask, and joined the dancers immediately, taking care to keep always in the most crowded corner of the apartment. For some time this plan of action proved successful, and he saw no more of the mysterious yellow domino. Erelong, however, some new dances were arranged, in which the great majority of the persons in the ball-room took part; the figures resembling the old English country dances in this respect, that the ladies and gentlemen were placed in long rows apposite to each other. The sets consisted of about twenty couples each, placed sometimes across, and sometimes along the apartment; and the spectators were all required to move away on either side, and range themselves close to the walls. As Fabio among others complied with this necessity, he looked down a row of dancers waiting during the performance of the orchestral prelude; and there, watching him again, from the opposite end of the lane formed by the gentlemen on one side and the ladies on the other, he saw the Yellow Mask.

He moved abruptly back towards another row of dancers, placed at right angles to the first row; and there again, at the opposite end of the gay lane of brightly-dressed figures, was the Yellow Mask. He slipped into the middle of the room; but it was only to find her occupying his former position near the wall, and still, in spite of his disguise, watching him through row after row of dancers. The persecution began to grow intolerable; he felt a kind of angry curiosity mingling now with the vague dread that had hitherto oppressed him. Finello's advice recurred to his memory; and he determined to make the woman unmask at all hazards. With this intention he returned to the supper-room in which he had left his friends.

They were gone, probably to the ball-room, to look for him. Plenty of wine was still left on the sideboard, and he poured himself out a glass. Finding that his hand trembled as he did so, he drank several more glasses in quick succession, to nerve himself for the approaching encounter with the Yellow Mask. While he was drinking he expected every moment to see her in the looking-glass again; but she never appeared – and yet he felt almost certain that he had detected her gliding out after him when he left the ball-room.

He thought it possible that she might be waiting for him in one of the smaller apartments, and, taking off his mask, walked through several of them without meeting her, until he came to the door of the refreshment-room in which Nanina and he had recognized each other. The waiting-women behind the table, who had first spoken to him, caught sight of him now, and ran round to the door.

'Don't come in and speak to Nanina again,' she said, mistaking the purpose which had brought him to the door. 'What with frightening her first, and making her cry after-wards, you have rendered her quite unfit for her work. The steward is in there at this moment, very good-natured, but not very sober. He says she is pale and red-eyed, and not fit to be a shepherdess any longer, and that, as she will not be missed now, she may go home if she likes. We have got her an old cloak, and she is going to try and slip through the rooms unobserved, to get down stairs and change her dress. Don't speak to her, pray – or you will only make her cry again, and what is worse, make the steward fancy —'

She stopped at that last word, and pointed suddenly over Fabio's shoulder.

'The Yellow Mask!' she exclaimed. 'Oh, sir, draw her away into the ball-room, and give Nanina a chance of getting out!'

Fabio turned directly, and approached the Mask, who, as they looked at each other, slowly retreated before him. The waiting-woman, seeing the yellow figure retire, hastened back to Nanina in the refreshment-room.

Slowly the masked woman retreated from one apartment to another till she entered a corridor brilliantly lit up and

beautifully ornamented with flowers. On the right hand this
corridor led to the ball-room; on the left to an ante-chamber at
the head of the palace staircase. The Yellow Mask went on a
few paces towards the left; then stopped. The bright eyes fixed
themselves as before on Fabio's face, but only for a moment.
He heard a light step behind him, and then he saw the eyes
move. Following the direction they took, he turned round,
and discovered Nanina, wrapped up in the old cloak which
was to enable her to get down stairs unobserved.

'Oh, how can I get out! how can I get out!' cried the girl,
shrinking back affrightedly as she saw the Yellow Mask.

'That way,' said Fabio, pointing in the direction of the
ball-room. 'Nobody will notice you in the cloak: it will only
be thought some new disguise.' He took her arm as he spoke
to reassure her, and continued in a whisper, – 'Don't forget
to-morrow.'

At the same moment he felt a hand laid on him. It was the
hand of the masked woman, and it put him back from Nanina.

In spite of himself, he trembled at her touch, but still
retained presence of mind enough to sign to the girl to make
her escape. With a look of eager inquiry in the direction of the
Mask, and a half suppressed exclamation of terror, she obeyed
him, and hastened away towards the ball-room.

'We are alone,' said Fabio, confronting the gleaming black
eyes, and reaching out his hand resolutely towards the Yellow
Mask. 'Tell me who you are, and why you follow me, or I
will uncover your face, and solve the mystery for myself.'

The woman pushed his hand aside, and drew back a few
paces, but never spoke a word. He followed her. There was
not an instant to be lost, for just then the sound of footsteps
hastily approaching the corridor became audible.

'Now or never.' he whispered to himself, and snatched at
the mask.

His arm was again thrust aside; but this time the woman
raised her disengaged hand at the same moment, and removed
the yellow mask.

The lamps shed their soft light full on her face.

It was the face of his dead wife.

CHAPTER IV

Signor Andrea d'Arbino, searching vainly through the various rooms in the palace for Count Fabio d'Ascoli, and trying, as a last resource, the corridor leading to the ball-room and grand staircase, discovered his friend lying on the floor in a swoon, without any living creature near him. Determining to avoid alarming the guests, if possible, d'Arbino first sought help in the ante-chamber. He found there the marquis's valet, assisting the Cavaliere Finello (who was just taking his departure) to put on his cloak.

While Finello and his friend carried Fabio to an open window in the ante-chamber, the valet procured some iced water. This simple remedy, and the change of atmosphere, proved enough to restore the fainting man to his senses, but hardly – as it seemed to his friends – to his former self. They noticed a change to blankness and stillness in his face, and when he spoke, an indescribable alteration in the tone of his voice.

'I found you in a room in the corridor,' said d'Arbino. What made you faint? Don't you remember? Was it the heat?'

Fabio waited for a moment, painfully collecting his ideas. He looked at the valet; and Finello signed to the man to withdraw.

'Was it the heat?' repeated d'Arbino.

'No.' answered Fabio, in strangely hushed, steady tones. 'I have seen the face that was behind the Yellow Mask.'

'Well?'

'It was the face of my dead wife.'

'Your dead wife!'

'When the mask was removed I saw her face. Not as I remember it in the pride of her youth and beauty – not even as I remember her on her sick-bed – but as I remember her in her coffin.'

'Count! for God's sake rouse yourself! Collect your

thoughts – remember where you are – and free your mind of its horrible delusion.'

'Spare me all remonstrances – I am not fit to bear them. My life has only one object now – the pursuing of this mystery to the end. Will you help me? I am scarcely fit to act for myself.'

He still spoke in the same unnaturally hushed, deliberate tones. D'Arbino and Finello exchanged glances behind him as he rose from the sofa on which he had hitherto been lying.

We will help you in everything,' said d'Arbino, soothingly. 'Trust in us to the end. What do you wish to do first?'

'The figure must have gone through this room. Let us descend the staircase and ask the servants if they have seen it pass.'

(Both d'Arbino and Finello remarked that he did not say her.)

They inquired down to the very court-yard. Not one of the servants had seen the Yellow Mask.

The last resource was the porter at the outer gate. They applied to him; and in answer to their questions, he asserted that he had most certainly seen a lady in a yellow domino and mask drive away, about half an hour before, in a hired coach.

'Should you remember the coachman again?' asked d'Arbino.

'Perfectly; he is an old friend of mine.'

'And you know where he lives?'

'Yes, as well as I know where I do.'

'Any reward you like, if you can get somebody to mind your lodge, and can take us to that house.'

In a few minutes they were following the porter through the dark, silent streets. 'We had better try the stables first,' said the man. 'My friend the coachman will hardly have had time to do more than set the lady down. We shall most likely catch him just putting up his horses.'

The porter turned out to be right. On entering the stable-yard, they found that the empty coach had just driven into it.

'You have been taking home a lady in a yellow domino from the masquerade?' said d'Arbino, putting some money into the coachman's hand.

'Yes, sir; I was engaged by that lady for an evening – engaged to drive her to the ball, as well as to drive her home.'

'Where did you take her from?'

'From a very extraordinary place – from the gate of the Campo Santo burial-ground.'

During this colloquy, Finello and d'Arbino had been standing with Fabio between them, each giving him an arm. The instant the last answer was given, he reeled back with a cry of horror.

'Where have you taken her to now?" asked d'Arbino. He looked about him nervously as he put the question, and spoke for the first time in a whisper.

'To the Campo Santo again,' said the coachman.

Fabio suddenly drew his arms out of the arms of his friends, and sank to his knees on the ground, hiding his face. From some broken ejaculations which escaped him, it seemed as if he dreaded that his senses were leaving him, and that he was praying to be preserved in his right mind.

'Why is he so violently agitated?' said Finello, eagerly, to his friend.

'Hush!' returned the other. 'You heard him say that when he saw the face behind the Yellow Mask, it was the face of his dead wife?'

'Yes! But what then?'

'His wife was buried in the Campo Santo.'

CHAPTER V

Of all the persons who had been present, in any capacity, at the Marquis Melani's ball, the earliest riser on the morning after it was Nanina. The agitation produced by the strange events in which she had been concerned destroyed the very idea of sleep. Through the hours of darkness she could not even close her eyes; and, as soon as the new day broke, she rose to breathe the early morning air at her window, and to think in perfect tranquillity over all that had passed since she entered the Melani Palace to wait on the guests at the masquerade.

On reaching home the previous night, all her other sensations had been absorbed in a vague feeling of mingled dread and curiosity, produced by the sight of the weird figure in the yellow mask, which she had left standing alone with Fabio in the palace corridor. The morning light, however, suggested new thoughts. She now opened the note which the young nobleman had pressed into her hand, and read over and over again the hurried pencil lines scrawled on the paper. Could there be any harm, any forgetfulness of her own duty, in using the key enclosed in the note, and keeping her appointment in the Ascoli gardens at ten o'clock? Surely not – surely the last sentence he had written – 'Believe in my truth and honour, Nanina, for I believe implicity in yours' – was enough to satisfy her this time that she could not be doing wrong in listening for once to the pleading of her own heart. And besides, there, in her lap, lay the key of the wicket-gate. It was absolutely necessary to use that, if only for the purpose of giving it back safely into the hands of its owner.

As this last thought was passing through her mind, and plausibly overcoming any faint doubts and difficulties which she might still have felt, she was startled by a sudden knocking at the street door; and, looking out of the window immediately, saw a man in livery standing in the street,

84

anxiously peering up at the house to see if his knocking had aroused anybody.

'Does Marta Angrisani, the sick-nurse, live here?' inquired the man, as soon as Nanina showed herself at the window.

'Yes,' she answered. 'Must I call her up? Is there some person ill?'

'Call her up directly,' said the servant, 'She is wanted at the Ascoli Palace. My master, Count Fabio —'

Nanina waited to hear no more. She flew to the room in which the sick-nurse slept, and awoke her, almost roughly, in an instant.

'He is ill!' she cried, breathlessly. 'Oh, make haste! make haste! – he is ill, and he has sent for you!'

Marta inquired who had sent for her; and on being informed, promised to lose no time. Nanina ran down stairs to tell the servant that the sick-nurse was getting on her clothes. The man's serious expression, when she came close to him, terrified her. All her usual self-distrust vanished; and she entreated him, without attempting to conceal her anxiety, to tell her particularly what his master's illness was, and how it had affected him so suddenly after the ball.

'I know nothing about it,' answered the man, noticing Nanina's manner as she put her question, with some surprise, 'except that my master was brought home by some gentlemen, friends of his, about a couple of hours ago, in a very bad state; half out of his mind, as it seemed to me. I gathered from what was said that he had got a dreadful shock from seeing some woman take off her mask and show her face to him at the ball. How that could be I don't in the least understand; but I know that when the doctor was sent for, he looked very serious, and talked about fearing brain-fever.'

Here the servant stopped; for to his astonishment he saw Nanina suddenly turn away from him, and then heard her crying bitterly as she went back into the house.

Marta Angrisani had huddled on her clothes, and was looking at herself in the glass, to see that she was sufficiently presentable to appear at the palace, when she felt two arms flung round her neck; and, before she could say a word, found Nanina sobbing on her bosom.

'He is ill – he is in danger!' cried the girl. 'I must go with

you to help him. You have always been kind to me, Marta –
be kinder than ever now. Take me with you! – Take me with
you to the palace!'

'You, child!' exclaimed the nurse, gently unclasping her
arms.

'Yes – yes! if it is only for an hour,' pleaded Nanina – 'if it
only for one little hour every day. You have only to say that I
am your helper, and they would let me in. Marta! I shall break
my heart if I can't see him, and help him to get well again.'

The nurse still hesitated. Nanina clasped her round the neck
once more, and laid her cheek – burning hot now, through the
tears had been streaming down it but an instant before – close
to the good woman's face.

'I love him, Marta – great as he is, I love him with all my
heart and soul and strength,' she went on, in quick, eager,
whispering tones. 'And he loves me. He would have married
me if I had not gone away to save him from it. I could keep
my love for him secret while he was well – I could stifle it, and
crush it down, and wither it up by absence. But now he is ill,
it gets beyond me; I can't master it. Oh, Marta! don't break
my heart by denying me! I have suffered so much for his sake
that I have earned the right to nurse him!'

Marta was not proof against the last appeal. She had one
great and rare merit for a middle-aged woman – she had not
forgotten her own youth.

'Come, child,' said she, soothingly; 'I won't attempt to
deny you. Dry your eyes, put on your mantilla, and, when we
get face to face with the doctor, try to look as old and ugly as
you can, if you want to be let into the sick-room along with
me.'

The ordeal of medical scrutiny was passed more easily than
Marta Angrisani had anticipated. It was of great importance,
in the doctor's opinion, that the sick man should see familiar
faces at his bedside. Nanina had only, therefore, to state that
he knew her well, and that she had sat to him as a model in the
days when he was learning the art of sculpture, to be
immediately accepted as Marta's privileged assistant in the
sick-room.

The worst apprehensions felt by the doctor for the patient
were soon realized. The fever flew to his brain. For nearly six

weeks he lay prostrate, at the mercy of Death; now raging with the wild strength of delirium, and now sunk in the speechless, motionless, sleepless exhaustion which was his only repose. At last the blessed day came when he enjoyed his first sleep, and when the doctor began, for the first time, to talk of the future with hope. Even then, however, the same terrible peculiarity marked his light dreams, which had previously shown itself in his fierce delirium. From the faintly-uttered, broken phrases which dropped from him when he slept, as from the wild words which burst from him when his senses were deranged, the one sad discovery inevitably resulted – that his mind was still haunted, day and night, hour after hour, by the figure in the yellow mask.

As his bodily health improved, the doctor in attendance on him grew more and more anxious as to the state of his mind. There was no appearance of any positive derangement of intellect, but there was a mental depression – an unaltering, invincable prostration, produced by his absolute belief in the reality of the dreadful vision that he had seen at the masked ball – which suggested to the physician the gravest doubts about the case. He saw with dismay that the patient showed no anxiety, as he got stronger, except on one subject. He was eagerly desirous of seeing Nanina every day by his bedside; but, as soon as he was assured that his wish should be faithfully complied with, he seemed to care for nothing more. Even when they proposed, in the hope of rousing him to an exhibition of something like pleasure, that the girl should read to him for an hour every day out of one of his favourite books, he only showed a languid satisfaction. Weeks passed away, and still, do what they would, they could not make him so much as smile.

One day, Nanina had begun to read to him as usual, but had not proceeded far before Marta Angrisani informed her that he had fallen into a doze. She ceased, with a sigh, and sat looking at him sadly, as he lay near her, faint and pale and mournful in his sleep – miserably altered from what he was when she first knew him. It had been a hard trial to watch by his bedside in the terrible time of his delirium; but it was a harder trial still to look at him now, and to feel less and less hopeful with each succeeding day.

While her eyes and thoughts were still compassionately
fixed on him, the door of the bedroom opened, and the doctor
came in, followed by Andrea d'Arbino, whose share in the
strange adventure with the Yellow Mask caused him to feel a
special interest in Fabio's progress towards recovery.

'Asleep, I see; and sighing in his sleep,' said the doctor,
going to the bedside. 'The grand difficulty with him,' he
continued, turning to d'Arbino, 'remains precisely what it
was. I have hardly left a single means untried of rousing him
from that fatal depression; yet, for the last fortnight, he has
not advanced a single step. It is impossible to shake his
conviction of the reality of that face which he saw (or rather
which he thinks he saw) when the yellow mask was removed;
and, as long as he persists in his own shocking view of the
case, so long he will lie there, getting better, no doubt, as to
his body, but worse as to his mind.'

'I suppose, poor fellow, he is not in a fit state to be reasoned
with?'

'On the contrary, like all men with fixed delusion, he has
plenty of intelligence to appeal to on every point, except the
one point on which he is wrong. I have argued with him
vainly by the hour together. He possesses, unfortunately, an
acute nervous sensibility and a vivid imagination; and besides,
he has, as I suspect, been superstitiously brought up as a child.
It would be probably useless to argue rationally with him on
certain spiritual subjects, even if his mind was in perfect
health. He has a good deal of the mystic and the dreamer in his
composition; and science and logic are but broken reeds to
depend upon with men of that kind.'

'Does he merely listen to you when you reason with him, or
does he attempt to answer?'

'He has only one form of answer, and that is unfortunately
the most difficult of all to dispose of. Whenever I try to
convince him of his delusion, he invariably retorts by asking
me for a rational explanation of what happened to him at the
masked ball. Now, neither you nor I, though we believe
firmly that he has been the dupe of some infamous conspiracy,
have been able as yet to penetrate thoroughly into this mystery
of the Yellow Mask. Our common sense tells us that he must
be wrong in taking his view of it, and that we must be right in

taking ours; but if we cannot give him actual, tangible proof of that – if we can only theorize, when he asks us for an explanation – it is but too plain, in his present condition, that every time we remonstrate with him on the subject we only fix him in his delusion more and more firmly.'

'It is not for want of perseverance on my part,' said d'Arbino, after a moment of silence, 'that we are still left in the dark. Ever since the extraordinary statement of the coachman who drove the woman home, I have been inquiring and investigating. I have offered a reward of two hundred scudi for the discovery of her; I have myself examined the servants at the palace, the night-watchman at the Campo Santo, the police-books, the lists of keepers of hotels and lodging-houses, to hit on some trace of this woman; and I have failed in all directions. If my poor friend's perfect recovery does indeed depend on his delusion being combated by actual proof, I fear we have but little chance of restoring him. So far as I am concerned, I confess myself at the end of my resources.'

'I hope we are not quite conquered yet,' returned the doctor. 'The proofs we want may turn up when we least expect them. It is certainly a miserable case,' he continued, mechanically laying his fingers on the sleeping man's pulse. 'There he lies, wanting nothing now but to recover the natural elasticity of his mind; and here we stand at his bedside, unable to relieve him of the weight that is pressing his faculties down. I repeat it, Signor Andrea, nothing will rouse him from his delusion that his is the victim of the supernatural interposition, but the production of some startling, practical proof of his error. At present he is in the position of a man who has been imprisoned from his birth in a dark room, and who denies the existence of daylight. If we cannot open the shutters, and show him the sky outside, we shall never convert him to a knowledge of the truth.'

Saying these words, the doctor turned to lead the way out of the room, and observed Nanina, who had moved from the bedside on his entrance, standing near the door. He stopped to look at her, shook his head good-humouredly, and called to Marta, who happened to be occupied in an adjoining room.

'Signora Marta, said the doctor, 'I think you told me some time ago, that your pretty and careful little assistant lives in your house. Pray does she take much walking exercise?'

'Very little, Signor Dottore. She goes home to her sister when she leaves the palace. Very little walking exercise indeed.'

'I thought so! Her pale cheeks and heavy eyes told me as much. Now, my dear,' said the doctor, addressing Nanina, 'you are a very good girl, and I am sure you will attend to what I tell you. Go out every morning before you come here, and take a walk in the fresh air. You are too young not to suffer by being shut up in close rooms every day, unless you get some regular exercise. Take a good long walk in the morning, or you will fall into my hands as a patient, and be quite unfit to continue your attendance here. – Now, Signor Andrea, I am ready for you.–Mind, my child, a walk every day in the open air, outside the town, or you will fall ill, take my word for it!'

Nanina promised compliance; but she spoke rather absently, and seemed scarcely conscious of the kind familiarity which marked the doctor's manner. The truth was, that all her thoughts were occupied with what he had been saying by Fabio's bedside. She had not lost one word of the conversation while the doctor was talking of his patient, and of the conditions on which his recovery depended. 'Oh, if that proof which would cure him could only be found!' she thought to herself, as she stole back anxiously to the bedside when the room was empty.

On getting home that day she found a letter waiting for her, and was greatly surprised to see that it was written by no less a person than the master-sculptor, Luca Lomi. It was very short; simply informing her that he had just returned to Pisa; and that he was anxious to know when she could sit to him for a new bust – a commission from a rich foreigner at Naples.

Nanina debated with herself for a moment whether she should answer the letter in the hardest way, to her, by writing, or, in the easiest way, in person; and decided on going to the studio and telling the master-sculptor that it would be impossible for her to serve him as a model, at least for some time to come. It would have taken her a long hour to say this with due propriety on paper; it would only take her a few minutes to say it with her own lips – so she put on her mantilla again, and departed for the studio.

On arriving at the gate and ringing the bell, a thought suddenly occurred to her, which she wondered had not struck her before. Was it not possible that she might meet Father Rocco in his brother's workroom? It was too late to retreat now, but not too late to ask, before she entered, if the priest was in the studio. Accordingly, when one of the workmen opened the door to her, she inquired first, very confusedly and anxiously, for Father Rocco. Hearing that he was not with his brother then, she went tranquilly enough to make her apologies to the master-sculptor.

She did not think it necessary to tell him more than that she was now occupied every day by nursing duties in a sick-room, and that it was consequently out of her power to attend at the studio. Luca Lomi expressed, and evidently felt, great disappointment at her failing him as a model, and tried hard to persuade her that she might find time enough, if she chose, to sit to him, as well as to nurse the sick person. The more she resisted his arguments and entreaties, the more obstinately he reiterated them. He was dusting his favourite busts and statues after his long absence with a feather-brush when she came in; and he continued this occupation all the while he was talking – urging a fresh plea to induce Nanina to reconsider her refusal to sit, at every fresh piece of sculpture he came to; and always receiving the same resolute apology from her, as she slowly followed him down the studio towards the door.

Arriving thus at the lower end of the room, Luca stopped with fresh argument on his lips before his statue of Minerva. He had dusted it already, but he lovingly returned to dust it again. It was his favourite work – the only good likeness (although it did assume to represent a classical subject) of his dead daughter that he possessed. He had refused to part with it for Maddalena's sake; and, as he now approached it with his brush for the second time, he absently ceased speaking, and mounted on a stool to look at the face near and blow some specks of dust off the forehead. Nanina thought this a good opportunity of escaping from further importunities. She was on the point of slipping away to the door with a word of farewell when a sudden exclamation from Luca Lomi arrested her.

'Plaster!' cried the master-sculptor, looking intently at the part of the hair of the statue which lay lowest on the forehead.

'Plaster here!' He took out his penknife, as he spoke, and removed a tiny morsel of some white substance from an interstice between two folds of the hair where it touched the face. 'It *is* plaster!' he exclaimed excitedly. 'Somebody has been taking a cast from the face of my statue!'

He jumped off the stool, and looked all round the studio with an expression of suspicious inquiry. 'I must have this cleared up,' he said 'My statues were left under Rocco's care, and he is answerable if there has been any stealing of casts from any one of them. I must question him directly.'

Nanina seeing that he took no notice of her, felt that she might now easily effect her retreat. She opened the studio door, and repeated, for the twentieth time at least, that she was sorry she could not sit to him.

'I am sorry too, child,' he said, irritably looking about for his hat. He found it apparently just as Nanina was going out; for she heard him call to one of the workmen in the inner studio, and order the man to say, if anybody wanted him, that he had gone to Father Rocco's lodgings.

CHAPTER VI

The next morning, when Nanina arose, a bad attack of headache, and sense of languor and depression, reminded her of the necessity of following the doctor's advice, and preserving her health by getting a little fresh air and exercise. She had more than two hours to spare before the usual time when her daily attendance began at the Ascoli Palace; and she determined to employ the interval of leisure in taking a morning walk outside the town. La Biondella would have been glad enough to go too, but she had a large order for dinner-mats on hand, and was obliged, for that day, to stop in the house and work. Thus it happened, that when Nanina set forth from home, the learned Poodle, Scarammuccia, was her only companion.

She took the nearest way out of the town; the dog trotting along in his usual steady, observant way, close at her side, pushing his great rough muzzle, from time to time, affectionately into her hand, and trying hard to attract her attention, at intervals, by barking and capering in front of her. He got but little notice, however, for his pains. Nanina was thinking again of all that the physician had said the day before by Fabio's bedside: and these thoughts brought with them others, equally absorbing, that were connected with the mysterious story of the young nobleman's adventure with the Yellow Mask. Thus preoccupied, she had little attention left for the gambols of the dog. Even the beauty of the morning appealed to her in vain. She felt the refreshment of the cool, fragrant air, but she hardly noticed the lovely blue of the sky, or the bright sunshine that gave a gaiety and an interest to the commonest objects around her.

After walking nearly an hour, she began to feel tired, and looked about for a shady place to rest in.

Beyond and behind her there was only the high road and the flat country; but by her side stood a little wooden building,

93

half inn, half coffee-house, backed by a large, shady pleasure-garden, the gates of which stood invitingly open. Some workmen in the garden were putting up a stage for fireworks, but the place was otherwise quiet and lonely enough. It was only used at night as a sort of rustic Ranelagh, to which the citizens of Pisa resorted for pure air and amusement after the fatigues of the day. Observing that there were no visitors in the grounds, Nanina ventured in, intending to take a quarter of an hour's rest in the coolest place she could find, before returning to Pisa.

She had passed the back of a wooden summer-house in a secluded part of the gardens, when she suddenly missed the dog from her side; and, looking round after him, saw that he was standing behind the summer-house with his ears erect and his nose to the ground, having evidently that instant scented something that excited his suspicion.

Thinking it possible that he might be meditating an attack on some unfortunate cat, she turned to see what he was watching. The carpenters engaged on the firework stage were just then hammering at it violently. The noise prevented her from hearing that Scarammuccia was growling, but she could feel that he was, the moment she laid her hand on his back. Her curiosity was excited, and she stooped down close to him, to look through a crack in the boards, before which he stood, into the summer-house.

She was startled at seeing a lady and gentleman sitting inside. The place she was looking through was not high enough up to enable her to see their faces; but she recognized, or thought she recognized, the pattern of the lady's dress, as one which she had noticed in former days in the Demoiselle Grifoni's show-room. Rising quickly, her eye detected a hole in the boards about the level of her own height, caused by a knot having been forced out of the wood. She looked through it to ascertain, without being discovered, if the wearer of the familiar dress was the person she had taken her to be; and saw, not Brigida only, as she had expected, but Father Rocco as well. At the same moment, the carpenters left off hammering and began to saw. The new sound from the firework stage was regular and not loud. The voices of the occupants of the summer-house reached her through it, and she heard Brigida pronounce the name of Count Fabio.

Instantly stooping down once more by the dog's side, she caught his muzzle firmly in both her hands. It was the only way to keep Scarammuccia from growling again, at a time when there was no din of hammering to prevent him from being heard. Those two words, 'Count Fabio,' in the mouth of another woman, excited a jealous anxiety in her. What could Brigida have to say in connexion with that name? She never came near the Ascoli Palace – what right, or reason, could she have to talk of Fabio?

'Did you hear what I said?' she heard Brigida ask, in her coolest, hardest tone.

'No,' the priest answered. 'At least, not all of it.'

I will repeat it then. I asked what had so suddenly determined you to give up all idea of making any future experiments on the superstitious fears of Count Fabio?'

'In the first place, the result of the experiment already tried has been so much more serious than I had anticipated, that I believe the end I had in view in making it has been answered already.'

'Well; that is not your only reason?'

'Another shock to his mind might be fatal to him. I can use what I believe to be a justifiable fraud to prevent his marrying again; but I cannot burden myself with a crime.'

'That is your second reason; but I believe you have another yet. The suddenness with which you sent to me last night, to appoint a meeting in this lonely place; the emphatic manner in which you requested – I may almost say ordered – me to bring the wax mask here, suggest to my mind that something must have happened. What is it? I am a woman, and my curiosity must be satisfied. After the secrets you have trusted to me already, you need not hesitate, I think, to trust me with one more.'

'Perhaps not. The secret this time is, moreover, of no great importance. You know that the wax mask you wore at the ball was made in a plaster mould taken off the face of my brother's statue.'

'Yes, I know that.'

'My brother has just returned to his studio; has found a

morsel of the plaster I used for the mould sticking in the hair of the statue; and has asked me, as the person left in charge of his work-rooms, for an explanation. Such an explanation as I could offer has not satisfied him, and he talks of making further inquiries. Considering that it will be used no more, I think it safest to destroy the wax mask; and I asked you to bring it here that I might see it burnt or broken up, with my own eyes. Now you know all you wanted to know; and now, therefore, it is my turn to remind you that I have not yet had a direct answer to the first question I addressed to you when we met here. Have you brought the wax mask with you, or have you not?'

'I have not.'

'And why?'

Just as that question was put, Nanina felt the dog dragging himself free of her grasp on his mouth. She had been listening hitherto with such painful intensity, with such all-absorbing emotions of suspense, terror, and astonishment, that she had not noticed his efforts to get away, and had continued mechanically to hold his mouth shut. But now she was aroused by the violence of his struggles to the knowledge that, unless she hit upon some new means of quieting him, he would have his mouth free, and would betray her by a growl.

In an agony of apprehension lest she should lose a word of the momentous conversation, she made a desperate attempt to appeal to the dog's fondness for her, by suddenly flinging both her arms round his neck, and kissing his rough hairy cheek. The stratagem succeeded. Scarammuccia had, for many years past, never received any greater marks of his mistress's kindness for him than such as a pat on the head or a present of a lump of sugar might convey. His dog's nature was utterly confounded by the unexpected warmth of Nanina's caress, and he struggled up vigorously in her arms to try and return it by licking her face. She could easily prevent him from doing this, and could so gain a few minutes more to listen behind the summer-house without danger of discovery.

She had lost Brigida's answer to Father Rocco's question; but she was in time to hear her next words.

'We are alone here,' said Brigida. 'I am a woman, and I don't know that you may not have come armed. It is only the commonest precaution on my part not to give you a chance of getting at the wax mask till I have made my conditions.'

'You never said a word about conditions before.'

'True. I remember telling you that I wanted nothing but the novelty of going to the masquerade in the character of my dead enemy, and the luxury of being able to terrify the man who had brutally ridiculed me in old days in the studio. That was the truth. But it is not the less the truth, that our experiment on Count Fabio has detained me in this city much longer than I ever intended, that I am all but penniless, and that I deserve to be paid. In plain words, will you buy the mask of me for two hundred scudi?'

'I have not twenty scudi in the world, at my own free disposal.'

'You must find two hundred if you want the wax mask. I don't wish to threated – but money I must have. I mention the sum of two hundred scudi, because that is the exact amount offered in the public handbills by Count Fabio's friends for the discovery of the woman who wore the yellow mask at the Marquis Melani's ball. What have I to do but to earn that money if I please, by going to the palace, taking the wax mask with me, and telling them that I am the woman. Suppose I confess in that way! they can do nothing to hurt me, and I should be two hundred scudi the richer. You might be injured, to be sure, if they insisted on knowing who made the wax model, and who suggested the ghastly disguise —'

'Wretch! do you believe that my character could be injured on the unsupported evidence of any words from your lips?'

'Father Rocco! for the first time since I have enjoyed the pleasure of your acquaintance, I find you committing a breach of good manners. I shall leave you until you become more like yourself. If you wish to apologize for calling me a wretch, and if you want to secure the wax mask, honour me with a visit before four o'clock this afternoon, and bring two hundred scudi with you. Delay till after four, and it will be too late.'

An instant of silence followed; and then Nanina judged that Brigida must be departing, for she heard the rustling of a dress on the lawn in front of the summer-house. Unfortunately Scarammuccia heard it too. He twisted himself round in her arms and growled.

The noise disturbed Father Rocco. She heard him rise and leave the summer-house. There would have been time enough, perhaps, for her to conceal herself among some trees, if she could have recovered her self-possession at once; but she was incapable of making an effort to regain it. She could neither think nor move – her breath seemed to die away on her lips – as she saw the shadow of the priest stealing over the grass slowly, from the front to the back of the summer-house. In another moment they were face to face.

He stopped a few paces from her, and eyed her steadily in dead silence. She still crouched against the summer-house, and still with one hand mechanically kept her hold of the dog. It was well for the priest that she did so. Scarammuccia's formidable teeth were in full view, his shaggy coat was bristling, his eyes were starting, his growl had changed from the surly to the savage note; he was ready to tear down, not Father Rocco only, but all the clergy in Pisa, at a moment's notice.

'You have been listening,' said the priest, calmly. 'I see it in your face. You have heard all.'

She could not answer a word: she could not take her eyes from him. There was an unnatural stillness in his face, a steady, unrepentant, unfathomable, despair in his eyes, that struck her with horror. She would have given worlds to be able to rise to her feet and fly from his presence.

'I once distrusted you and watched you in secret,' he said, speaking after a short silence, thoughtfully, and with a strange tranquil sadness in his voice. 'And now, what I did by you, you do by me. You put the hope of your life once in my hands. It is because they were not worthy of the trust that discovery and ruin overtake me, and that you are the instrument of the retribution? Can this be the decree of Heaven? or is it nothing but the blind justice of chance?'

He looked upward, doubtingly, to the lustrous sky above him, and sighed. Nanina's eyes still followed his mechanically. He seemed to feel their influence, for he suddenly looked down at her again.

'What keeps you silent? Why are you afraid?' he said. 'I can do you no harm, with your dog at your side, and the workmen yonder within call. I can do you no harm, and I wish to do you none. Go back to Pisa; tell what you have heard, restore the man you love to himself, and ruin me. That is your work; do it! I was never your enemy even when I distrusted you. I am not your enemy now. It is no fault of yours that a fatality has been accomplished through you – no fault of yours that I am rejected as the instrument of securing a righteous restitution to the Church. Rise, child, and go your way, while I go mine, and prepare for what is to come. If we never meet again, remember that I parted from you without one hard saying or one harsh look – parted from you so, knowing that the first words you speak in Pisa will be death to my character, and destruction to the great purpose of my life.'

Speaking these works, always with the same calmness which had marked his manner from the first, he looked fixedly at her for a little while – sighed again – and turned away. Just before he disappeared among the trees, he said 'Farewell;' but so softly that she could barely hear it. Some strange confusion clouded her mind as she lost sight of him. Had she injured him? or had he injured her? His words bewildered and oppressed her simple heart. Vague doubts and fears, and a sudden antipathy to remaining any longer near the summer-house, overcame her. She started to her feet, and, keeping the dog still at her side, hurried from the garden to the high road. There, the wide glow of sunshine, the sight of the city lying before her, changed the current of her thoughts, and directed them all to Fabio and to the future.

A burning impatience to be back in Pisa now possessed her. She hastened towards the city at her utmost speed. The doctor was reported to be in the palace when she passed the servants lounging in the courtyard. He saw, the moment she came into his presence, that something had happened; and led her away from the sick-room into Fabio's empty study. There she told him all.

'You have saved him,' said the doctor, joyfully, 'I will answer for his recovery. Only let that woman come here for the reward; and leave me to deal with her as she deserves. In the mean time, my dear, don't go away from the palace on any account until I give you permission. I am going to send a message immediately to Signor Andrea d'Arbino to come and hear the extraordinary disclosure that you have made to me.

Go back to read to the Count, as usual, until I want you again; but, remember you must not drop a word to him yet of what you have said to me. He must be carefully prepared for all that we have to tell him; and must be kept quite in the dark until those preparations are made.'

D'Arbino answered the doctor's summons in person; and Nanina repeated her story to him. He and the doctor remained closeted together for some time after she had concluded her narrative and had retired. A little before four o'clock they sent for her again into the study. The doctor was sitting by the table with a bag of money before him, and d'Arbino was telling one of the servants that if a lady called at the palace on the subject of the handbill which he had circulated, she was to be admitted into the study immediately.

As the clock struck four Nanina was requested to take possession of a window-seat, and to wait there until she was summoned. When she had obeyed, the doctor loosened one of the window-curtains, to hide her from the view of any one entering the room.

About a quarter of an hour elapsed; and then the door was thrown open, and Brigida herself was shown into the study. The doctor bowed, and d'Arbino placed a chair for her. She was perfectly collected, and thanked them for their politeness with her best grace.

'I believe I am addressing confidential friends of Count Fabio d'Ascoli?' Brigida began, 'May I ask if you are authorized to act for the Count, in relation to the reward which this handbill offers?'

The doctor, having examined the handbill, said that the lady was quite right, and pointed significantly to the bag of money.

'You are prepared then,' pursued Brigida, smiling, 'to give a reward of two hundred scudi to any one able to tell you who the woman is who wore the yellow mask at the Marquis Melani's ball, and how she contrived to personate the face and figure of the late Countess d'Ascoli?'

'Of course we are prepared,' answered d'Arbino, a little irritably. 'As men of honour, we are not in the habit of promising anything that we are not perfectly willing, under proper conditions, to perform.'

'Pardon me, my dear friend,' said the doctor; 'I think you speak a little too warmly to the lady. She is quite right to take every precaution. We have the two hundred scudi here, madam,' he continued, patting the money-bag. 'And we are prepared to pay that sum for the information we want. But' (here the doctor suspiciously moved the bag of scudi from the table to his lap) 'we must have proofs that the person claiming the reward is really entitled to it.'

Brigida's eyes followed the money-bag greedily.

'Proofs!' she exclaimed, taking a small flat box from under her cloak, and pushing it across to the doctor. 'Proofs! there you will find one proof that establishes my claim beyond the possibility of doubt.'

The doctor opened the box, and looked at the wax mask inside it; then handed it to d'Arbino, and replaced the bag of scudi on the table.

'The contents of that box seem certainly to explain a great deal,' he said, pushing the bag gently towards Brigida, but always keeping his hand over it. 'The woman who wore the yellow domino was, I presume, of the same height as the late Countess?'

'Exactly,' said Brigida. 'Her eyes were also of the same colour as the late Countess's; she wore yellow of the same shade as the hangings in the late Countess's room, and she had on, under her yellow mask, the colourless wax model of the late Countess's face, now in your friend's hand. So much for that part of the secret. Nothing remains now to be cleared up but the mystery of who the lady was. Have the goodness, sir, to push that bag an inch or two nearer my way, and I shall be delighted to tell you.'

'Thank you madam,' said the doctor, with a very perceptible change in his manner. 'We know who the lady was already.'

He moved the bag of scudi while he spoke back to his own side of the table. Brigida's cheeks reddened, and she rose from her seat.

'Am I to understand, sir,' she said, haughtily, 'that you take advantage of my position here, as a defenceless woman, to cheat me out of the reward?'

'By no means, madam,' rejoined the doctor. 'We have

covenanted to pay the reward to the person who could give us the information we required.'

'Well, sir! have I not given you part of it? And am I not prepared to give you the whole?'

'Certainly; but the misfortune is, that another person has been beforehand with you. We ascertained who the lady in the yellow domino was, and how she contrived to personate the face of the late Countess d'Ascoli, several hours ago, from another informant. That person has consequently the prior claim; and, on every principle of justice, that person must also have the reward. Nanina, this bag belongs to you – come and take it.'

Nanina appeared from the window-seat. Brigida, thunderstruck, looked at her in silence for a moment; gasped out, 'That girl!' – then stopped again, breathless.

'That girl was at the back of the summer-house this morning, while you and your accomplice were talking together,' said the doctor.

D'Arbino had been watching Brigida's face intently from the moment of Nanina's appearance, and had quietly stolen close to her side. This was a fortunate movement; for the doctor's last words were hardly out of his mouth before Brigida seized a heavy ruler lying, with some writing materials, on the table. In another instant, if d'Arbino had not caught her arm, she would have hurled it at Nanina's head.

'You may let go your hold, sir," she said, dropping the ruler, and turning towards d'Arbino with a smile on her white lips and wicked calmness in her steady eyes. 'I can wait for a better opportunity.'

With those words, she walked to the door; and, turning round there, regarded Nanina fixedly.

'I wish I had been a moment quicker with the ruler,' she said, and went out.

'There!' exclaimed the doctor: 'I told you I knew how to deal with her as she deserved. One thing I am certainly obliged to her for: she has saved us the trouble of going to her house, and forcing her to give up the mask. And now, my child,' he continued, addressing Nanina, you can go home, and one of the men servants shall see you safe to your own door, in case that woman should still be lurking about the palace. Stop! you are leaving the bag of scudi behind you."

'I can't take it, sir.'

'And why not?'

'*She* would have taken money!' Saying those words, Nanina reddened, and looked towards the door.

The doctor glanced approvingly at d'Arbino. 'Well, well, we won't argue about that now,' he said. 'I will lock up the money with the mask for to-day. Come here to-morrow morning as usual, my dear. By that time I shall have made up my mind on the right means for breaking your discovery to Count Fabio. Only let us proceed slowly and cautiously, and I answer for success.'

CHAPTER VII

The next morning, among the first visitors at the Ascoli Palace was the master-sculptor, Luca Lomi. He seemed, as the servants thought, agitated, and said he was especially desirous of seeing Count Fabio. On being informed that this was impossible, he reflected a little, and then inquired if the medical attendant of the Count was at the palace, and could be spoken with. Both questions were answered in the affirmative, and he was ushered into the doctor's presence.

'I know not how to preface what I want to say,' Luca began, looking about him confusedly. 'May I ask you, in the first place, if the work-girl named Nanina was here yesterday?'

'She was,' said the doctor.

'Did she speak in private with any one?'

'Yes; with me.'

'Then, you know everything?'

'Absolutely everything.'

'I am glad at least to find that my object in wishing to see the Count can be equally well answered by seeing you. My brother, I regret to say —' He stopped perplexedly, and drew from his pocket a roll of papers.

'You may speak of your brother in the plainest terms,' said the doctor. 'I know what share he has had in promoting the infamous conspiracy of the Yellow Mask.'

'My petition to you, and through you to the Count, is, that your knowledge of what my brother has done may go no further. If this scandal becomes public it will ruin me in my profession. And I make little enough by it already,' said Luca, with his old sordid smile breaking out again faintly on his face.

'Pray, do you come from your brother with this petition?' inquired the doctor.

'No; I come solely on my own account. My brother seems careless what happens. He has made a full statement of his share in the matter from the first; has forwarded it to his

104

ecclesiastical superior (who will send it to the archbishop), and is now awaiting whatever sentence they choose to pass on him. I have a copy of the document, to prove that he has at least been candid, and that he does not shrink from consequences which he might have avoided by flight. The law cannot touch him, but the church can – and to the church he has confessed. All I ask is, that he may be spared a public exposure. Such an exposure would do no good to the Count, and it would do dreadful injury to me. Look over the papers yourself, and show them, whenever you think proper, to the master of this house. I have every confidence in his honour and kindness, and in yours.'

He laid the roll of papers open on the table, and then retired with great humility to the window. The doctor looked over them with some curiosity.

The statement or confession began by boldly avowing the writer's conviction that part of the property which the Count Fabio d'Ascoli had inherited from his ancestors had been obtained by fraud and misrepresentation from the church. The various authorities on which this assertion was based were then produced in due order; along with some curious particles of evidence culled from old manuscripts, which it must have cost much trouble to collect and decipher.

The second section was devoted, at great length, to the reasons which induced the writer to think it his absolute duty, as an affectionate son and faithful servant of the church, not to rest until he had restored to the successors of the apostles, in his day, the property which had been fraudulently taken from them in days gone by. The writer held himself justified, in the last resort, and in that only, in using any means for effecting this restoration, except such as might involve him in mortal sin.

The third section described the priest's share in promoting the marriage of Maddelena Lomi with Fabio; and the hopes he entertained of securing the restitution of the church property through his influence over his niece, in the first place, and, when she had died, through his influence over her child, in the second. The necessary failure of all his projects, if Fabio married again, was next glanced at; and the time at which the first suspicion of the possible occurrence of this catastrophe occurred to his mind, was noted with scrupulous accuracy.

The fourth section narrated the manner in which the conspiracy of the Yellow Mask had originated. The writer described himself as being in his brother's studio, on the night of his niece's death, harassed by forebodings of the likelihood of Fabio's marrying again, and filled with the resolution to prevent any such disastrous second union at all hazards. He asserted that the idea of taking the wax mask from his brother's statue flashed upon him on a sudden, and that he knew of nothing to lead to it, except, perhaps, that he had been thinking, just before, of the superstitious nature of the young man's character, as he had himself observed it in the studio. He further declared that the idea of the wax mask terrified him at first; that he strove against a temptation of the devil; that, from fear of yielding to this temptation, he abstained even from entering the studio during his brother's absence at Naples, and that he first faltered in his good resolution when Fabio returned to Pisa, and when it was rumoured, not only that the young nobleman was going to the ball, but that he would certainly marry for the second time.

The fifth section related, that the writer, upon this, yielded to temptation rather than forego the cherished purpose of his life by allowing Fabio a chance of marrying again – that he made the wax mask in a plaster mould taken from the face of his brother's statue – and that he then had two separate interviews with a woman named Brigida (of whom he had some previous knowledge) who was ready and anxious, from motives of private malice, to personate the deceased Countess at the masquerade. This woman had suggested that some anonymous letters to Fabio would pave the way in his mind for the approaching impersonation, and had written the letters herself. However, even when all the preparations were made, the writer declared that he shrank from proceeding to extremities; and that he would have abandoned the whole project, but for the woman Brigida informing him one day that a work-girl named Nanina was to be one of the attendants at the ball. He knew the Count to have been in love with this girl, even to the point of wishing to marry her; he suspected that her engagement to wait at the ball was preconcerted; and, in consequence, he authorized his female accomplice to perform her part in the conspiracy.

The sixth section detailed the proceedings at the masquerade, and contained the writer's confession that, on the night before it, he had written to the Count proposing the reconciliation of a difference that had taken place between them, solely for the purpose of guarding himself against suspicion. He next acknowledged that he had borrowed the key of the Campo Santo gate, keeping the authority to whom it was intrusted in perfect ignorance of the purpose for which he wanted it. That purpose was to carry out the ghastly delusion of the wax mask (in the very probable event of the wearer being followed and inquired after) by having the woman Brigida taken up and set down at the gate of the cemetery in which Fabio's wife had been buried.

The seventh section solemnly averred that the sole object of the conspiracy was to prevent the young nobleman from marrying again, by working on his superstitious fears; the writer repeating, after this avowal, that any such second marriage would necessarily destroy his project for promoting the ultimate restoration of the church possessions, by diverting Count Fabio's property in great part, from his first wife's child, over whom the priest would always have influence, to another wife and probably other children, over whom he could not hope to have any.

The eighth and last section expressed the writer's contrition for having allowed his zeal for the church to mislead him into actions liable to bring scandal on his cloth; reiterated in the strongest language his conviction, that whatever might be thought of the means employed, the end he had proposed to himself was a most righteous one; and concluded by asserting his resolution to suffer with humility any penalties, however severe, which his ecclesiastical superiors might think fit to inflict on him.

Having looked over this extraordinary statement, the doctor addressed himself again to Luca Lomi.

'I agree with you,' he said, 'that no useful end is to be gained now by mentioning your brother's conduct in public – always provided, however, that his ecclesiastical superiors do their duty. I shall show these papers to the Count as soon as he is fit to peruse them, and I have no doubt that he will be ready to take my view of the matter.'

This assurance relieved Luca Lomi of a great weight of anxiety. He bowed and withdrew.

The doctor placed the papers in the same cabinet in which he had secured the wax mask. Before he locked the doors again he took out the flat box, opened it, and looked thoughtfully for a few minutes at the mask inside, then sent for Nanina.

'Now, my child,' he said, when she appeared, 'I am going to try our first experiment with Count Fabio; and I think it of great importance that you should be present while I speak to him.'

He took up the box with the mask in it, and beckoning to Nanina to follow him, led the way to Fabio's chamber.

CHAPTER VIII

About six months after the events already related, Signor Andrea d'Arbino and the Cavaliere Finello happened to be staying with a friend, in a seaside villa on the Castellamare shore of the Bay of Naples. Most of their time was pleasantly occupied on the sea, in fishing and sailing. A boat was placed entirely at their disposal. Sometimes they loitered whole days along the shore; sometimes made trips to the lovely islands in the bay.

One evening they were sailing near Sorrento, with a light wind. The beauty of the coast tempted them to keep the boat close in shore. A short time before sunset, they rounded the most picturesque headland they had yet passed; and a little bay, with a white sand beach, opened on their view. They noticed first a villa surrounded by orange and olive trees on the rocky heights inland – then a path in the cliffside leading down to the sands – then a little family party on the beach, enjoying the fragrant evening air.

The elders of the group were a lady and gentleman, sitting together on the sand. The lady had a guitar in her lap, and was playing a simple dance melody. Close at her side, a young child was rolling on the beach in high glee: in front of her a little girl was dancing to the music, with a very extraordinary partner in the shape of a dog, who was capering on his hind legs in the most grotesque manner. The merry laughter of the girl, and the lively notes of the guitar were heard distinctly across the still water.

'Edge a little nearer in shore,' said d'Arbino to his friend, who was steering; 'and keep as I do in the shadow of the sail. I want to see the faces of those persons on the beach without being seen by them.'

Finello obeyed. After approaching just near enough to see the countenances of the party on shore, and to be barked at lustily by the dog, they turned the boat's head again towards the offing.

'A pleasant voyage, gentlemen,' cried the clear voice of the little girl. They waved their hats in return; and then saw her run to the dog and take him by the fore-legs. 'Play, Nanina,' they heard her say. 'I have not half done with my partner yet.' The guitar sounded once more, and the grotesque dog was on his hind legs in a moment.

'I had heard that he was well again, that he had married her lately, and that he was away with her and her sister, and his child by the first wife,' said d'Arbino. 'But I had no suspicion that their place of retirement was so near us. It is too soon to break in upon their happiness, or I should have felt inclined to run the boat on shore.'

'I never heard the end of that strange adventure of the Yellow Mask,' said Finello. 'There was a priest mixed up in it, was there not?'

'Yes; but nobody seems to know exactly what has become of him. He was sent for to Rome, and has never been heard of since. One report is, that he has been condemned to some mysterious penal seclusion by his ecclesiastical superiors – another, that he has volunteered, as a sort of Forlorn Hope, to accept a colonial curacy among rough people, and in a pestilential climate. I asked his brother, the sculptor, about him a little while ago, but he only shook his head, and said nothing.'

'And the woman who wore the yellow mask?'

'She, too, has ended mysteriously. At Pisa she was obliged to sell off everything she possessed to pay her debts. Some friends of hers at a milliner's shop, to whom she applied for help, would have nothing to do with her. She left the city alone and penniless.'

The boat had approached the next headland on the coast while they were talking. They looked back for a last glance at the beach. Still the notes of the guitar came gently across the quiet water; but there mingled with them now the sound of the lady's voice. She was singing. The little girl and the dog were at her feet, and the gentleman was still in his old place close at her side.

In a few minutes more the boat rounded the next headland, the beach vanished from view, and the music died away softly in the distance.

THE FRENCH GOVERNESS'S STORY
OF SISTER ROSE

PROLOGUE

It was a sad day for me when Mr Lanfray of Rockleigh Place, discovering that his youngest daughter's health required a warm climate, removed from his English establishment to the South of France. Roving from place to place, as I am obliged to do, though I make many acquaintances, I keep but few friends. The nature of my calling is, I am quite aware, mainly answerable for this. People cannot be blamed for forgetting a man who, on leaving their houses, never can tell them for certain when he is likely to be in their neighbourhood again.

Mr Lanfray was one of the few exceptional persons who always remembered me. I have proofs of his friendly interest in my welfare in the shape of letters which I treasure with grateful care. The last of these is an invitation to his house in the South of France. There is little chance at present of my being able to profit by his kindness; but I like to read his invitation from time to time, for it makes me fancy, in my happier moments, that I may one day really be able to accept it.

My introduction to this gentleman, in my capacity of portrait-painter, did not promise much for me in a professional point of view. I was invited to Rockleigh – or to 'The Place,' as it was more frequently called among the people of the county – to take a likeness in water-colours, on a small scale, of the French governess who lived with Mr Lanfray's daughters. My first idea on hearing of this was, that the governess was about to leave her situation, and that her pupils wished to have a memorial of her in the shape of a portrait. Subsequent inquiry, however, informed me that I was in error. It was the eldest of Mr Lanfray's daughters, who was on the point of leaving the house to accompany her husband to India; and it was for her that the portrait had been ordered, as a home remembrance of her best and dearest friend. Besides these particulars, I discovered that the governess, though still called 'Mademoiselle,' was an old lady; that Mr Lanfray had been introduced to her many years since in France, after the death of his wife; that she was absolute mistress in the house; and that her three pupils had always looked up to her as a second mother, from the time when their father first placed them under her charge.

These scraps of information made me rather anxious to see Mademoiselle Clairfait, the governess.

On the day appointed for my attendance at the comfortable country-house of Rockleigh, I was detained on the road, and did not arrive at my destination until late in the evening. The welcome accorded to me by Mr Lanfray gave an earnest of the unvarying kindness that I was to experience at his hands in after-life. I was received at once on equal terms, as if I had been a friend of the family, and was presented the same evening to my host's daughters. They were not merely three elegant and attractive young women, but – what means much more than that – three admirable subjects for pictures, the bride particularly. Her young husband did not strike me much at first sight: he seemed rather shy and silent. After I had been introduced to him, I looked round for Mademoiselle Clairfait, but she was not present; and I was soon afterwards informed by Mr Lanfray that she always spent the latter part of the evening in her own room.

At the breakfast-table the next morning I again looked for my sitter, and once more in vain. 'Mamma, as we call her,' said one of the ladies, 'is dressing expressly for her picture, Mr Kerby. I hope you are not above painting silk, lace, and jewellery. The dear old lady, who is perfection in everything else, is perfection also in dress, and is bent on being painted in all her splendour.'

This explanation prepared me for something extraordinary; but I found that my anticipations had fallen far below the reality when Mademoiselle Clairfait at last made her appearance, and announced that she was ready to sit for her portrait.

Never before or since have I seen such perfect dressing and such active old age in combination. 'Mademoiselle' was short and thin; her face was perfectly white all over, the skin being puckered up in an infinite variety of the smallest possible wrinkles. Her bright black eyes were perfect marvels of youthfulness and and vivacity. They sparkled, and beamed, and ogled, and moved about over everybody and everything as such a rate, that the plain grey hair above them looked unnaturally venerable, and the wrinkles below an artful piece of masquerade to represent old age. As for her dress, I remember few harder pieces of work than the painting of it. She wore a silver-grey silk gown, that seemed always flashing out into some new light whenever she moved. It was as stiff as a board, and rustled like the wind. Her head, neck, and bosom were enveloped in clouds of the airiest-looking lace I ever saw, disposed about each part of her with the most exquisite grace and propriety, and glistening at all sorts of unexpected places with little fairy-like toys in gold and precious stones. On her right wrist she wore three small bracelets with the hair of her three pupils worked into them; and on her left, one large bracelet with a miniature let in over the clasp. She had a dark crimson and gold scarf thrown coquettishly over her shoulders, and held a lovely little feather-fan in her hand. When she first presented herself before me in this costume, with a brisk curtsy and a bright smile, filling the room with perfume, and gracefully flirting the feather-fan, I lost all confidence in my powers as a portrait-painter immediately. The brightest colours in my box looked dowdy and dim, and I myself felt like an unwashed, unbrushed, unpresentable sloven.

'Tell me, my angels,' said Mademoiselle, apostrophizing her pupils in the prettiest foreign English, 'am I the cream of all creams this morning? Do I carry my sixty years resplendently? Will the savages in India, when my own love exhibits my picture among them, say,'Ah! smart! this was a great dandy?' And the gentleman, the skilful artist, whom it is even more an honour than a happiness to meet, does he approve of me for a model? Does he find me pretty and paintable from top to toe?' Here she dropped me another brisk curtsy, placed herself in a languishing position in the sitter's chair, and asked us all if she looked like a shepherdess in Dresden china.

The young ladies burst out laughing, and Mademoiselle, as gay as any of them and a great deal shriller, joined in the merriment. Never before had I contended with any sitter half as restless as that wonderful old lady. No sooner had I begun than she jumped out of the chair, and exclaiming, '*Grand Dieu*! I have forgotten to embrace my angels this morning,' ran up to her pupils, raised herself on tiptoe before them in quick succession, put the two first fingers of each hand under their ears, kissed them lightly on both cheeks, and was back again in the chair before an English governess could have said, 'Good morning, my dears, I hope you all slept well last night.'

I began again. Up jumped Mademoiselle for the second time, and tripped across the room to a cheval glass. 'No!' I heard her say to herself, 'I have not discomposed my head in kissing my angels. I may come back and pose for my picture.'

Back she came. I worked from her for five minutes at the most. 'Stop!' cries Mademoiselle, jumping up for the third time; 'I must see how this skilful artist is getting on. *Grand Dieu*! why he has done nothing!'

For the fourth time I began, and for the fourth time the old lady started out of her chair. 'Now I must repose myself,' said Mademoiselle, walking lightly from end to end of the room, and humming a French air, by way of taking a rest.

I was at my wits end, and the young ladies saw it. They all surrounded my unmanagable sitter, and appealed to her compassion for me. 'Certainly!' said Mademoiselle, expressing astonishment by flinging up both her hands with all the fingers spread out in the air. 'But why apostrophize me thus? I am here, I am ready, I am at the service of this skilful artist. Why apostrophize me?'

A fortunate chance-question of mine steadied her for some time. I inquired if I was expected to draw the whole of my sitter's figure as well as her face. Mademoiselle replied by a comic scream of indignation. If I was the brave and gifted man for whom she took me, I ought to be ready to perish rather than leave out an inch of her anywhere. Dress was her passion, and it would be an outrage on her sentiments if I did not do full justice to everything she had on – to her robe, to her lace, to her scarf, to her fan, to her rings, her jewels, and, above all, to her bracelets. I groaned in spirit at the task before me, but made my best bow of acquiescence. Mademoiselle was not to be satisfied by a mere bow: she desired the pleasure of specially directing my attention, if I would be so amiable as to get up and approach her, to one of her bracelets in particular – the bracelet with the miniature, on her left wrist. It had been the gift of the dearest friend she ever had, and the miniature represented that friend's beloved and beautiful face. Could I make a tiny, tiny copy of that likeness in my drawing? Would I only be so obliging as to approach for one little moment, and see if such a thing were possible?

I obeyed unwillingly enough, expecting, from Mademoiselle's expression, to see a common-place portrait of some unfortunate admirer whom she had treated with unmerited severity in the days of her youth. To my astonishment, I found that the miniature, which was very beautifully painted, represented a woman's face – a young woman with kind, sad eyes, pale delicate cheeks, light hair, and such a pure, tender, lovely expression, that I thought of Raphael's Madonnas the moment I looked at her portrait.

The old lady observed the impression which the miniature produced on me, and nodded her head in silence. 'What a beautiful, innocent, pure face!' I said.

Mademoiselle Clairfait gently brushed a particle of dust from the miniature with her handkerchief, and kissed it. 'I have three angels still left,' she said, looking at her pupils. 'They console me for the fourth, who has gone to heaven.'

She patted the face on the miniature gently with her little withered white fingers, as if it had been a living thing. 'Sister Rose!' she sighed to herself, then, looking up again at me, said:– 'I should like it put into my portrait, sir, because I have always worn it since I was a young woman, for 'Sister Rose's sake.'

The sudden change in her manner from the extreme of flighty gaiety to the extreme of quiet sadness, would have looked theatrical in a woman of any other nation. It seemed, however, perfectly natural and appropriate in her. I went back to my drawing, rather perplexed. Who was 'Sister Rose?' Not one of the Lanfray family apparently. The composure of the young ladies when the name was mentioned showed plainly enough that the original of the miniature had been no relation of theirs.

I tried to stifle my curiosity on the subject of Sister Rose, by giving myself entirely to my work. For a full half-hour, Mademoiselle Clairfait sat quietly before me with her hands crossed on her lap, and her eyes fixed on the bracelet. This happy alteration enabled me to do something towards completing the outline of her face and figure. I might even under fortunate circumstances have vanquished the preliminary difficulties of my task at one effort; but the fates were against me that day. While I was still working rapidly and to my satisfaction, a servant knocked at the door, to announce luncheon, and Mademoiselle lightly roused herself from her serious reflections and her quiet position in a moment.

'Ah me!' she said, turning the miniature round on her wrist till it was out of sight. 'What animals we are after all! The spiritual part of us is at the mercy of the stomach. My heart is absorbed by tender thoughts, yet I am not the less ready for luncheon! Come, my children and fellow-mortals. '*Allons cultiver notre jardin!*'

With this quotation from *Candide*, plaintively delivered, the old lady led the way out of the room, and was followed by her younger pupils. The eldest sister remained behind for a moment, and reminded me that the lunch was ready.

'I am afraid you have found the dear old soul rather an unruly sitter,' she said, noticing the look of dissatisfaction with which I was regarding my drawing. 'But she will improve as you go on. She has done better already for the last half-hour, has she not?'

'Much better,' I answered. 'My admiration of the miniature on the bracelet seemed – I suppose, by calling up some old associations – to have a strangely soothing effect on Mademoiselle Clairfait.'

'Ah, yes! only remind her of the original of that portrait, and you change her directly, whatever she may have been saying or doing the moment before. Sometimes she talks of *Sister Rose*, and of all that she went through in the time of the French Revolution, by the hour together. It is wonderfully interesting – at least we all think so.'

'I presume that the lady described as 'Sister Rose,' was a relation of Mademoiselle Clairfait's?'

'No, only a very dear friend. Mademoiselle Clairfait is the daughter of a silk-mercer, once established at Chalons-ser-Marne. Her father happened to give asylum in his office to a lonely old man, to whom 'Sister Rose' and her brother had been greatly indebted in the revolutionary time; and out of a train of circumstances connected with that, the first acquaintance between Mademoiselle and the friend whose portrait she wears, arose. After the time of her father's bankruptcy, and for many years before we were placed under her charge, our good old governess lived entirely with 'Sister Rose' and her brother. She must then have heard all the interesting things that she has since often repeated to my sisters and myself.'

'Might I suggest,' said I, after an instant's consideration, 'that the best way to give me a fair chance of studying Mademoiselle Clairfait's face at the next sitting, would be to lead her thoughts again to that quieting subject of the miniature, and to the events which the portrait recalls? It is really the only plan, after what I have observed this morning, that I can think of for enabling me to do myself and my sitter justice.'

'I am delighted to hear you say so,' replied the lady; 'for the execution of you plan, by me or by my sisters, will be the easiest thing in the world. A word from us at any time, will set Mademoiselle thinking, and talking too, of the friend of her youthful days. Depend on our assistance so far. And now, let me show you the way to the luncheon table.'

Two good results followed the ready rendering of the help I had asked from my host's daughters. I succeeded with my portrait of Mademoiselle Clairfait, and I heard the story which occupies the following pages.

In the case of the preceding narratives, I repeated what was related to me, as nearly as possible in the very words of my sitters. In the case of this third story, it is impossible for me to proceed upon the same plan. The circumstances of 'Sister Rose's' eventful history were narrated to me at different times, and in the most fragmentary and discursive manner. Mademoiselle Clairfait characteristically mixed up with the direct interest of her story, not only references to places and people which had no recognisable connexion with it, but outbursts of passionate political declamation, on the extreme liberal side – to say nothing of little tender apostrophes to her beloved friend, which sounded very prettily as she spoke them, but which would lose their effect altogether by being transferred to paper. Under these circumstances, I have thought it best to tell the story in my own way – rigidly adhering to the events of it exactly as they were related; and never interfering on my own responsibility except to keep order in the march of the incidents, and to present them to the best of my ability variously as well as interestingly to the reader.

PART FIRST

CHAPTER I

'Well, Monsieur Guillaume, what is the news this evening?'

'None that I know of, Monsieur Justin, except that Mademoiselle Rose is to be married to-morrow.'

'Much obliged, my respectable old friend, for so interesting and unexpected a reply to my question. Considering that I am the valet of Monsieur Danville, who plays the distinguished part of bridegroom in the little wedding comedy to which you refer, I think I may assure you, without offence, that your news is, so far as I am concerned, of the stalest possible kind. Take a pinch of snuff, Monsieur Guillaume, and excuse me if I inform you that my question referred to public news, and not to the private affairs of the two families whose household interests we have the pleasure of promoting.'

'I don't understand what you mean by such a phrase as promoting household interests, Monsieur Justin. I am the servant of Monsieur Louis Trudaine, who lives here with his sister, Mademoiselle Rose. You are the servant of Monsieur Danville, whose excellent mother has made up the match for him with my young lady. As servants, both of us, the pleasantest news we can have any concern with is news that is connected with the happiness of our masters. I have nothing to do with public affairs; and, being one of the old school, I make it my main object in life to mind my own business. If our homely domestic politics have no interest for you, allow me to express my regret, and to wish you a very good evening.'

'Pardon me, my dear sir, I have not the slightest respect for the old school, or the least sympathy with people who only mind their own business. However, I accept you expressions of regret; I reciprocate your Good evening; and I trust to find you improved in temper, dress, manners, and appearance the next time I have the honour of meeting you. Adieu, Monsieur

Guillaume, and *Vive la bagatelle!*'

These scraps of dialogue were interchanged on a lovely summer evening in the year seventeen hundred and eighty-nine, before the back-door of a small house which stood on the banks of the Seine, about three miles westward of the city of Rouen. The one speaker was lean, old, crabbed, and slovenly; the other was plump, young, oily-mannered, and dressed in the most gorgeous livery costume of the period. The last days of genuine dandyism were then rapidly approaching all over the civilized world; and Monsieur Justin was, in his own way, dressed to perfection, as a living illustration of the expiring glories of his epoch.

After the old servant had left him, he occupied himself for a few minutes in contemplating, superciliously enough, the back view of the little house before which he stood. Judging by the windows, it did not contain more than six or eight rooms in all. Instead of stables and outhouses, there was a conservatory attached to the building on one side, and a low long room, built of wood gaily painted, on the other. One of the windows of this room was left uncurtained, and through it could be seen, on a sort of dresser inside, bottles filled with strangely-coloured liquids, oddly-shaped utensils of brass and copper, one end of a large furnace, and other objects, which plainly proclaimed that the apartment was used as a chemical laboratory.

'Think of our bride's brother amusing himself in such a place as that with cooking drugs in saucepans,' muttered Monsieur Justin, peeping into the room. 'I am the least particular man in the universe, but I must say I wish we were not going to be connected by marriage with an amateur apothecary. Pah! I can smell the place through the window.'

With these words Monsieur Justin turned his back on the laboratory in disgust, and sauntered towards the cliffs overhang-ing the river.

Leaving the garden attached to the house, he ascended some gently-rising ground by a winding path. Arrived at the summit, the whole view of the Seine with its lovely green islands, its banks fringed with trees, its gliding boats, and little scattered waterside cottages opened before him. Westward, where the level country appeared beyond the further bank of the river, the landscape was all a-glow with the crimson of the setting sun. Eastward, the long shadows and mellow intervening lights, the red glory that quivered on the rippling water, the steady ruby-fire glowing on cottage windows that reflected the level sunlight, led the eye onward and onward, along the windings of the Seine, until it rested upon the spires, towers, and broadly-massed houses of Rouen, with the wooded hills rising beyond them for background. Lovely to look on at any time, the view was almost supernaturally beautiful now under the gorgeous evening light that glowed upon it. All its attractions, however, were lost on the valet; he stood yawning with his hands in his pockets, looking neither to the right nor to the left, but staring straight before him at a little hollow, beyond which the ground sloped away smoothly to the brink of the cliff. A bench was placed here, and three persons – an old lady, a gentleman, and a young girl – were seated on it, watching the sunset, and by consequence turning their backs on Monsieur Justin. Near them stood two gentlemen, also looking towards the river and the distant view. These five figures attracted the valet's attention, to the exclusion of every other object around him.

'There they are still,' he said to himself discontentedly. 'Madame Danville in the same place on the seat; my master, the bridegroom, dutifully next to her; Mademoiselle Rose, the bride, bashfully next to him; Monsieur Trudaine, the amateur apothecary brother, affectionately next to her; and Monsieur Lomaque, our queer land-steward, officially in the waiting on the whole party. There they all are indeed, incomprehensibly wasting their time still in looking at nothing! Yes,' continued Monsieur Justin, lifting his eyes wearily, and staring hard, first up the river at Rouen, then down the river at the setting sun; 'yes, plague take them, looking at nothing, absolutely and positively at nothing, all this while.

Here Monsieur Justin yawned again, and, returning to the garden, sat himself down in an arbour and resignedly went to sleep.

If the valet had ventured near the five persons whom he had been apostrophizing from a distance, and if he had been possessed of some little refinement of observation, he could hardly have failed to remark that the bride and bridegroom of the morrow, and their companions on either side, were all, in a greater or less degree, under the influence of some secret restraint, which affected their conversation, their gestures, and even the expression of their faces. Madame Danville – a handsome, richly-dressed old lady, with very bright eyes, and a quick suspicious manner – looked composedly and happily enough, as long as her attention was fixed on her son. But when she turned from him towards the bride, a hardly-perceptible uneasiness passed over her face – an uneasiness which only deepened to positive distrust and dissatisfaction whenever she looked towards Mademoiselle Trudaine's brother. In the same way, her son, who was all smiles and happiness while he was speaking with his future wife, altered visibly in manner and look, exactly as his mother altered, whenever the presence of Monsieur Trudaine specially impressed itself on his attention. Then, again, Lomaque the land-steward – quiet, sharp, skinny Lomaque, with the submissive manner, and the red-rimmed eyes – never looked up at his master's future brother-in-law without looking away again rather uneasily, and thoughtfully drilling holes in the grass with his long sharp-pointed cane. Even the bride herself, the pretty innocent girl, with her childish shyness of manner, seemed to be affected like the others. Doubt, if not distress, overshadowed her face from time to time, and the hand which her lover held trembled a little, and grew restless, when she accidentally caught her brother's eye.

Strangely enough there was nothing to repel, but, on the contrary, everything to attract in the look and manner of the person whose mere presence seemed to exercise such a curiously constraining influence over the wedding-party. Louis Trudaine was a remarkably handsome man. His expression was singularly kind and gentle; his manner irresistibly winning in its frank, manly firmness and composure. His words, when he occasionally spoke, seemed as unlikely to give offence as his looks; for he only opened his lips in courteous reply to questions directly addressed to him. Judging by a latent mournfulness in the tones of his voice, and by the sorrowful tenderness which clouded his kind earnest eyes whenever they rested on his sister, his thoughts were certainly not of the happy or the hopeful kind. But he gave them no direct expression; he intruded his secret sadness, whatever it might be, on no one of his companions. Nevertheless, modest and self-restrained as he was, there was evidently some reproving or saddening influence in his presence which affected the spirits of everyone near him, and darkened the eve of the wedding to bride and bridegroom alike.

As the sun slowly sank in the heaven, the conversation flagged more and more. After a long silence the bridegroom was the first to start a new subject.

'Rose, love,' he said, 'that magnificent sunset is a good omen for our marriage; it promises another lovely day to-morrow.'

The bride laughed and blushed.

'Do you really believe in omens, Charles?' she said.

'My dear,' interposed the old lady, before her son could answer, 'if Charles does believe in omens, it is nothing to laugh at. You will soon know better, when you are his wife, than to confound him, even in the slightest things, with the common herd of people. All his convictions are well founded – so well, that if I thought he really did believe in omens, I should most assuredly make up my mind to believe in them too.'

'I beg your pardon, madam,' Rose began tremulously, 'I only meant —'

'My dear child, have you so little knowledge of the world as to suppose that I could be offended —'

'Let Rose speak,' said the young man.

He turned round petulantly, almost with the air of a spoilt child, to his mother, as he said those words. She had been looking fondly and proudly on him the moment before. Now her eyes wandered disconcertedly from his face; she hesitated an instant with a sudden confusion which seemed quite foreign to her character, then whispered in his ear:

'Am I to blame, Charles, for trying to make her worthy of you?'

Her son took no notice of the question. He only reiterated sharply, – 'Let Rose speak.'

'I really had nothing to say,' faltered the young girl, growing more and more confused.

'Oh, but you had!'

There was such an ungracious sharpness in his voice, such an outburst of petulance in his manner as he spoke, that his

mother gave him a warning touch on the arm, and whispered
'Hush!'

Monsieur Lomaque the land-steward, and Monsieur
Trudaine the brother, both glanced searchingly at the bride, as
the words passed the bridegroom's lips. She seemed to be
frightened and astonished, rather than irritated or hurt. A
curious smile puckered up Lomaque's lean face, as he looked
demurely down on the ground, and began drilling a fresh hole
in the turf with the sharp point of his cane. Trudaine turned
aside quickly, and, sighing, walked away a few paces; then
came back, and seemed about to speak, but Danville interrupted him.

'Pardon me, Rose,' he said; 'I am so jealous of even the
appearance of any want of attention towards you, that I was
nearly allowing myself to be irritated about nothing.'

He kissed her hand very gracefully and tenderly as he made
his excuse; but there was a latent expression in his eye which
was at variance with the apparent spirit of his action. It was
noticed by nobody but observant and submissive Monsieur
Lomaque, who smiled to himself again, and drilled harder
than ever at his hole in the grass.

'I think Monsieur Trudaine was about to speak,' said
Madame Danville. 'Perhaps he will have no objection to let us
hear what he was going to say.'

'None, madame,' replied Trudaine politely. 'I was about to
take upon myself the blame of Rose's want of respect for
believers in omens, by confessing that I have always encouraged her to laugh at superstitions of every kind.'

'You a ridiculer of superstitions!' said Danville, turning
quickly on him. 'You who have built a laboratory; you who
are an amateur professor of the occult arts of chemistry, a
seeker after the Elixir of Life. On my word of honour, you
astonish me!'

There was an ironical politeness in his voice, look, and
manner as he said this, which his mother and his land-steward,
Monsieur Lomaque, evidently knew how to interpret. The
first touched his arm again and whispered 'Be careful!' the
second suddenly grew serious, and left off drilling his hole in
the grass. Rose neither heard the warning of Madame
Danville, nor noticed the alteration in Lomaque. She was

looking round at her brother, and was waiting with a bright affectionate smile to hear his answer. He nodded, as if to reassure her, before he spoke again to Danville.

'You have rather romantic ideas about experiments in chemistry,' he said quietly. 'Mine have so little connexion with what you call the occult arts, that all the world might see them, if all the world thought it worth while. The only Elixirs of Life that I know of are a quiet heart and contented mind. Both those I found, years and years ago, when Rose and I first came to live together in the house yonder.'

He spoke with a quiet sadness in his voice, which meant far more to his sister than the simple words he uttered. Her eyes filled with tears: she turned for a moment from her lover and took her brother's hand. 'Don't talk, Louis, as if you thought you were going to lose your sister, because —' Her lip began to tremble, and she stopped suddenly.

More jealous than ever of your taking her away from him!' whispered Madame Danville in her son's ear. 'Hush! don't, for God's sake, take any notice of it,' she added hurriedly, as he rose from the seat and faced Trudaine with undisguised irritation and impatience in his manner. Before he could speak, the old servant Guillaume made his appearance, and announced that coffee was ready. Madame Danville again said 'Hush!' and quickly took one of his arms, while he offered the other to Rose. 'Charles!' said the young girl, amazedly, 'how flushed your face is, and how your arm trembles!'

He controlled himself in a moment, smiled, and said to her, 'Can't you guess why, Rose? I am thinking of to-morrow.' While he was speaking, he passed close by the land-steward, on his way back to the house with the ladies. The smile returned to Monsieur Lomaque's lean face, and a curious light twinkled in his red-rimmed eyes, as he began a fresh hole in the grass.

'Won't you go indoors, and take some coffee?' asked Trudaine, touching the land-steward on the arm.

Monsieur Lomaque started a little, and left his cane sticking in the ground. 'A thousand thanks, monsieur,' he said: 'may I be allowed to follow you?'

'I confess the beauty of the evening makes me a little unwilling to leave this place just yet.'

'Ah! the beauties of nature – I feel them with you, Monsieur Trudaine: I feel them here.' Saying this, Lomaque laid one hand on his heart, and with the other pulled stick out of the grass. He had looked as little at the landscape or the setting sun as Monsieur Justin himself.

They sat down, side by side, on the empty bench; and then there followed an awkward pause. Submissive Lomaque was too discreet to forget his place, and venture on starting a new topic. Trudaine was pre-occupied, and disinclined to talk. It was necessary, however, in common politeness, to say something. Hardly attending himself to his own words, he began with a common-place phrase, – 'I regret, Monsieur Lomaque, that we have not had more opportunities of bettering our acquaintance.'

'I feel deeply indebted,' rejoined the land-steward, 'to the admirable Madame Danville for having chosen me as her escort hither from her son's estate near Lyons, and having thereby procured for me the honour of this introduction.' Both Monsieur Lomaque's red-rimmed eyes were seized with a sudden fit of winking, as he made this polite speech. His enemies were accustomed to say, that whenever he was particularly insincere, or particularly deceitful, he always took refuge in the weakness of his eyes, and so evaded the trying ordeal of being obliged to look steadily at the person whom he was speaking with.

'I was pleased to hear you mention my late father's name, at dinner, in terms of high respect,' continued Trudaine, resolutely keeping up the conversation. 'Did you know him?'

'I am indirectly indebted to your excellent father,' answered the land-steward, 'for the very situation which I now hold. At a time when the good word of a man of substance and reputation was needed to save me from poverty and ruin, your father spoke that word. Since then, I have, in my own very small way, succeeded in life, until I have risen to the honour of superintending the estate of Monsieur Danville.

'Excuse me – but your way of speaking of your present situation rather surprises me. Your father, I believe, was a merchant, just as Danville's father was a merchant; the only difference between them was, that one failed, and the other realized a large fortune. Why should you speak of yourself as honoured by holding your present place?'

'Have you never heard?' exclaimed Lomaque, with an appearance of great astonishment, 'or can you have heard, and forgotten, that Madame Danville is descended from one of the noble houses of France? Has she never told you, as she has often told me, that she condescended when she married her late husband; and that her great object in life is to get the title of her family (years since extinct in the male line) settled on her son?'

'Yes,' replied Trudaine; 'I remember to have heard something of this, and to have paid no great attention to it at the time, having little sympathy with such aspirations as you describe. You have lived many years in Danville's service, Monsieur Lomaque, have you' – he hesitated for a moment, then continued, looking the land-steward full in the face, 'have you found him a good and kind master?'

Lomaque's thin lips seemed to close instinctively at the question, as if he were never going to speak again. He bowed – Trudaine waited – he only bowed again. Trudaine waited a third time. Lomaque looked at his host with perfect steadiness for an instant, then his eyes began to get weak again. 'You seem to have some special interest,' he quietly remarked, 'if I may say so without offence, in asking me that question.

'I deal frankly, at all hazards, with every one,' returned Trudaine; 'and stranger as you are, I will deal frankly with you. I acknowledge that I have an interest in asking that question – the dearest, the tenderest of all interests.' At those last words, his voice trembled for a moment, but he went on firmly; 'from the beginning of my sister's engagement with Danville, I made it my duty not to conceal my own feelings: my conscience and my affection for Rose counselled me to be candid to the last, even though my candour should distress or offend others. When we first made the acquaintance of Madame Danville, and when I first discovered that her son's attentions to Rose were not unfavourably received, I felt astonished, and, though it cost me a hard effort, I did not conceal that astonishment from my sister —'

Lomaque, who had hitherto been all attention, started here, and threw up his hands in amazement. 'Astonished, did I hear you say? Astonished, Monsieur Trudaine, that the attentions of a young gentleman possessed of all the graces and accomplishments of a highly-bred Frenchman should be favourably received by a young lady! Astonished that such a dancer, such a singer, such a talker, such a notoriously fascinating ladies' man as Monsieur Danville should, by dint of respectful assiduity, succeed in making some impression on the heart of Mademoiselle Rose! Oh! Monsieur Trudaine, venerated Monsieur Trudaine, this is almost too much to credit!' Lomaque's eyes grew weaker than ever, and winked incessantly, as he uttered this apostrophe. At the end, he threw up his hands again, and blinked inquiringly all round him, in mute appeal to universal nature.

'When, in the course of time, matters were farther advanced,' continued Trudaine, without paying any attention to the interruption; 'when the offer of marriage was made, and when I knew that Rose had in her own heart accepted it, I objected, and I did not conceal my objections —'

'Heavens!' interposed Lomaque again, clasping his hands this time with a look of bewilderment; 'what objections? what possible objections to a man young and well-bred, with an immense fortune and an uncompromised character? I have heard of these objections: I know they have made bad blood; and I ask myself again and again, what can they be?'

'God knows I have often tried to dismiss them from my mind, as fanciful and absurd,' said Trudaine, 'and I have always failed. It is impossible, in your presence, that I can describe in detail what my own impressions have been, from the first, of the master whom you serve. Let it be enough if I confide to you that I cannot, even now, persuade myself of the sincerity of his attachment to my sister, and that I feel – in spite of myself, in spite of my earnest desire to put the most implicit confidence in Rose's choice – a distrust of his character and temper, which now, on the eve of the marriage, amounts to positive terror. Long secret suffering, doubt and suspense, wring this confession from me, Monsieur Lomaque, almost unawares, in defiance of caution, in defiance of all the conventionalities of society. You have lived for years under the same roof with this man; you have seen him in his most unguarded and private moments. I tempt you to betray no confidence – I only ask you if you can make me happy by telling me that I have been doing your master grievous injustice by my opinion of him? I ask you to take my hand, and tell me if you can, in all honour, that my sister is not risking the happiness of her whole life by giving herself in marriage to Danville tomorrow!'

He held out his hand while he spoke. By some strange chance, Lomaque happened just at that moment to be looking away towards those beauties of nature which he admired so greatly. 'Really, Monsieur Trudaine, really such an appeal from you, at such a time, amazes me.' Having got so far, he stopped and said no more.

'When we first sat down together here, I had no thought of making this appeal, no idea of talking to you as I have talked,' pursued the other. 'My words have escaped me, as I told you, almost unawares – you must make allowances for them and for me. I cannot expect others, Monsieur Lomaque, to appreciate and understand my feelings for Rose. We two have lived alone in the world together: father, mother, kindred, they all died years since and left us. I am so much older than my sister, that I have learnt to feel towards her more as a father than as a brother. All my life, all my dearest hopes, all my highest expectations have centred in her. I was past the period of my boyhood when my mother put my little child-sister's hand in mine, and said to me on her death-bed, 'Louis, be all to her that I have been, for she has no one left to look to but you.' Since then the loves and ambitions of other men have not been my loves or my ambitions. Sister Rose – as we all used to call her in those past days, as I love to call her still – Sister Rose has been the one aim, the one happiness, the one precious trust, the one treasured reward of all my life. I have lived in this poor house, in this dull retirement, as in a Paradise, because Sister Rose, my innocent, happy, bright-faced Eve, has lived here with me. Even if the husband of her choice had been the husband of mine, the necessity of parting with her would have been the hardest, the bitterest of trials. As it is, thinking what I think, dreading what I dread, judge what my feelings must be on the eve of her marriage; and know why, and with what object, I made the appeal which surprised you a moment since, but which cannot surprise you now. Speak if you will – I can say no more.' He sighed bitterly; his head dropped on his breast, and the hand which he had extended to Lomaque trembled as he withdrew it and let it fall at his side.

The land-steward was not a man accustomed to hesitate, but he hesitated now. He was not usually at a loss for phrases in which to express himself, but he stammered at the very outset of his reply. 'Suppose I answered,' he began slowly; 'suppose I told you that you wronged him, would my testimony really be strong enough to shake opinions, or rather presumptions, which have been taking firmer and firmer hold of you for months and months past? Suppose, on the other hand, that my master had his little' – (Lomaque hesitated before he pronounced the next word) – 'his little – infirmities, let me say; but only hypothetically, mind that – infirmities; and suppose I had observed them, and was willing to confide them to you, what purpose would such a confidence answer now, at the eleventh hour, with Mademoiselle Rose's heart engaged, with the marriage fixed for to-morrow? No! no! trust me —'

Trudaine looked up suddenly. 'I thank you for reminding me, Monsieur Lomaque, that it is too late now to make inquiries, and by consequence too late also to trust in others. My sister has chosen; and on the subject of that choice my lips shall be hence-forth sealed. The events of the future are with God: whatever they may be, I hope I am strong enough to bear my part in them with the patience and the courage of a man! I apologize, Monsieur Lomaque, for having thoughtlessly embarrassed you by questions which I had no right to ask. Let us return to the house – I will show you the way.'

Lomaque's lips opened, then closed again: he bowed uneasily, and his sallow complexion whitened for a moment.

Trudaine led the way in silence back to the house: the land-steward following slowly at a distance of several paces, and talking in whispers to himself. 'His father was the saving of me,' muttered Lomaque; 'that is truth, and there is no getting over it: his father was the saving of me; and yet here am I – no! it's too late! – too late to speak – too late to act – too late to do anything!'

Close to the house they were met by the old servant. 'My young lady had just sent me to call you in to coffee, Monsieur,' said Guillaume. 'She has kept a cup hot for you, and another cup for Monsieur Lomaque.'

The land-steward stared – this time with genuine astonishment. 'For me!' he exclaimed. 'Mademoiselle Rose has troubled herself to keep a cup of coffee hot for me?' The old servant started; Trudaine stopped and looked back. 'What is there so very surprising,' he asked, 'in such an ordinary act of politeness on my sister's part?'

'Excuse me, Monsieur Trudaine,' answered Lomaque: 'you have not passed such an existence as mine – you are not a friendless old man – you have a settled position in the world, and are used to be treated with consideration. I am not. This is the first occasion in my life on which I find myself an object for the attention of a young lady, and it takes me by surprise. I repeat my excuses – pray let us go in.'

Trudaine made no reply to this curious explanation. He wondered at it a little, however, and he wondered still more, when, on entering the drawing-room, he saw Lomaque walk straight up to his sister, and – apparently not noticing that Danville was sitting at the harpsichord and singing at the time – address her confusedly and earnestly with a set speech of thanks for his hot cup of coffee. Rose looked perplexed and half inclined to laugh, as she listened to him. Madame Danville, who sat by her side, frowned, and tapped the land-steward contemptuously on the arm with her fan.

'Be so good as to keep silent until my son has done singing,' she said. Lomaque made a low bow, and retiring to a table in a corner, took up a newspaper lying on it. If Madame Danville had seen the expression that came over his face when he turned away from her, proud as she was, her aristocratic composure might possibly have been a little ruffled.

Danville had finished his song, had quitted the harpsichord, and was talking in whispers to his bride; Madame Danville was adding a word to the conversation every now and then; Turdaine was seated apart at the far-end of the room, thoughtfully reading a letter which he had taken from his pocket – when an exclamation from Lomaque, who was still engaged with the newspaper, caused all the other occupants of the apartment to suspend their employment and look up.

'What is it?' asked Danville, impatiently.

'Shall I be interrupting, if I explain?' inquired Lomaque, getting very weak in the eyes again, as he deferentially addressed himself to Madame Danville.

'You have already interrupted us,' said the old lady sharply; 'so you may now just as well explain.'

'It is a passage from the Scientific Intelligence, which has given me great delight, and which will be joyful news for every one here.' Saying this, Lomaque looked significantly at Trudaine, and then read from the newspaper these lines:-

"ACADEMY OF SCIENCES, PARIS. – The vacant sub-professorship of chemistry has been offered, we are rejoiced to hear, to a gentleman whose modesty has hitherto prevented his scientific merits from becoming sufficiently prominent in the world. To the members of the academy he has been long since known as the originator of some of the most remarkable improvements in chemistry which have been made of late years – improvements, the credit of which he has, with rare, and we were almost about to add, culpable moderation, allowed others to profit by with impunity. No man in any profession is more thoroughly entitled to have a position of trust and distinction conferred on him by the state than the gentleman to whom we refer – M. Louis Trudaine."

Before Lomaque could look up from the paper to observe the impression which his news produced, Rose had gained her brother's side, and was kissing him in a flutter of delight.

'Dear Louis,' she cried, clapping her hands, 'let me be the first to congratulate you! How proud and glad I am! You accept the professorship, of course?'

Trudaine, who had hastily and confusedly put his letter back in his pocket the moment Lomaque began to read, seemed at a loss for an answer. He patted his sister's hand rather absently, and said,

'I have not made up my mind; don't ask me why, Rose – at least not now, not just now.' An expression of perplexity and distress came over his face, as he gently motioned her to resume her chair.

'Pray, is a sub-professor of chemistry supposed to hold the rank of a gentleman?' asked Madame Danville, without the slightest appearance of any special interest in Lomaque's news.

'Of course not,' replied her son, with a sarcastic laugh; 'he is expected to work and make himself useful. What gentleman does that?'

'Charles!' exclaimed the old lady, reddening with anger.

'Bah!' cried Danville, turning his back on her, 'enough of chemistry. Lomaque! now you have begun reading the newspaper, try if you can't find something interesting to read about. What are the last accounts from Paris? Any more symptoms of a general revolt?'

Lomaque turned to another part of the paper. 'Bad, very bad prospects for the restoration of tranquillity,' he said. 'Necker, the people's minister, is dismissed. Placards against popular gatherings are posted all over Paris. The Swiss Guards have been ordered to the Champs Elysées, with four pieces of artillery. No more is yet known, but the worst is dreaded. The breach between the aristocracy and the people is widening fatally almost hour by hour.'

Here he stopped and laid down the newspaper. Trudaine took it from him, and shook his head forebodingly, as he looked over the paragraph which had just been read.

'Bah!' cried Madame Danville. 'The People, indeed! Let those four pieces of artillery be properly loaded, let the Swiss Guards do their duty, and we shall hear no more of the People!'

'I advise you not to be sure of that,' said her son, carelessly, 'there are rather too many people in Paris for the Swiss Guards to shoot conveniently. Don't hold your head too aristocratically high, mother, till we are quite certain which way the wind really does blow. Who knows if I may not have to bow just as low one of these days to King Mob, as ever you curtsyed in your youth to King Louis the Fifteenth!'

He laughed complacently as he ended, and opened his snuff-box. His mother rose from her chair, her face crimson with indignation.

'I won't hear you talk so – it shocks, it horrifies me!' she exclaimed with vehement gesticulation. 'No, no! I decline to hear another word. I decline to sit by patiently, while my son, whom I love, jests at the most sacred principles, and sneers at the memory of an anointed king. This is my reward, is it, for having yielded and having come here, against all the laws of etiquette, the night before the marriage? I comply no longer; I resume my own will and my own way. I order you, my son, to accompany me back to Rouen. We are the bridegroom's party, and we have no business overnight at the house of the bride. You meet no more till you meet at the church. Justin! my coach! Lomaque, pick up my hood. Monsieur Trudaine! thanks for your hospitality; I shall hope to return it with interest the first time you are in our neighbourhood. Mademoiselle! put on your best looks to-morrow, along with your wedding finery; and remember that my son's bride must do honour to my son's taste. Justin! my coach – drone, vagabond, idiot, where is my coach!'

'My mother looks handsome when she is in a passion, does she not, Rose?' said Danville, quietly putting up his snuff-box as the old lady sailed out of the room. 'Why you seem quite frightened, love,' he added, taking her hand with his easy graceful air, 'frightened, let me assure you, without the least cause. My mother has but that one prejudice, and that one weak point, Rose. You will find her a very dove for gentleness, as long as you do not wound her pride of caste. Come, come! on this night, of all others, you must not send me away with such a face as that.'

He bent down and whispered to her a bridegroom's compliment, which brought the blood back to her cheek in an instant.

'Ah! how she loves him – how dearly she loves him,' thought her brother, watching her from his solitary corner of the room, and seeing the smile that brightened her blushing face when Danville kissed her hand at parting.

Lomaque, who had remained imperturbably cool during the outbreak of the old lady's anger; Lomaque, whose observant eyes had watched sarcastically the effect of the scene between mother and son on Trudaine and his sister, was the last to take leave. After he had bowed to Rose with a certain gentleness in his manner, which contrasted strangely with his wrinkled haggard face, he held out his hand to her brother. 'I did not take your hand when we sat together on the bench,' he said, 'may I take it now?'

Trudaine met his advance courteously, but in silence. 'You may alter your opinion of me one of these days.' Adding those words in a whisper, Monsieur Lomaque bowed once more to the bride and went out.

For a few minutes after the door had closed, the brother and sister kept silence. 'Our last night together at home!' that was the thought which now filled the heart of each. Rose was the first to speak. Hesitating a little, as she approached her brother, she said to him anxiously:

'I am sorry for what happened with Madame Danville, Louis. Does it make you think the worse of Charles?'

'I can make allowance for Madame Danville's anger,' returned Trudaine, evasively, 'because she spoke from honest conviction.'

'Honest?' echoed Rose sadly – 'honest? – ah, Louis! I know you are thinking disparagingly of Charles's convictions, when you speak so of his mother's.'

Trudaine smiled and shook his head; but she took no notice of the gesture of denial – only stood looking earnestly and wistfully into his face. Her eyes began to fill; she suddenly threw her arms round his neck, and whispered to him. 'Oh, Louis, Louis! how I wish I could teach you to see Charles with my eyes!'

He felt her tears on his cheek as she spoke, and tried to reassure her.

'You shall teach me, Rose – you shall indeed. Come, come! we must keep up our spirits, or how are you to look your best to-morrow.'

He unclasped her arms, and led her gently to a chair. At the same moment, there was a knock at the door, and Rose's maid appeared, anxious to consult her mistress on some of the preparations for the wedding ceremony. No interruption could have been more welcome just at that time. It obliged Rose to think of present trifles, and it gave her brother an excuse for retiring to his study.

He sat down by his desk, doubting and heavy-hearted, and placed the letter from the Academy of Sciences open before him.

Passing over all the complimentary expressions which it contained, his eye rested only on these lines at the end: – 'During the first three years of your Professorship, you will be required to reside in or near Paris nine months out of the year, for the purpose of delivering lectures, and superintending experiments from time to time in the laboratories.' The letter in which these lines occurred offered him such a position as in his modest self-distrust he had never dreamed of before: the lines themselves contained the promise of such vast facilities for carrying on his favourite experiments, as he could never hope to command in his own little study, with his own limited means; and yet there he now sat, doubting whether he should accept or reject the tempting honours and advantages that were offered to him – doubting for his sister's sake!

'Nine months of the year in Paris,' he said to himself, sadly, 'and Rose is to pass her married life at Lyons. Oh! if I could clear my heart of its dread on her account – if I could free my mind of its forebodings for her future – how gladly I would answer this letter by accepting the trust it offers me!'

He paused for a few minutes and reflected. The thoughts that were in him marked their ominous course in the growing paleness of his cheek, in the dimness that stole over his eyes. 'If this cleaving distrust from which I cannot free myself should be in very truth the mute prophecy of evil to come – to come, I know not when – if it be so (which God forbid), how soon she may want a friend, a protector near at hand, a ready refuge in the time of her trouble! Where shall she then find protection or refuge. With that passionate woman? With her husband's kindred and friends?'

He shuddered as the thought crossed his mind, and, opening a blank sheet of paper, dipped his pen in the ink. 'Be all to her, Louis, that I have been,' he murmured to himself, repeating his mother's last words, and beginning the letter while he uttered them. It was soon completed. It expressed, in the most respectful terms, his gratitude for the offer made to him, and his inability to accept it, in consequence of domestic circumstances which it was needless to explain. The letter was directed, sealed: it only remained for him to place it in the post-bag, lying near at hand. At this last decisive act he hesitated. He had told Lomaque, and he had firmly believed himself, that he had conquered all ambitions for his sister's sake. He knew now, for the first time, that he had only lulled them to rest – he knew that the letter from Paris had aroused them. His answer was written, his hand was on the post-bag, and at that moment the whole struggle had to be risked over again – risked when he was most unfit for it! He was not a man under any ordinary circumstances to procrastinate, but he procrastinated now.

'Night brings counsel: I will wait till to-morrow,' he said to himself, and put the letter of refusal in his pocket, and hastily quitted the laboratory.

CHAPTER II

Inexorably the important morrow came: irretrievably, for good or for evil, the momentous marriage-vow was pronounced. Charles Danville and Rose Trudaine were now man and wife. The prophecy of the magnificent sunset overnight had not proved false. It was a cloudless day on the marriage morning. The nuptial ceremonies had proceeded smoothly throughout, and had even satisfied Madame Danville. She returned with the wedding-party to Trudaine's house, all smiles and serenity. To the bride she was graciousness itself. 'Good girl,' said the old lady, following Rose into a corner, and patting her approvingly on the cheek with her fan, 'Good girl! you have looked well this morning – you have done credit to my son's taste. Indeed, you have pleased me, child! Now go up stairs, and get on your travelling-dress, and count on my maternal affection as long as you make Charles happy.

It had been arranged that the bride and bridegroom should pass their honeymoon in Brittany, and then return to Danville's estate near Lyons. The parting was hurried over, as all such partings should be. The carriage had driven off- Trudaine, after lingering long to look after it, had returned hastily to the house – the very dust of the whirling wheels had all dispersed – there was absolutely nothing to see – and yet, there stood Monsieur Lomaque at the outer gate; idly, as if he was an independent man – calmly, as if no such responsibilities as the calling of Madame Danville's coach, and the escorting of Madame Danville back to Lyons, could possibly rest on his shoulders.

Idly and calmly, slowly rubbing his hands one over the other, slowly nodding his head in the direction by which the bride and bridegroom had departed, stood the eccentric land-steward at the outer gate. On a sudden, the sound of footsteps approaching from the house seemed to arouse him. Once more he looked out into the road, as if he expected still

140

to see the carriage of the newly married couple. 'Poor girl!-ah, poor girl!' said Monsieur Lomaque softly to himself, turning round to ascertain who was coming from the house.

It was only the postman with a letter in his hand, and the post-bag crumpled up under his arm.

'Any fresh news from Paris, friend?' asked Lomaque.

'Very bad, monsieur,' answered the postman. 'Camille Desmoulins has appealed to the people in the Palais Royal – there are fears of a riot.'

'Only a riot!' repeated Lomaque, sarcastically.

'Oh, what a brave government not to be afraid of anything worse! Any letters?' he added, hastily dropping the subject.

'None *to* the house,' said the postman – 'only one *from* it, given me my Monsieur Trudaine. Hardly worth while,' he added, twirling the letter in his hand, 'to put it into the bag, is it?'

Lomaque looked over his shoulder as he spoke, and saw that the letter was directed to the President of the Academy of Sciences, Paris.

'I wonder whether he accepts the place or refuses it?' thought the land-steward, nodding to the postman, and continuing on his way back to the house.

At the door, he met Trudaine, who said to him rather hastily, 'You are going back to Lyons with Madame Danville, I suppose?'

'This very day,' answered Lomaque.

'If you should hear of a convenient bachelor-lodging at Lyons, or near it,' continued the other, dropping his voice and speaking more rapidly than before, 'you would be doing me a favour if you would let me know about it.'

Lomaque assented; but before he could add a question which was on the tip of his tongue, Trudaine had vanished in the interior of the house.

'A bachelor-lodging!' repeated the land-steward, standing alone on the door-step. 'At or near Lyons! Aha! Monsieur Trudaine, I put your bachelor-lodging and your talk to me last night together, and I make out a sum-total which is, I think, pretty near the mark. You have refused that Paris appointment, my friend; and I fancy I can guess why.'

He paused thoughtfully, and shook his head with ominous

frowns and bitings of his lips.

'All clear enough in that sky,' he continued, after a while, looking up at the lustrous mid-day heaven. 'All clear enough there; but I think I see a little cloud rising in a certain household firmament already – a little cloud which hides much, and which I for one shall watch carefully.'

PART SECOND

CHAPTER I

Five years have elapsed since Monsieur Lomaque stood thoughtfully at the gate of Trudaine's house, looking after the carriage of the bride and bridegroom, and seriously reflecting on the events of the future. Great changes have passed over that domestic firmament in which he prophetically discerned the little warning cloud. Greater changes have passed over the firmament of France.

What was Revolt five years ago, is Revolution now – revolution which has engulfed thrones and principalities and powers; which has set up crownless, inhereditary kings and counsellors of its own, and has bloodily torn them down again by dozens; which has raged and raged on unrestrainedly in fierce earnest, until but one king can still govern and control it for a little while. That King is named Terror, and seventeen hundred and ninety-four is the year of his reign.

Monsieur Lomaque, land-steward no longer, sits alone in an official-looking room in one of the official buildings of Paris. It is another July evening, as fine as that evening when he and Trudaine sat talking together on the bench overlooking the Seine. The window of the room is wide open, and a faint, pleasant breeze is beginning to flow through it. But Lomaque breathes uneasily, as if still oppressed by the sultry mid-day heat; and there are signs of perplexity and trouble in his face as he looks down absently now and then into the street.

The times he lives in are enough of themselves to sadden any man's face. In the Reign of Terror no living being in all the city of Paris can rise in the morning and be certain of escaping the spy, the denunciation, the arrest, or the guillotine, before night. Such times are trying enough to oppress any man's spirits; but Lomaque is not thinking of them or caring for them now. Out of a mass of papers which lie before him on his old writing-table, he has just taken up and read one, which has carried his thoughts back to the past, and to the changes which have taken place since he stood alone on the door-step of Trudaine's house, pondering on what might happen.

More rapidly, even than he had foreboded, those changes had occurred. In less time even than he had anticipated, the sad emergency for which Rose's brother had prepared, as for a barely possible calamity, overtook Trudaine, and called for all the patience, the courage, the self-sacrifice, which he had to give for his sister's sake. By slow gradations downward, from bad to worse, her husband's character manifested itself less and less disguisedly almost day by day. Occasional slights ending in habitual neglect; careless estrangement turning to cool enmity; small insults which ripened evilly to great injuries – these were the pitiless signs which showed her that she had risked all and lost all while still a young woman – these were the unmerited afflictions which found her helpless, and would have left her helpless, but for the ever-present comfort and support of her brother's self-denying love. From the first, Trudaine had devoted himself to meet such trials as now assailed him; and, like a man, he met them, in defiance alike of persecution from the mother and of insult from the son.

The hard task was only lightened when, as time advanced, public trouble began to mingle itself with private grief. Then absorbing political necessities came as a relief to domestic misery. Then it grew to be the one purpose and pursuit of Danville's life cunningly to shape his course so that he might move safely onward with the advancing revolutionary tide – he cared not whither, as long as he kept his possessions safe and his life out of danger. – His mother, inflexibly true to her old-world convictions through all peril, might entreat and upbraid, might talk of honour, and courage, and sincerity – he heeded her not, or heeded only to laugh. As he had taken the false way with his wife, so he was now bent on taking it with the world.

The years passed on: destroying changes swept hurricane-like over the old governing system of France; and still Danville shifted successfully with the shifting times. The first days of the Terror approached; in public and in private – in high places and in low – each man now suspected his brother. Crafty as Danville was, even he fell under suspicion at last, at head-quarters in Paris, principally on his mother's account. This was his first political failure, and, in a moment of thoughtless rage and disappointment, he wreaked the irritation caused by it on Lomaque. Suspected himself, he in turn suspected the land-steward. His mother fomented the suspicion – Lomaque was dismissed.

In the old times the victim would have been ruined – in the new times he was simply rendered eligible for a political vocation in life. Lomaque was poor, quick-witted, secret, not scrupulous. He was a good patriot, he had good patriot friends, plenty of ambition, a subtle, cat-like courage, nothing to dread – and he went to Paris. There were plenty of small chances there for men of his calibre. He waited for one of them. It came; he made the most of it; attracted favourably the notice of the terrible Fouquier-Tinville; and won his way to a place in the office of the Secret Police.

Meanwhile, Danville's anger cooled down: he recovered the use of that cunning sense which had hitherto served him well, and sent to recall the discarded servant. It was too late. Lomaque was already in a position to set him at defiance – nay, to put his neck, perhaps, under the blade of the guillotine. Worse than this, anonymous letters reached him, warning him to lose no time in proving his patriotism by some indisputable sacrifice, and in silencing his mother, whose imprudent sincerity was likely erelong to cost her her life. Danville knew her well enough to know that there was but one way of saving her, and thereby saving himself. She had always refused to emigrate; but he now insisted that she should seize the first opportunity he could procure for her of quitting France until calmer times arrived.

Probably she would have risked her own life ten times over rather than have obeyed him; but she had not the courage to risk her son's too; and she yielded for his sake. Partly by secret influence, partly by unblushing fraud, Danville procured for her such papers and permits as would enable her to leave France by way of Marseilles. Even then she refused to depart, until she knew what her son's plans were for the future. He showed her a letter which he was about to despatch to

Robespierre himself, vindicating his suspected patriotism, and indignantly demanding to be allowed to prove it by filling some office, no matter how small, under the redoubtable triumvirate which then governed, or more properly terrified, France. The sight of this document reassured Madame Danville. She bade her son farewell, and departed at last, with one trusty servant, for Marseilles.

Danville's intention in sending his letter to Paris, had been simply to save himself by patriotic bluster. He was thunderstruck at receiving a reply, taking him at his word, and summoning him to the capital to accept employment there under the then existing government. There was no choice but to obey. So to Paris he journeyed; taking his wife with him into the very jaws of danger. He was then at open enmity with Trudaine; and the more anxious and alarmed he could make the brother feel on the sister's account, the better he was pleased. True to his trust and his love, through all dangers as through all persecutions, Trudaine followed them; and the street of their sojourn at Paris, in the perilous days of the Terror, was the street of his sojourn too.

Danville had been astonished at the acceptance of his proffered services – he was still more amazed when he found that the post selected for him was one of the superintendent's places in that very office of Secret Police in which Lomaque was employed as Agent. Robespierre and his colleagues had taken the measure of their man – he had money enough, and local importance enough, to be worth studying. They knew where he was to be distrusted, and how he might be made useful. The affairs of the Secret Police were the sort of affairs which an unscrupulously cunning man was fitted to help on; and the faithful exercise of that cunning in the service of the state was ensured by the presence of Lomaque in the office. The discarded servant was just the right sort of spy to watch the suspected master. Thus it happened that, in the office of the Secret Police of Paris, and under the Reign of Terror, Lomaque's old master was, nominally, his master still – the superintendent to whom he was ceremonially accountable, in public – the suspected man, whose slightest words and deeds he was officially set to watch, in private.

Ever sadder and darker grew the face of Lomaque as he now pondered alone over the changes and misfortunes of the past five years. A neighbouring church-clock striking the hour of seven aroused him from his meditations. He arranged the confused mass of papers before him – looked towards the door as if expecting some one to enter – then, finding himself still alone, recurred to the one special paper which had first suggested his long train of gloomy thoughts. The few lines it contained were signed in cipher, and ran thus:–

"You are aware that your superintendent, Danville, obtained leave of absence, last week, to attend to some affairs of his at Lyons, and that he is not expected back just yet for a day or two. While he is away, push on the affair of Trudaine. Collect all the evidence, and hold yourself in readiness to act on it at a moment's notice. Don't leave the office till you have heard from me again. If you have a copy of the Private Instructions respecting Danville, which you wrote for me, sent to to my house. I wish to refresh my memory. Your original letter is burnt."

Here the note abruptly terminated. As he folded it up, and put it in his pocket, Lomaque sighed. This was a very rare expression of feeling with him. He leaned back in his chair, and beat his nails impatiently on the table. Suddenly there was a faint little tap at the room door, and eight or ten men – evidently familiars of the new French Inquisition – quietly entered, and ranged themselves against the wall.

Lomaque nodded to two of them. 'Picard and Magloire, go and sit down at that desk. I shall want you after the rest are gone.' Saying this, Lomaque handed certain sealed and dock-eted papers to the other men waiting in the room, who received them in silence, bowed, and went out. Innocent spectators might have thought them clerks taking bills of lading from a merchant. Who could have imagined that the giving and receiving of Denunciations, Arrest Orders, and Death Warrants, – the providing of its doomed human meal for the all-devouring guillotine – could have been managed so coolly and quietly, with such unruffled calmness of official routine!

'Now,' said Lomaque, turning to the two men at the desk, as the door closed, 'have you got those notes about you?' (They answered in the affirmative). 'Picard, you have the first particulars of this affair of Trudaine: so you must begin reading. I have sent in the reports; but we may as well go over the evidence again from the commencement, to make sure that nothing has been left out. If any corrections are to be made, now is the time to make them. Read, Picard, and lose as little time as you possibly can.'

Thus admonished, Picard drew some long slips of paper from his pocket, and began reading from them as follows:–

"Minutes of evidence collected concerning Louis Trudaine, suspected, on the denunciation of Citizen Superintendent Danville, of hostility to the sacred cause of liberty, and of disaffection to the sovereignty of the people. (1) The suspected person is placed under secret observation, and these facts are elicited: – He is twice seen passing at night from his own house to a house in the Rue de Cléry. On the first night he carries with him money, – on the second, papers. He returns without either. These particulars have been obtained through a citizen engaged to help Trudaine in housekeeping (one of the sort called Servants in the days of the Tyrants). This man is a good patriot, who can be trusted to watch Trudaine's actions. (2) The inmates of the house in the Rue de Cléry are numerous, and in some cases not so well known to the government as could be wished. It is found difficult to gain certain information about the person or persons visited by Trudaine without having recourse to an arrest. (3) An arrest is thought premature at this preliminary stage of the proceedings, being likely to stop the development of conspiracy, and give warning to the guilty to fly. Order thereupon given to watch and wait for the present. (4) Citizen-Superintendent Danville quits Paris for a short time. The office of watching Trudaine is then taken out of the hands of the undersigned, and is confided to his comrade, Magloire. – Signed, PICARD. Countersigned, LOMAQUE."

Having read so far, the police-agent placed his papers on the writing-table, waited a moment for orders, and, receiving none, went out. No change came over the sadness and perplexity of Lomaque's face. He still beat his nails anxiously on the writing-table, and did not even look at the second agent, as he ordered the man to read his report. Magloire produced some slips of paper precisely similar to Picard's, and read from them in the same rapid, business-like, unmodulated tones:–

"Affair of Trudaine. Minutes continued. Citizen-Agent Magloire having been appointed to continue the surveillance of Trudaine, reports the discovery of additional facts of importance. (1) Appearances make it probable that Trudaine, meditates a third secret visit to the house in the Rue de Cléry. The proper measures are taken for observing him closely, and the result is the implication of another person discovered to be connected with the supposed conspiracy. This person is the sister of Trudaine, and the wife of Citizen-Superintendent Danville."

'Poor, lost creature! – ah, poor lost creature!' muttered Lomaque to himself, sighing again, and shifting uneasily from side to side, in his mangy old leathern arm-chair. Apparently, Magloire was not accustomed to sighs, interruptions, and expressions of regret, from the usually imperturbable chief agent. He looked up from his papers with a stare of wonder. 'Go on, Magloire!' cried Lomaque with a sudden outburst of irritability. 'Why the devil don't you go on?' – 'All ready, citizen,' returned Magloire submissively, and proceeded:–

"(2) It is at Trudaine's house that the woman Danville's connexion with her brother's secret designs is ascertained, through the vigilance of the before-mentioned patriot-citizen. The interview of the two suspected persons is private; their conversation is carried on in whispers. Little can be overheard; but that little suffices to prove that Trudaine's sister is perfectly aware of his intention to proceed for the third time to the house in the Rue de Cléry. It is further discovered that she awaits his return, and that she then goes back privately to her own house. (3) Meanwhile, the strictest measures are taken for watching the house in the Rue de Cléry. It is discovered that

Trudaine's visits are paid to a man and woman known to the landlord and lodgers by the name of Dubois. They live on the fourth floor. It is impossible, at the time of the discovery, to enter this room, or to see the citizen and citoyenne Dubois, without producing an undesirable disturbance in the house and neighbourhood. A police-agent is left to watch the place, while search and arrest-orders are applied for. The granting of these is accidentally delayed. When they are ultimately obtained, it is discovered that the man and woman are both missing. They have not hitherto been traced. (4) The landlord of the house is immediately arrested, as well as the police-agent appointed to watch the premises. The landlord protests that he knows nothing of his tenants. It is suspected, however, that he has been tampered with, as also that Trudaine's papers, delivered to the citizen and citoyenne Dubois, are forged passports. With these and with money, it may not be impossible that they have already succeeded in escaping from France. The proper measures have been taken for stopping them, if they have not yet passed the frontiers. No further report in relation to them has yet been received. (5) Trudaine and his sister are under perpetual surveillance; and the undersigned holds himself ready for further orders.– Signed, MAGLOIRE. Countersigned, LOMAQUE."

Having finished reading his notes, Magloire placed them on the writing-table. He was evidently a favoured man in the office, and he presumed upon his position; for he ventured to make a remark, instead of leaving the room in silence, like his predecessor Picard.

'When citizen Danville returns to Paris,' he began, 'he will be rather astonished to find that in denouncing his 's brother, he has also unconsciously denounced his wife.'

Lomaque looked up quickly, with that old weakness in his eyes which affected them in such a strangely irregular manner on certain occasions. Magloire knew what this symptom meant, and would have become confused, if he had not been a police agent. As it was, he quietly backed a step or two from the table, and held his tongue.

'Friend Magloire,' said Lomaque, winking mildly, 'your last remark looks to me like a question in disguise. I put questions constantly to others, – I never answer questions myself. You want to know, citizen, what our superintendent's secret motive is for denouncing his wife's brother? Suppose you try and find that out for yourself. It will be famous practice for you, friend Magloire – famous practice after office hours.'

'Any further orders?' inquired Magloire, sulkily.

'None in relation to the reports,' returned Lomaque. 'I find nothing to alter or add on a revised hearing. But I shall have a little note ready for you immediately. Sit down at the other desk, friend Magloire; I am very fond of you when you are not inquisitive, – pray sit down.'

While addressing this polite invitation to the agent in his softest voice, Lomaque produced his pocket-book, and drew from it a little note, which he opened and read through attentively. It was headed, 'Private Instructions relative to Superintendent Danville,' and proceeded thus: –

"The undersigned can confidently assert, from long domestic experience in Danville's household, that his motive for denouncing his wife's brother is purely a personal one, and is not in the most remote degree connected with politics. Briefly, the facts are these: – Louis Trudaine, from the first, opposed his sister's marriage with Danville; distrusting the latter's temper and disposition. The marriage, however, took place, and the brother resigned himself to await results, – taking the precaution of living in the same neighbourhood as his sister, to interpose, if need be, between the crimes which the husband might commit, and the sufferings which the wife might endure. The results soon exceeded his worst anticipations, and called for the interposition for which he had prepared himself. He is a man of inflexible firmness, patience, and integrity, and he makes the protection and consolation of his sister the business of his life. He gives his brother-in-law no pretext for openly quarrelling with him. He is neither to be deceived, irritated, nor tired out, and he is Danville's superior every way, – in conduct, temper, and capacity. Under these circumstances, it is unnecessary to say that his brother-in-law's enmity towards him is of the most implacable kind, and equally unnecessary to hint at the perfectly plain motive of the denunciation."

"As to the suspicious circumstances affecting not Trudaine only, but his sister as well, the undersigned regrets his inability, thus far, to offer either explanation or suggestion. At this preliminary stage, the affair seems involved in impenetrable mystery."

Lomaque read these lines through, down to his own signature at the end. They were the duplicate Secret Instructions demanded from him in the paper which he had been looking over before the entrance of the two police agents. Slowly and, as it seemed, unwillingly, he folded the note up in a fresh sheet of paper, and was preparing to seal it when a tap at the door stopped him. 'Come in,' he cried, irritably, and a man in travelling costume, covered with dust, entered, quietly whispered a word or two in his ear, and then went out. Lomaque started at the whisper, and, opening his note again, hastily wrote under his signature: – "I have just heard that Danville has hastened his return to Paris, and may be expected back to-night." Having traced these lines, he closed, sealed, and directed the letter, and gave it to Magloire. The police-agent looked at the address as he left the room – it was 'To Citizen Robespierre, Rue Saint-Honoré.'

Left alone again, Lomaque rose, and walked restlessly backwards and forwards, biting his nails.

'Danville comes back to-night,' he said to himself, 'and the crisis comes with him. Trudaine a conspirator! Sister Rose (as he used to call her) a conspirator! Bah! conspiracy can hardly be the answer to the riddle this time. What is?'

He took a turn or two in silence – then stopped at the open window, looking out on what little glimpse the street afforded him of the sunset sky.

'This time five years,' he said, 'Trudaine was talking to me on that bench overlooking the river; and Sister Rose was keeping poor hatchet-faced old Lomaque's cup of coffee hot for him! Now, I am officially bound to suspect them both; perhaps to arrest them; perhaps – I wish this job had fallen into other hands. I don't want it – I don't want it at any price!'

He returned to the writing-table and sat down to his papers with the dogged air of a man determined to drive away vexing thoughts by dint of sheer hard work. For more than an hour he laboured on resolutely, munching a bit of dry bread from

time to time. Then he paused a little, and began to think again.
Gradually the summer twilight faded, and the room grew
dark.

'Perhaps we shall tide over to-night, after all – who knows?'
said Lomaque, ringing his hand-bell for lights. They were
brought in; and with them ominously returned the police-
agent Magloire with a small sealed packet. It contained an
arrest-order and a tiny three-cornered note, looking more like
a love-letter or a lady's invitation to a party than anything else.
Lomaque opened the note eagerly and read these lines, neatly
written, and signed with Robespierre's initials – M. R. –
formed elegantly in cipher: –

'Arrest Trudaine and his sister to-night. On second
thoughts I am not sure, if Danville comes back in time to be
present, that it may not be all the better. He is unprepared for
his wife's arrest. Watch him closely when it takes place, and
report privately to me. I am afraid he is a vicious man; and of
all things I abhor Vice.'

'Any more work for me to-night?' asked Magloire, with a
yawn.

'Only an arrest,' replied Lomaque. 'Collect our men, and
when you're ready, get a coach at the door.'

'We were just going to supper,' grumbled Magloire to
himself, as he went out. 'The devil seize the Aristocrats!
They're all in such a hurry to get to the guillotine that they
won't even give a man time to eat his victuals in peace!'

'There's no choice now,' muttered Lomaque, angrily thrus-
ting the arrest-order and the three-cornered note into his
pocket. 'His father was the saving of me; he himself welcomed
me like an equal; his sister treated me like a gentleman, as the
phrase went in those days; and now —'

He stopped and wiped his forehead – then unlocked his
desk, produced a bottle of brandy, and poured himself out a
glass of the liquor, which he drank by sips, slowly.

'I wonder whether other men get softer-hearted as they
grow older?' he said 'I seem to do so at any rate. Courage!
courage! what must be, must. If I risked my head to do it, I
couldn't stop this arrest. Not a man in the office but would be
ready to execute it, if I wasn't.'

Here the rumble of carriage-wheels sounded outside.

'There's the coach!' exclaimed Lomaque, locking up the brandy-bottle, and taking his hat. 'After all, as this arrest is to be made, it's as well for them that I should make it.'

Consoling himself as he best could with this reflection, Chief Police-Agent Lomaque blew out the candles, and quitted the room.

CHAPTER II

Ignorant of the change in her husband's plans, which was to bring him back to Paris a day before the time that had been fixed for his return, Sister Rose had left her solitary home to spend the evening with her brother. They had sat talking together long after sunset, and had let the darkness steal on them insensibly, as people will who are only occupied with quiet familiar conversation. Thus it happened, by a curious coincidence, that just as Lomaque was blowing out his candles at the office, Rose was lighting the reading-lamp at her brother's lodgings.

Five years of disappointment and sorrow had sadly changed her to outward view. Her face looked thinner and longer; the once delicate red and white of her complexion was gone; her figure had wasted under the influence of some weakness which already made her stoop a little when she walked. Her manner had lost its maiden shyness only to become unnaturally quiet and subdued. Of all the charms which had so fatally, yet so innocently, allured her heartless husband, but one remained – the winning gentleness of her voice. It might be touched now and then with a note of sadness; but the soft attraction of its even, natural tone still remained. In the marring of all other harmonies, this one harmony had been preserved unchanged! Her brother, though his face was care-worn, and his manner sadder than of old, looked less altered from his former self. It is the most fragile material which soonest shows the flaw. The world's idol, Beauty, holds its frailest tenure of existence in the one Temple where we most love to worship it.

'And so you think, Louis, that our perilous undertaking has really ended well by this time?' said Rose, anxiously, as she lit the lamp and placed the glass shade over it. 'What a relief it is only to hear you say you think we have succeeded at last!'

'I said I hoped, Rose,' replied her brother.

'Well, even hoped is a great word from you, Louis – a great

155

word from any one in this fearful city, and in these days of Terror.'

She stopped suddenly, seeing her brother raise his hand in warning. They looked at each other in silence, and listened. The sound of footsteps going slowly past the house – ceasing for a moment just beyond it – then going on again – came through the open window. There was nothing else, out of doors or in, to disturb the silence of the night – the deadly silence of Terror which, for months past, had hung over Paris. It was a significant sign of the times, that even a passing footstep, sounding a little strangely at night, was subject for suspicion, both to brother and sister – so common a subject that they suspended their conversation as a matter of course, without exchanging a word of explanation, until the tramp of the strange footsteps had died away.

'Louis,' continued Rose, dropping her voice to a whisper, after nothing more was audible, 'when may I trust our secret to my husband?'

'Not yet!' rejoined Trudaine earnestly. 'Not a word, not a hint of it, till I give you leave. Remember, Rose, you promised silence from the first. Everything depends on your holding that promise sacred till I release you from it.'

'I will hold it sacred; I will indeed, at all hazards, under all provocations,' she answered.

'That is quite enough to reassure me – and now, love, let us change the subject. Even these walls may have ears, and the closed door yonder may be no protection.' He looked towards it uneasily while he spoke. 'By-the-by, I have come round to your way of thinking, Rose, about that new servant of mine – there is something false in his face. I wish I had been as quick to detect it as you were.'

Rose glanced at him affrightedly. 'Has he done anything suspicious? Have you caught him watching you? Tell me the worst, Louis.'

'Hush! hush! my dear, not so loud. Don't alarm yourself; he has done nothing suspicious.'

'Turn him off – pray, pray turn him off, before it is too late!'

'And be denounced by him, in revenge, the first night he goes to his Section. You forget that servants and masters are equal now. I am not supposed to keep a servant at all. I have a

citizen living with me who lays me under domestic obligations, for which I make a pecuniary acknowledgment. No!
no! if I do anything, I must try if I can't entrap him into giving
me warning. But we have got to another unpleasant subject
already – suppose I change the topic again? You will find a
little book on that table there, in the corner – tell me what you
think of it.'

The book was a copy of Corneille's Cid, prettily bound in
blue morrocco. Rose was enthusiastic in her praises. 'I found it
in a bookseller's shop, yesterday,' said her brother, 'and
bought it as a present for you. Corneille is not an author to
compromise any one, even in these times. Don't you remember saying the other day, that you felt ashamed of knowing
but little of our greatest dramatist?' Rose remembered well,
and smiled almost as happily as in the old times over her
present. 'There are some good engravings at the beginning of
each act,' continued Trudaine, directing her attention rather
earnestly to the illustrations, and then suddenly leaving her
side when he saw that she became interested in looking at
them.

He went to the window – listened – then drew aside the
curtain, and looked up and down the street. No living soul
was in sight. 'I must have been mistaken,' he thought,
returning hastily to his sister; 'but I certainly fancied I was
followed in my walk to-day by a spy.'

'I wonder,' asked Rose, still busy over her book, 'I wonder,
Louis, whether my husband would let me go with you to see
Le Cid the next time it is acted?'

'No!' cried a voice at the door; 'not if you went on your
knees to ask him?'

Rose turned round with a scream. There stood her husband
on the threshold, scowling at her, with his hat on, and his
hands thrust doggedly into his pockets. Trudaine's servant
announced him, with an insolent smile, during the pause that
followed the discovery. 'Citizen-Superintendent Danville, to
visit the citoyenne, his wife,' said the fellow, making a mock
bow to his master.

Rose looked at her brother, then advanced a few paces
towards the door. 'This is a surprise,' she said faintly; 'has
anything happened? We – we didn't expect you.' — Her voice

failed her, as she saw her husband advancing, pale to his very lips with suppressed anger.

'How dare you come here, after what I told you?' he asked in quick low tones.

She shrank at his voice almost as if he had struck her. The blood flew into her brother's face as he noticed the action, but he controlled himself, and, taking her hand, led her in silence to a chair.

'I forbid you to sit down in his house,' said Danville, advancing still; "I order you to come back with me! Do you hear? I order you."

He was approaching nearer to her, when he caught Trudaine's eye fixed on him, and stopped. Rose started up, and placed herself between them.

'Oh, Charles! Charles!' she said to her husband, 'be friends with Louis to-night, and be kind again to me – I have a claim to ask that much of you, though you may not think it!'

He turned away from her, and laughed contemptuously. She tried to speak again, but Trudaine touched her on the arm, and gave her a warning look.

'Signals!' exclaimed Danville; 'secret signals between you!'

His eye, as he glanced suspiciously at his wife, fell on Trudaine's gift-book, which she still held unconsciously.

'What book is that?' he asked.

Only a play of Corneille's,' answered Rose; 'Louis has just made me a present of it.'

At this avowal, Danville's suppressed anger burst beyond all control.

'Give it him back!' he cried, in voice of fury. 'You shall take no presents from him; the venom of the household spy soils everything he touches. Give it him back!' She hesitated. 'You won't?' He tore the book from her with an oath – threw it on the floor, and set his foot on it.

'Oh, Louis! Louis! for God's sake remember!'

Trudaine was stepping forward as the book fell to the floor. At the same moment his sister threw her arms round him. He stopped, turning from fiery red to ghastly pale.

'No! no! Louis,' she said, clasping him closer; 'Not after five years' patience No – No!'

He gently detached her arms.

'You are right, love. Don't be afraid, it is all over now.'

Saying that, he put her from him, and in silence took up the book from the floor.

'Won't *that* offend you even?' said Danville, with an insolent smile. 'You have a wonderful temper – any other man would have called me out!'

Trudaine looked back at him steadily; and, taking out his handkerchief, passed it over the soiled cover of the book.

'If I could wipe the stain of your blood off my conscience as easily as I can wipe the stain of your boot off this book,' he said quietly, 'you should not live another hour. Don't cry, Rose,' he continued, turning again to his sister; 'I will take care of your book for you until you can keep it yourself.'

'You will do this! you will do that!' cried Danville, growing more and more exasperated, and letting his anger get the better even of his cunning now. 'Talk less confidently of the future – you don't know what it has in store for you. Govern your tongue when you are in my presence; a day may come when you will want my help – my help, do you hear that?'

Trudaine turned his face from his sister, as if he feared to let her see it when those words were spoken.

'The man who followed me to-day was a spy – Danville's spy!' That thought flashed across his mind, but he gave it no utterance. There was an instant's pause of silence; and through it there came heavily on the still night-air the rumbling of distant wheels. The sound advanced nearer and nearer – advanced, and ceased under the window.

Danville hurried to it, and looked out eagerly.

'I have not hastened my return without reason. I wouldn't have missed this arrest for anything!' thought he, peering into the night.

The stars were out; but there was no moon. He could not recognize either the coach or the persons who got out of it; and he turned again into the interior of the room. His wife had sunk into a chair – her brother was locking up in a cabinet the book which he had promised to take care of for her. The dead silence made the noise of slowly ascending footsteps on the stairs painfully audible. At last the door opened softly.

'Citizen Danville, health and fraternity!' said Lomaque, appearing in the doorway, followed by his agents. 'Citizen

Louis Trudaine?' he continued, beginning with the usual form.

Rose started out of her chair; but her brother's hand was on her lips before she could speak.

'My name is Louis Trudaine,' he answered.

'Charles!' cried his sister, breaking from him and appealing to her husband, 'who are these men? What are they here for?'

He gave her no answer.

'Louis Trudaine,' said Lomaque, slowly drawing the order from his pocket, 'in the name of the Republic, I arrest you.'

'Rose, come back,' cried Trudaine.

It was too late; she had broken from him, and in the recklessness of terror had seized her husband by the arm.

'Save him!' she cried. 'Save him, by all you hold dearest in the world! You are that man's superior, Charles – order him from the room!'

Danville roughly shook her hand off his arm.

'Lomaque is doing his duty. Yes,' he added, with a glance of malicious triumph at Trudaine – 'Yes, doing his duty. Look at me as you please – your looks won't move me. I denounced you! I admit it – I glory in it! I have rid myself of an enemy, and the State of a bad citizen. Remember your secret visits to the house in the Rue de Cléry!'

His wife uttered a cry of horror. She seized his arm again with both hands – frail, trembling hands – that seemed suddenly nerved with all the strength of a man's.

'Come here – come here! I must and will speak to you!'

She dragged him by main force a few paces back, towards an unoccupied corner of the room. With deathly cheeks and wild eyes she raised herself on tiptoe, and put her lips to her husband's ear. At that instant, Trudaine called to her:

'Rose, if you speak I am lost!'

She stopped at the sound of his voice, dropped her hold on her husband's arm, and faced her brother, shuddering.

'Rose,' he continued, 'you have promised, and your promise is sacred. If you prize your honour, if you love me, come here – come here, and be silent.'

He held out his hand. She ran to him; and, laying her head on his bosom, burst into a passion of tears.

Danville turned uneasily towards the police-agents.

'Remove your prisoner,' he said. 'You have done your duty here.'

'Only half of it,' retorted Lomaque, eyeing him attentively. 'Rose Danville' —

'My wife!' exclaimed the other. 'What about my wife!'

'Rose Danville,' continued Lomaque, impassibly, 'you are included in the arrest of Louis Trudaine.'

Rose raised her head quickly from her brother's breast. His firmness had deserted him – he was trembling. She heard him whispering to himself, 'Rose, too! Oh, my God! I was not prepared for that.' She heard these words, and dashed the tears from her eyes, and kissed him, saying –

'I am glad of it, Louis. We risked all together – we shall now suffer together. I am glad of it!'

Deville looked incredulously at Lomaque, after the first shock of astonishment was over.

'Impossible!' he exclaimed, 'I never denounced my wife. There is some mistake: you have exceeded your orders.'

'Silence!' retorted Lomaque, imperiously. 'Silence, citizen, and respect to a decree of the Republic!'

'You blackguard! show me the arrest-order!' said Danville. 'Who has dared to denounce my wife?'

'You have!' said Lomaque, turning on him with a grin of contempt. 'You! – and blackguard back in your teeth! You, in denouncing her brother! Aha! we work hard in our office: we don't waste time in calling names – we make discoveries. If Trudaine is guilty, your wife is implicated in his guilt. We know it; and we arrest her.'

'I resist the arrest,' cried Danville. 'I am the authority here. Who opposes me?'

The impassible chief-agent made no answer. Some new noise in the street struck his quick ear. He ran to the window, and looked out eagerly.

'Who opposes me?' reiterated Danville.

'Hark!' exclaimed Lomaque, raising his hand. 'Silence, and listen!'

The heavy dull tramp of men marching together became audible as he spoke. Voices humming low and in unison the Marseillaise hymn, joined solemnly with the heavy regular footfalls. Soon the flare of torchlight began to glimmer redder and redder under the dim starlight sky.

'Do you hear that? Do you see the advancing torchlight?' cried Lomaque, pointing exultingly into the street. 'Respect to the national hymn, and to the man who holds in the hollow of his hand the destinies of all France! Hat off, citizen Danville! Robespierre is in the street. His body-guard, the Hard-hitters, are lighting him on his way to the Jacobin club! – Who shall oppose you, did you say? Your master and mine; the man whose signature is at the bottom of this order – the man who, with a scratch of his pen, can send both our heads rolling together into the sack of the guillotine! Shall I call to him as he passes the house? Shall I tell him that Superintendent Danville resists me in making an arrest? Shall I? Shall I?' And in the immensity of his contempt, Lomaque seemed absolutely to rise in stature, as he thrust the arrest-order under Danville's eyes, and pointed to the signature with the head of his stick.

Rose looked round in terror, as Lomaque spoke his last words – looked round, and saw her husband recoil before the signature on the arrest-order, as if the guillotine itself had suddenly arisen before him. Her brother felt her shrinking back in his arms, and trembled for the preservation of her self-control if the terror and suspense of the arrest lasted any longer.

'Courage, Rose; courage!' he said. 'You have behaved nobly: you must not fail now. No, no! Not a word more. Not a word till I am able to think clearly again, and to decide what is best. Courage, love: our lives depend on it. Citizen,' he continued, addressing himself to Lomaque, 'proceed with your duty – we are ready.'

The heavy marching footsteps outside were striking louder and louder on the ground; the chanting voices were every moment swelling in volume; the dark street was flaming again with the brightening torchlight, as Lomaque, under pretext of giving Trudaine his hat, came close to him, and, turning his back towards Danville, whispered, 'I have not forgotten the eve of the wedding and the bench on the river-bank.'

Before Trudaine could answer, he had taken Rose's cloak and hood from one of his assistants, and was helping her on with it. Danville, still pale and trembling, advanced a step when he was these preparations for departure, and addressed a word or two to his wife; but he spoke in low tones, and the fast-advancing march of feet and sullen low roar of singing outside drowned his voice. An oath burst from his lips, and he struck his fist, an impotent fury on a table near him.

'The seals are set on everything in this room and in the bedroom,' said Magloire, approaching Lomaque, who nodded, and signed to him to bring up the other police-agents at the door.

'Ready,' cried Magloire, coming forward immediately with his men, and raising his voice to make himself heard, 'Where to?'

Robespierre and his Hard-hitters were passing the house. The smoke of the torchlight was rolling in at the window; the tramping footsteps struck heavier and heavier on the ground; the low sullen roar of the Marseillaise was swelling to its loudest, as Lomaque referred for a moment to his arrest-order, and then answered –

'To the prison of St Lazare!'

CHAPTER III

The head-gaoler of St Lazare stood in the outer hall of the
prison, two days after the arrest at Trudaine's lodgings,
smoking his morning pipe. Looking towards the court-yard
gate, he saw the wicket opened, and a privileged man let in,
whom he soon recognised as the chief-agent of the second
section of Secret Police. 'Why, friend Lomaque,' cried the
gaoler, advancing towards the court-yard, 'what brings you
here this morning, business or pleasure?'

'Pleasure, this time, citizen. I have an idle hour or two to
spare for a walk. I find myself passing the prison, and I can't
resist calling in to see how my friend the head-gaoler is getting
on.' Lomaque spoke in a surprisingly brisk and airy manner.
His eyes were suffering under a violent fit of weakness and
winking; but he smiled, notwithstanding, with an air of the
most inveterate cheerfulness. Those old enemies of his, who
always distrusted him most when his eyes were most affected,
would have certainly disbelieved every word of the friendly
speech he had just made, and would have assumed it as a
matter of fact that his visit to the head-gaoler had some
specially underhand business at the bottom of it.

'How am I getting on?' said the gaoler, shaking his head.
'Overworked, friend – overworked. No idle hours in our
department. Even the guillotine is getting too slow for us!'

'Sent off your batch of prisoners for trial this morning?'
asked Lomaque, with an appearance of perfect unconcern.

'No; they're just going,' answered the other. 'Come and
have a look at them.' He spoke as if the prisoners were a
collection of pictures on view, or a set of dresses just made up.
Lomaque nodded his head, still with his air of happy holiday
carelessness. The gaoler led the way to an inner hall; and,
pointing lazily with his pipe-stem, said: 'Our morning batch,
citizen, just ready for the baking.'

In one corner of the hall were huddled together more than

thirty men and women of all ranks and ages; some staring round them with looks of blank despair; some laughing and gossiping recklessly. Near them lounged a guard of "Patriots," smoking, spitting, and swearing. Between the patriots and the prisoners sat, on a rickety stool, the second gaoler – a humpbacked man, with an immense red moustachio – finishing his breakfast of broad beans, which he scooped out of a basin with his knife, and washed down with copious draughts of wine from the bottle. Carelessly as Lomaque looked at the shocking scene before him, his quick eyes contrived to take note of every prisoner's face, and to descry in a few minutes Trudaine and his sister standing together at the back of the group.

'Now then, Apollo!' cried the head-gaoler, addressing his subordinate by a facetious prison nick-name, 'don't be all day starting that trumpery batch of yours! And hark ye, friend, I have leave of absence, on business, at my Section this afternoon. So it will by your duty to read the list for the guillotine, and chalk the prisoners' doors before the cart comes to-morrow morning. 'Ware the bottle, Apollo, to-day; 'ware the bottle, for fear of accidents with the death-list to-morrow.'

'Thirsty July weather, this, – eh, citizen?' said Lomaque, leaving the head-gaoler, and patting the hunchback in the friendliest manner on the shoulder. 'Why, how you have got your batch huddled up together this morning! Shall I help you to shove them into marching order? My time is quite at your disposal. This is a holiday morning with me!'

'Ha! ha! ha! what a jolly dog he is on his holiday morning!' exclaimed the head-gaoler, as Lomaque – apparently taking leave of his natural character altogether in the exhilaration of an hour's unexpected leisure – began pushing and pulling the prisoners into rank, with humorous mock apologies, at which, not the officials only, but many of the victims themselves – reckless victims of a reckless tyranny – laughed heartily. Persevering to the last in his practical jest, Lomaque contrived to get close to Trudaine for a minute, and to give him one significant look before he seized him by the shoul-ders, like the rest. 'Now, then, rear-guard,' cried Lomaque, pushing Trudaine on. 'Close the line of march, and mind you keep step with your young woman there. Pluck up your spirits, citoyenne! one gets used to everything in this world, even to the guillotine!'

While he was speaking and pushing at the same time, Trudaine felt a piece of paper slip quickly between his neck and his cravat. 'Courage!' he whispered, pressing his sister's hand, as he saw her shuddering under the assumed brutality of Lomaque's joke.

Surrounded by the guard of "Patriots," the procession of prisoners moved slowly into the outer court-yard, on its way to the revolutionary tribunal, the humpbacked gaoler bringing up the rear. Lomaque was about to follow at some little distance, but the head-gaoler hospitably expostulated. 'What a hurry you're in!' said he. 'Now that incorrigible drinker, my second in command, has gone off with his batch, I don't mind asking you to step in and have a drop of wine.'

'Thank you,' answered Lomaque; 'but I have rather a fancy for hearing the trial this morning. Suppose I come back afterwards? What time do you go to your Section? At two o'clock, eh? Good! I shall try if I can't get here soon after one.' With these words he nodded and went out. The brilliant sunlight in the court-yard made him wink faster than ever. Had any of his old enemies been with him, they would have whispered within themselves – 'If you mean to come back at all citizen Lomaque, it will not be soon after one!'

On his way through the streets, the chief-agent met one or two police-office friends, who delayed his progress; so that when he arrived at the revolutionary tribunal, the trials of the day were just about to begin.

The principal article of furniture in the Hall of Justice was a long clumsy deal table covered with green baize. At the head of this table sat the president and his court, with their hats on, backed by a heterogeneous collection of patriots officially connected in various ways with the proceedings what were to take place. Below the front of the table, a railed-off space, with a gallery beyond, was appropriated to the general public – mostly represented, as to the gallery, on this occasion, by women, all sitting together on forms, knitting, shirt-mending, and baby-linen-making, as coolly as if they were at home. Parallel with the side of the table farthest from the great door of entrance, was a low platform railed off, on which the prisoners, surrounded by their guard, were now assembled to await their trial. The sun shone in brightly from a high window, and a hum of ceaseless talking pervaded the hall cheerfully, as Lomaque entered it. He was a privileged man here, as at the prison; and he made his way in by a private door, so as to pass the prisoners' platform, and to walk round it, before he got to a place behind the president's chair. Trudaine, standing with his sister on the outermost limits of the group, nodded significantly as Lomaque looked up at him for an instant. He had contrived, on his way to the tribunal, to get an opportunity of reading the paper which the chief-agent had slipped into this cravat. It contained these lines:-

'I have just discovered who the citizen and citoyenne Dubois are. There is no chance for you but to confess everything. By that means you may inculpate a certain citizen holding authority and may make it his interest, if he loves his own life, to save yours and your sister's.'

Arriving at the back of the president's chair, Lomaque recognized his two trusty subordinates, Magloire and Picard, waiting among the assembled patriot officials, to give their evidence. Beyond them, leaning against the wall, addressed by no one, and speaking to no one, stood the superintendent Danville. Doubt and suspense were written in every line of his face; the fretfulness of an uneasy mind expressed itself in his slightest gestures – even in his manner of passing a handkerchief from time to time over his face, on which the perspiration was gathering thick and fast already.

'Silence!' cried the usher of the court for the time being – a hoarse-voiced man in top-boots, with a huge sabre buckled to his side, and a bludgeon in his hand. 'Silence for the citizen-president!' he reiterated, striking his bludgeon on the table.

The president rose and proclaimed that the sitting for the day had begun then sat down again.

The momentary silence which followed was interrupted by a sudden confusion among the prisoners on the platform. Two of the guards sprang in among them. There was the thump of a heavy fall – a scream of terror from some of the female prisoners – then another dead silence, broken by one of the guards, who walked across the hall with a bloody knife in his hand, and laid it on the table. 'Citizen-president,' he said, 'I have to report that one of the prisoners has just stabbed himself.' There was a murmuring exclamation – 'Is that all?' among the women-spectators, as they resumed their work. Suicide at the bar of justice was no uncommon occurrence under the Reign of Terror.

'Name?' asked the president, quietly taking up his pen and opening a book.

'Martigné,' answered the humpbacked gaoler, coming forward to the table.

'Description?'

'Ex-royalist coachmaker to the tyrant Capet.'

'Accusation?'

'Conspiracy in prison.'

The president nodded, and entered in the book – "Martigné, coachmaker. Accused of conspiring in prison. Anticipated course of law by suicide. Action accepted as sufficient confession of guilt. Goods confiscated. 1st Thermidor, year two of the Republic."

'Silence!' cried the man with the bludgeon, as the president dropped a little sand on the entry, and signing to the gaoler that he might remove the dead body, closed the book.

'Any special cases this morning?' resumed the president, looking round at the group behind him.

'There is one,' said Lomaque, making his way to the back of the official chair. 'Will it be convenient to you, citizen, to take the case of Louis Trudaine and Rose Danville first? Two of my men are detained here as witnesses, and their time is valuable to the Republic.'

The president marked a list of names before him, and handed it to the crier or usher, placing the figures one and two against Louis Trudaine and Rose Danville.

While Lomaque was backing again to his former place behind the chair, Danville approached and whispered to him – 'There is a rumour that secret information has reached you about the citizen and citoyenne Dubois. Is it true? Do you know who they are?'

'Yes,' answered Lomaque; 'but I have superior orders to keep the information to myself just at present.'

The eagerness with which Danville put his question, and the disappointment he showed on getting no satisfactory answer to it, were of a nature to satisfy the observant chief agent that his superintendent was really as ignorant as he appeared to be on the subject of the man and woman Dubois. That one mystery, at any rate, was still, for Danville, a mystery unrevealed.

'Louis Trudaine! Rose Danville!' shouted the crier, with another rap of his bludgeon.

The two came forward, at the appeal, to the front railing of the platform. The first sight of her judges, the first shock on confronting the pitiless curiosity of the audience, seemed to overwhelm Rose. She turned from deadly pale to crimson, then to pale again, and hid her face on her brother's shoulder. How fast she heard his heart throbbing! How the tears filled her eyes as she felt that his fear was all for her!

'Now!' said the president, writing down their names. 'Denounced by whom?'

Magloire and Picard stepped forward to the table. The first answered – 'By citizen-superintendent Danville.'

The reply made a great stir and sensation among both prisoners and audience.

'Accused of what?' pursued the president.

'The male prisoner, of conspiracy against the Republic; the female prisoner, of criminal knowledge of the same.'

Produce your proofs in answer to this order.'

Picard and Magloire opened their minutes of evidence, and read to the president the same particulars which they had formerly read to Lomaque in the secret police office.

'Good,' said the president, when they had done; 'we need trouble ourselves with nothing more than the identifying of the citizen and citoyenne Dubois, which, of course, you are prepared for. Have you heard the evidence,' he continued, turning to the prisoners; while Picard and Magloire consulted together in whispers, looking perplexedly towards the chief-agent, who stood silent behind them, 'Have you heard the evidence, prisoners? Do you wish to say anything? If you do, remember that the time of this tribunal is precious, and that you will not be suffered to waste it.'

'I demand permission to speak for myself and for my sister,' answered Trudaine. 'My object is to save the time of the tribunal by making a confession.'

The faint whispering, audible among the women spectators a moment before, ceased instantaneously as he pronounced the word confession. In the breathless silence, his low quiet tones penetrated to the remotest corners of the hall; while, suppressing externally all evidences of the death-agony of hope within him, he continued his address in these words: –

'I confess my secret visits to the house in the Rue de Cléry. I confess that the persons whom I went to see are the persons pointed at in the evidence. And, lastly, I confess that my object in communicating with them as I did, was to supply them with the means of leaving France. If I had acted from political motives to the political prejudice of the existing government, I admit that I should be guilty of that conspiracy against the Republic with which I am charged. But no political purpose animated, no political necessity urged me, in performing the action which has brought me to the bar of this tribunal. The persons whom I aided in leaving France were without political influence or political con-nexions. I acted solely from private motives of humanity towards them and towards others – motives which a good republican may feel, and yet not turn traitor to the welfare of his country.'

'Are you ready to inform the court, next, who the man and woman Dubois really are?' inquired the president, impatiently.

'I am ready, answered Trudaine. 'But first I desire to say one word in reference to my sister, charged here at the bar with me.' His voice grew less steady, and, for the first time, his colour began to change, as Rose lifted her face from his shoulder and looked up at him eagerly, 'I implore the tribunal to consider my sister as innocent of all active participation in what is charged against me as a crime —' he went on. 'Having spoken with candour about myself, I have some claim to be believed when I speak of her; when I assert that she neither did help me nor could help me. If there be blame it is mine only; if punishment, it is I alone who should suffer.'

He stopped suddenly and grew confused. It was easy to guard himself from the peril of looking at Rose, but he could not escape the hard trial to his self-possession of hearing her, if she spoke. Just as he pronounced the last sentence, she raised her face again from his shoulder, and eagerly whispered to him:

'No, no, Louis! Not that sacrifice, after all the others – not that, through you should force me into speaking to them myself!'

She abruptly quitted her hold of him, and fronted the whole court in an instant. The railing in front of her shook with the quivering of her arms and hands as she held by it to support herself! Her hair lay tangled on her shoulders; her face had assumed a strange fixedness; her gentle blue eyes, so soft and tender at all other times, were lit up wildly. A low hum of murmured curiosity and admiration broke from the women of the audience. Some rose eagerly from the benches, others cried,

'Listen, listen! she is going to speak!'

She did speak. Silvery and pure the sweet voice, sweeter than ever in sadness, stole its way through the gross sounds – through the coarse humming and the hissing whispers.

'My lord the president' – began the poor girl, firmly. Her next words were drowned in a volley of hisses from the women.

'Ah! aristocrat, aristocrat! None of your accursed titles here!' was their shrill cry at her. She fronted that cry, she fronted the fierce gestures which accompanied it, with the steady light still in her eyes, with the strange rigidity still fastened on her face. She would have spoken again through the uproar and execration, but her brother's voice over-powered her.

'Citizen-president,' he cried, 'I have not concluded. I demand leave to complete my confession. I implore the tribunal to attach no importance to what my sister says. The trouble and terror of this day have shaken her intellects. She is not responsible for her words – I assert it solemnly, in the face of the whole court!'

The blood flew up into his white face as he made the asseveration. Even at that supreme moment the great heart of the man reproached him for yielding himself to a deception, though the motive of it was to save his sister's life.

'Let her speak! let her speak!' exclaimed the women, as Rose, without moving, without looking at her brother, without seeming even to have heard what he said, made a second attempt to address her judges, in spite of Trudaine's interposition.

'Silence!' shouted the man with the bludgeon. 'Silence, you women! the citizen-president is going to speak.'

'The prisoner Trudaine has the ear of the court,' said the president, 'and may continue his confession. If the female prisoner wishes to speak, she may be heard afterwards. I enjoin both the accused persons to make short work of it with their addresses to me, or they will make their case worse instead of better. I command silence among the audience, and if I am not obeyed, I will clear the hall. Now, prisoner Trudaine, I invite you to proceed. No more about your sister; let her speak for herself. Your business and ours is with the man and woman Dubois now. Are you, or are you not, ready to tell the court who they are?'

'I repeat that I am ready,' answered Trudaine. 'The citizen Dubois is a servant. The woman Dubois is the mother of the man who denounces me – superintendent Danville.'

A low, murmuring, rushing sound of hundreds of exclaiming voices, all speaking, half-suppressedly, at the same moment, followed the delivery of the answer. No officer of the court attempted to control the outburst of astonishment. The infection of it spread to the persons on the platform, to the crier himself, to the judges of the tribunal, lounging, but the moment before, so carelessly silent in their chairs. When the noise was at length quelled, it was subdued in the most instantaneous manner by one man, who shouted from the throng behind the president's chair,

'Clear the way there! Superintendent Danville is taken ill!'

A vehement whispering and contending of many voices interrupting each other, followed; then a swaying among the assembly of official people; then a great stillness; then the sudden appearance of Danville, alone, at the table.

The look of him, as he turned his ghastly face towards the audience, silenced and steadied them in an instant, just as they were on the point of falling into fresh confusion. Everyone stretched forward eagerly to hear what he would say. His lips moved; but the few words that fell from them were inaudible, except to the persons who happened to be close by him. Having spoken, he left the table supported by a police-agent, who was seen to lead him towards the private door of the court, and, consequently, also towards the prisoner's platform. He stopped, however, half-way, quickly turned his face from the prisoners, and pointing towards the public door at the opposite side of the hall, caused himself to be led out into the air by that direction. When he had gone, the president, addressing himself partly to Trudaine and partly to the audience, said, –

'The citizen-superintendent Danville has been overcome by the heat in the court. He has retired (by my desire, under the care of a police-agent) to recover in the open air; pledging himself to me to come back and throw a new light on the extraordinary and suspicious statement which the prisoner has just made. Until the return of citizen Danville, I order the accused, Trudaine, to suspend any further acknowledgment of complicity which he may have to address to me. This matter must be cleared up before other matters are entered on. Meanwhile, in order that the time of the tribunal may not be wasted, I authorize the female prisoner to take this opportunity of making any statement concerning herself which she may wish to address to the judges.'

'Silence him!' 'Remove him out of court!' 'Gag him!' 'Guillotine him!' These cries rose from the audience the moment the president had done speaking. They were all directed at Trudaine, who had made a last desperate effort to persuade his sister to keep silence, and had been detected in the attempt by the spectators.

'If the prisoner speaks another word to his sister, remove him,' said the president, addressing the guard round the platform.

'Good! we shall hear her at last. Silence! silence!' exclaimed the women, settling themselves comfortably on their benches, and preparing to resume their work.

'Rose Danville, the court is waiting to hear you,' said the president, crossing his legs and leaning back luxuriously in his large arm-chair.

Amid all the noise and confusion of the last few minutes, Rose had stood ever in the same attitude, with that strangely

fixed expression never altering on her face but once. When her
husband made his way to the side of the table, and stood there
prominently alone, her lips trembled a little, and a faint shade
of colour passed swiftly over her cheeks. Even that slight
change had vanished now – she was paler, stiller, more widely
altered from her former self than ever, as she faced the
president and said these words:–

'I wish to follow my brother's example, and make my
confession, as he has made his. I would rather he had spoken
for me; but he is too generous to say any words except such as
he thinks may save me from sharing his punishment. I refuse
to be saved, unless he is saved with me. Where he goes when
he leaves this place, I will go; what he suffers, I will suffer; if
he is to die, I believe God will grant me the strength to die
resignedly with him!'

She paused for a moment, and half turned towards Trudaine
– then checked herself instantly, and went on: —'This is what I
now wish to say, as to my share in the offence charged against
my brother: —some time ago, he told me one day that he had
seen my husband's mother in Paris disguised as a poor
woman; that he had spoken to her, and forced her to
acknowledge herself. Up to this time we had all felt certain
that she had left France, because she held old-fashioned
opinions, which it is dangerous for people to hold now – had
left France before we came to Paris. She told my brother that
she had indeed gone (with an old tried servant of the family to
help and protect her) as far as Marseilles; and that, finding
unforseen difficulty there in getting farther, she had taken it as
a warning from Providence not to desert her son, of whom
she was very passionately fond, and from whom she had been
most unwilling to depart. Instead of waiting in exile for
quieter times, she determined to go and hide herself in Paris,
knowing her son was going there too. She assumed the name
of her old and faithful servant, who declined to the last to leave
her unprotected; and she proposed to live in the strictest
secrecy and retirement, watching, unknown, the career of her
son, and ready at a moment's notice to disclose herself to him,
when the settlement of public affairs might reunite her safely
to her beloved child. My brother thought this plan full of
danger, both for herself, for her son, and for the honest old

man who was risking his head for his mistress's sake. I thought so too; and in an evil hour I said to Louis, "Will you try in secret to get my husband's mother away, and see that her faithful servant makes her really leave France this time?" I wrongly asked my brother to do this for a selfish reason of my own – a reason connected with my married life, which has not been a happy one. I had not succeeded in gaining my husband's affection, and was not treated kindly by him. My brother, who has always loved me far more dearly I am afraid than I have ever deserved; my brother increased his kindness to me, seeing me treated unkindly by my husband. This made ill-blood between them. My thought, when I asked my brother to do for me what I have said, was, that if we two in secret saved my husband's mother, without danger to him, from imperilling herself and her son, we should, when the time came for speaking of what we had done, appear to my husband in a new and better light. I should have shown how well I deserved his love, and Louis would have shown how well he deserved his brother-in-law's gratitude; and so we should have made home happy at last, and all three have lived together affectionately. This was my thought; and when I told it to my brother, and asked him if there would be much risk, out of his kindness and indulgence towards me he said "No!" He had so used me to accept sacrifices for my happiness, that I let him endanger himself to help me in my little household plan. I repent this bitterly now; I ask his pardon with my whole heart. If he is acquitted, I will try to show myself worthier of his love. If he is found guilty, I too will go the the scaffold, and die with my brother, who risked his life for my sake.'

She ceased as quietly as she had begun, and turned once more to her brother.

As she looked away from the court and looked at him, a few tears came into her eyes, and something of the old softness of form and gentleness of expression seemed to return to her face. He let her take his hand, but he seemed purposely to avoid meeting the anxious gaze she fixed on him. His head sunk on his breast; he drew his breath heavily; his countenance darkened and grew distorted, as if he were suffering some sharp pang of physical pain. He bent down a little, and, leaning his elbow on the rail before him, covered his face with his hands; and so quelled the rising agony, so forced back the scalding tears to his heart. The audience had heard Rose in silence, and they preserved the same tranquillity when she had done. This was a rare tribute to a prisoner from the people of the Reign of Terror.

The president looked round at his colleagues, and shook his head suspiciously.

'This statement of the female prisoner's complicates the matter very seriously,' said he. 'Is there anybody in court,' he added, looking at the persons behind his chair, 'who knows where the mother of Superintendent Danville and the servant are now?'

Lomaque came forward at the appeal, and placed himself by the table.

'Why, citizen agent!' continued the president, looking hard at him, 'are you overcome by the heat too?'

'The fit seemed to take him, citizen president, when the female prisoner had made an end of her statement,' explained Magloire, pressing forward officiously.

Lomaque gave his subordinate a look which sent the man back directly to the shelter of the official group; then said, in lower tones than were customary with him,

'I have received information relative to the mother of Superintendent Danville and the servant, and am ready to answer any questions that may be put to me.'

'Where are they now?' asked the president.

'She and the servant are known to have crossed the frontier, and are supposed to be on their way to Cologne. But, since they have entered Germany, their whereabouts is necessarily a matter of uncertainty to the republican authorities.'

'Have you any information relative to the conduct of the old servant while he was in Paris?'

'I have information enough to prove that he was not an object for political suspicion. He seems to have been simply animated by servile zeal for the woman's interests; to have performed for her all the menial offices of a servant in private; and to have misled the neighbours by affected equality with her in public.'

'Have you any reason to believe that Superintendent Danville was privy to his mother's first attempt at escaping from France?'

'I infer it from what the female prisoner has said, and for other reasons which it would be irregular to detail before the tribunal. The proofs can no doubt be obtained, if I am allowed time to communicate with the authorities at Lyons and Marseilles.'

At this moment Danville re-entered the court, and, advancing to the table, placed himself close by the chief-agent's side. They looked each other steadily in the face for an instant.

'He has recovered from the shock of Trudaine's answer,' thought Lomaque, retiring. 'His hand trembles, his face is pale, but I can see regained self-possession in his eye, and I dread the consequences already.'

'Citizen-president,' began Danville, 'I demand to know if anything has transpired affecting my honour and patriotism in my absence?'

He spoke apparently with the most perfect calmness, but he looked nobody in the face. His eyes were fixed steadily on the green baize of the table beneath him.

'The female prisoner has made a statement, referring principally to herself and her brother,' answered the president, 'but incidentally mentioning a previous attempt on your mother's part to break existing laws by emigrating from France. This portion of the confession contains in it some elements of suspicion which seriously affect you' –

'They shall be suspicions no longer – at my own peril I will change them to certainties!' exclaimed Danville, extending his arm theatrically and looking up for the first time. 'Citizen president, I avow it with the fearless frankness of a good patriot; I was privy to my mother's first attempt at escaping from France.'

Hisses and cries of execration followed this confession. He winced under them at first; but recovered his self-possession before silence was restored.

'Citizens, you have heard the confession of my fault,' he resumed, turning with desperate assurance towards the audience; 'now hear the atonement I have made for it at the altar of my country.'

He waited at the end of that sentence, until the secretary to the tribunal had done writing it down in the report-book of the court.

'Transcribe faithfully to the letter!' cried Danville, pointing solemnly to the open page of the volume. 'Life and death hang on my words.'

The secretary took a fresh dip of ink, and nodded to show that he was ready. Danville went on:

'In these times of glory and trial for France,' he proceeded, pitching his voice to a tone of deep emotion, 'what are all good citizens most sacredly bound to do? To immolate their dearest private affections and interests before their public duties! On the first attempt of my mother to violate the laws against emigration, by escaping from France, I failed in making the heroic sacrifice which inexorable patriotism demanded of me. My situation was more terrible than the situation of Brutus sitting in judgment on his own sons. I had not the Roman fortitude to rise equal to it. I erred, citizens – erred as Coriolanus did, when his august mother pleaded with him for the safety of Rome! For that error I deserved to be purged out of the republican community; but I escaped my merited punishment, – nay, I even rose to the honour of holding an office under the government. Time passed; and again my mother attempted an escape from France. Again inevitable fate brought my civic virtue to the test. How did I meet this second supremest trial? By an atonement for past weakness, terrible as the trial itself! Citizens, you will shudder; but you will applaud while you tremble. Citizens, look! and while you look, remember well the evidence given at the opening of this case. Yonder stands the enemy of his country, who intrigued to help my mother to escape; here stands the patriot son, whose voice was the first, the only voice, to denounce him for the crime!' As he spoke, he pointed to Trudaine, then struck himself on the breast, then folded his arms, and looked sternly at the benches occupied by the spectators.

'Do you assert,' exclaimed the president, 'that at the time when you denounced Trudaine, you knew him to be intriguing to aid your mother's escape?'

'I assert it,' answered Danville.

The pen which the president held, dropped from his hand at that reply; his colleagues started and looked at each other in blank silence.

A murmur of 'Monster! monster!' began with the prisoners on the platform, and spread instantly to the audience, who echoed and echoed it again; the fiercest woman-republican on the benches joined cause at last with the haughtiest woman-aristocrat on the platform. Even in the sphere of direst discords, in that age of sharpest enmities, the one touch of nature preserved its old eternal virtue, and roused the mother-instinct which makes the whole world kin!

Of the few persons in the court who at once foresaw the effect of Danville's answer on the proceedings of the tribunal, Lomaque was one. His sallow face whitened as he looked towards the prisoners' platform.

'They are lost,' he murmured to himself, moving out of the group in which he had hitherto stood. 'Lost! The lie which has saved that villain's head leaves them without the shadow of a hope. No need to stop for the sentence – Danville's infamous presence of mind has given them up to the guillotine!' Pronouncing these words, he went out hurriedly by a door near the platform, which led to the prisoners' waiting-room.

Rose's head sank again on her brother's shoulder. She shuddered, and leaned back faintly on the arm which he extended to support her. One of the female prisoners tried to help Trudaine in speaking consolingly to her; but the consummation of her husband's perfidy seemed to have paralyzed her at heart. She murmured once in her brother's ear, 'Louis! I am resigned to die – nothing but death is left for me after the degradation of having loved that man.' She said those words and closed her eyes wearily, and spoke no more.

'One other question, and you may retire,' resumed the president, addressing Danville. 'Were you cognizant of your wife's connexion with her brother's conspiracy?'

Danville reflected for a moment, remembered that there were witnesses in court who could speak to his language and behaviour on the evening of his wife's arrest, and resolved this time to tell the truth.

'I was not aware of it,' he answered. 'Testimony in my favour can be called which will prove that when my wife's complicity was discovered I was absent from Paris.'

Heartlessly self-possessed as he was, the public reception of his last reply had shaken his nerve. He now spoke in low tones, turning his back on the spectators, and fixing his eyes again on the green baize of the table at which he stood.

'Prisoners! have you any abjection to make, any evidence to call, invalidating the statement by which citizen Danville has cleared himself of suspicion?' inquired the president.

'He has cleared himself by the most execrable of all falsehoods,' answered Trudaine. 'If his mother could be traced and brought here, her testimony could prove it.'

'Can you produce any other evidence in support of you allegation?' asked the president.

'I cannot.'

'Citizen-superintendent Danville, you are at liberty to retire. Your statement will be laid before the authority to whom you are officially responsible. Either you merit a civic crown for more than Roman virtue, or '— Having got thus far, the president stopped abruptly, as if unwilling to commit himself too soon to an opinion, and merely repeated, – 'You may retire.'

Danville left the court immediately, going out again by the public door. He was followed by murmurs from the women's benches, which soon ceased, however, when the president was observed to close his note-book, and turn round towards his colleagues. 'The sentence!' was the general whisper now. 'Hush, hush – the sentence!'

After a consultation of a few minutes with the persons behind him, the president rose, and spoke the momentous words:–

'Louis Trudaine and Rose Danville, the revolutionary tribunal, having heard the charge against you, and having weighed the value of what you have said in answer to it, decides that you are both guilty, and condemns you to the penalty of death.'

Having delivered the sentence in those terms, he sat down again, and placed a mark against the two first condemned names on the list of prisoners. Immediately afterwards the next case was called on, and the curiosity of the audience was stimulated by a new trial.

CHAPTER IV

The waiting-room of the revolutionary tribunal was a grim,
bare place, with a dirty stone floor, and benches running
round the walls. The windows were high and barred; and at
the outer door, leading into the street, two sentinels kept
watch. On entering this comfortless retreat from the court,
Lomaque found it perfectly empty. Solitude was just then
welcome to him. He remained in the waiting-room, walking
slowly from end to end over the filthy pavement, talking
eagerly and incessantly to himself.

After a while, the door communicating with the tribunal
opened, and the humpbacked gaoler made his appearance,
leading in Trudaine and Rose.

'You will have to wait here,' said the little man, 'till the rest
of them have been tried and sentenced; and then you will all go
back to prison in a lump. Ha, citizen!' he continued, observing
Lomaque at the other end of the hall, and bustling up to him.
'Here still, eh? If you were going to stop much longer, I
should ask a favour of you.'

'I am in no hurry,' said Lomaque, with a glance at the two
prisoners.

'Good!' cried the hunchback, drawing his hand across his
mouth; 'I am parched with thirst, and dying to moisten my
throat at the wine-shop over the way. Just mind that man and
woman while I'm gone, will you? It's the merest form –
there's a guard outside, the windows are barred, the tribunal is
within hail. Do you mind obliging me?'

'On the contrary, I am glad of the opportunity.'

'That's a good fellow – and, remember, if I am asked for,
you must say I was obliged to quit the court for a few minutes,
and left you in charge.'

With these words, the humpbacked gaoler ran off to the
wine-shop.

He had scarcely disappeared before Trudaine crossed the

181

room, and caught Lomaque by the arm.

'Save her,' he whispered; 'there is an opportunity – save her!' His face was flushed – his eyes wandered – his breath on the chief-agent's cheek, while he spoke, felt scorching hot. 'Save her!' he repeated, shaking Lomaque by the arm, and dragging him towards the door. 'Remember all you owe to my father – remember our talk on that bench by the river – remember what you said to me yourself on the night of the arrest – don't wait to think – save her, and leave me without a word! If I die alone, I can die as a man should – if she goes to the scaffold by my side, my heart will fail me – I shall die the death of a coward! I have lived for her life – let me die for it, and I die happy!'

He tried to say more, but the violence of his agitation forbade it. He could only shake the arm he held again and again, and point to the bench on which Rose sat – her head sunk on her bosom, her hands crossed listlessly on her lap.

'There are two armed sentinels outside – the windows are barred – you are without weapons – and even if you had them, there is a guard-house within hail on one side of you, and the tribunal on the other. Escape from this room is impossible,' answered Lomaque.

'Impossible!' repeated the other furiously. 'You traitor! you coward! can you look at her sitting there helpless – her very life ebbing away already with every minute that passes, and tell me coolly that escape is impossible?'

In the frenzy of his grief and despair, he lifted his disengaged hand threateningly while he spoke. Lomaque caught him by the wrist, and drew him towards a window open at the top.

'You are not in your right senses,' said the chief-agent firmly; 'anxiety and apprehension on your sister's account have shaken your mind. Try to compose yourself, and listen to me. I have something important to say'— (Trudaine looked at him incredulously.) 'Important,' continued Lomaque, 'as affecting your sister's interests at this terrible crisis.'

That last appeal had an instantaneous effect. Trudaine's outstretched hand dropped to his side, and a sudden change passed over his expression.

'Give me a moment,' he said faintly; and, turning away, leaned against the wall, and pressed his burning forehead on the chill, damp stone. He did not raise his head again till he had mastered himself, and could say quietly, 'Speak – I am fit to hear you, and sufficiently in my senses to ask your forgiveness for what I said just now.'

'When I left the tribunal and entered this room,' Lomaque began in a whisper, 'there was no thought in my mind that could be turned to good account, either for your sister or for you. I was fit for nothing but to deplore the failure of the confession which I came to St Lazare to suggest to you as your best plan of defence. Since then, an idea has struck me, which may be useful – an idea so desperate, so uncertain – involving a proposal so absolutely dependent, as to its successful exec-ution, on the merest chance, that I refuse to confide it to you except on one condition.'

'Mention the condition! I submit to it beforehand.'

'Give me your word of honour that you will not mention what I am about to say to your sister until I grant you permission to speak. Promise me that when you see her shrinking before the terrors of death to-night, you will have self-restraint enough to abstain from breathing a word of hope to her. I ask this, because there are ten – twenty – fifty chances to one that there *is* no hope.'

'I have no choice but to promise,' answered Trudaine.

Lomaque produced his pocket-book and pencil before he spoke again.

'I will enter into particulars as soon as I have asked a strange question of you,' he said. 'You have been a great experimenter in chemistry in your time – is your mind calm enough at such a trying moment as this to answer a question which is connected with chemistry in a very humble way? You seem astonished. Let me put the question at once. Is there any liquid, or powder, or combination of more than one ingredient known, which will remove writing from paper, and leave no stain behind?'

'Certainly! But is that all the question? Is there no greater difficulty?'

'None. Write the prescription, whatever it may be, on that leaf,' said the other, giving him the pocket-book. 'Write it down with plain directions for use.' Trudaine obeyed. 'This is the first step,' continued Lomaque, putting the book in his pocket, 'towards the accomplishment of my purpose – my uncertain purpose, remember! Now listen; I am going to put my own head in danger for the chance of saving yours and your sister's by tampering with the death-list. Don't interrupt me! If I can save one, I can save the other. Not a word about gratitude! Wait till you know the extent of your obligation. I tell you plainly, at the outset, there is a motive of despair, as well as a motive of pity, at the bottom of the action in which I am now about to engage. Silence! I insist on it. Our time is short: it is for me to speak, and for you to listen. The president of the tribunal has put the death-mark against your names on the prison list of to-day. That list, when the trials are over, and it is marked to the end, will be called in this room before you are taken to St Lazare. It will then be sent to Robespierre, who will keep it, having a copy made of it the moment it is delivered, for circulation among his colleagues – St Just, and the rest. It is my business to make a duplicate of this copy in the first instance. The duplicate will be compared with the original, and possibly with the copy too, either by Robespierre himself, or by some one in whom he can place implicit trust, and will then be sent to St Lazare without passing through my hands again. It will be read in public the moment it is received, at the grating of the prison, and will afterwards be kept by the gaoler, who will refer to it as he goes round in the evening with a piece of chalk, to mark the cell-doors of the prisoners destined for the guillotine to-morrow. That duty happens, to-day, to fall to the hunchback whom you saw speaking to me. He is a confirmed drinker, and I mean to tempt him with such wine as he rarely tastes. If – after the reading of the list in public, and before the marking of the cell-doors – I can get him to sit down to the bottle, I will answer for making him drunk, for getting the list out of his pocket, and for wiping your names out of it with the prescription you have just written for me. I shall write all the names, one under another, just irregularly enough in my duplicate to prevent the interval left by the erasure from being easily observed. If I succeed in this, your door will not be marked, and your names will not be called to-morrow morning when the tumbrils come for the guillotine. In the present confusion of prisoners pouring in every day for trial, and prisoners pouring out every day for execution, you will have the best possible chance of security against awkward inquiries, if you play your cards properly, for a good fortnight or ten days at least. In that time—'

Well! well!' cried Trudaine eagerly.

Lomaque looked towards the tribunal door, and lowered his voice to a fainter whisper before he continued: 'In that time Robespierre's own head may fall into the sack! France is beginning to sicken under the Reign of Terror. Frenchmen of the Moderate faction, who have lain hidden for months in cellars and lofts, are beginning to steal out and deliberate by twos and threes together, under cover of the night. Robespierre has not ventured for weeks past to face the Convention committee. He only speaks among his own friends at the Jacobins. There are rumours of a terrible discovery made by Carnot, of a desperate resolution taken by Tallien. Men watching behind the scenes see that the last days of the Terror are at hand. If Robespierre is beaten in the approaching struggle, you are saved – for the new reign must be a Reign of Mercy. If he conquers, I have only put off the date of your death and your sister's, and have laid my own neck under the axe. Those are your chances – this is all I can do.'

He paused, and Trudaine again endeavoured to speak such words as might show that he was not unworthy of the deadly risk which Lomaque was prepared to encounter. But once more the chief-agent peremptorily and irritably interposed.

'I tell you, for the third time,' he said, 'I will listen to no expressions of gratitude from you, till I know when I deserve them. It is true that I recollect your father's timely kindness to me – true that I have not forgotten what passed, five years since, at your house by the river side. I remember everything, down to what you would only consider the veriest trifle – that cup of coffee, for instance, which your sister kept hot for me. I told you then that you would think better of me some day. I know that you do now. But this is not all. You want to glorify me to my face for risking my life for you. I won't hear you, because my risk is of the paltriest kind. I am weary of my life. I can't look back to it with pleasure. I am too old to look forward to what is left of it with hope. There was something in that night at your house before the wedding – something in what you said, in what your sister did – which altered me. I have had my days of gloom and self-reproach, from time to time, since then. I have sickened at my slavery, and subjection, and duplicity, and cringing, first under one master, then under another. I have longed to look back at my life, and comfort myself with the sight of some good action, just as a frugal man comforts himself with the sight of his little savings laid by in an old drawer. I can't do this, and I want to do it. The want takes me like a fit, at uncertain intervals, – suddenly, under the most incomprehensible influences. A glance up at the blue sky – starlight over the houses of this great city, when I look out at the night from my garret window – a child's voice coming suddenly, I don't know where from – the piping of my neighbour's linnet in his little cage – now one trifling thing, now another, wakes up that want in me a moment. Rascal as I am, those few simple words your sister spoke to the judge went through and through me like a knife. Strange, in a man like me, isn't it? I am amazed at it myself. *My* life? Bah! I've let it out for hire to be kicked about by rascals from one dirty place to another, like a football! It's my whim to give it a last kick myself, and throw it away decently before it lodges on the dunghill for ever. Your sister kept a good cup of coffee hot for me, and I give her a bad life in return for the compliment. You want to thank me for it? What folly! Thank me when I have done something useful. Don't thank me for that!'

He snapped his fingers contemptuously as he spoke, and walked away to the outer door to receive the gaoler, who returned at that moment.

'Well,' inquired the hunchback, 'has anybody asked for me?'

'No,' answered Lomaque; 'not a soul has entered the room. What sort of wine did you get?'

'So-so! Good at a pinch, friend – good at a pinch.'

'Ah! you should go to my shop and try a certain cask, filled with a particular vintage!'

'What shop? Which vintage?'

'I can't stop to tell you now; but we shall most likely meet again to-day. I expect to be at the prison this afternoon. Shall I ask for you? Good! I won't forget!' With those farewell words he went out, and never so much as looked back at the prisoners before he closed the door behind him.

Trudaine returned to his sister, fearful lest his face should betray what had passed during the extraordinary interview between Lomaque and himself. But, whatever change there might be in his expression, Rose did not seem to notice it. She was still strangely inattentive to all outward things. That spirit of resignation, which is the courage of women in all great emergencies, seemed now to be the one animating spirit that fed the flame of life within her.

When her brother sat down by her, she only took his hand gently and said – 'Let us stop together like this, Louis, till the time comes. I am not afraid of it, for I have nothing but you to make me love life, and you, too, are going to die. Do you remember the time when I used to grieve that I had never had a child to be some comfort to me? I was thinking a moment ago, how terrible it would have been now, if my wish had been granted. It is a blessing for me, in this great misery, that I am childless! Let us talk of old days, Louis, as long as we can – not of my husband, or my marriage – only of the old times, before I was a burden and a trouble to you.'

CHAPTER V

The day wore on. By ones and twos and threes at a time, the condemned prisoners came from the tribunal, and collected in the waiting-room. At two o'clock all was ready for the calling over of the death-list. It was read and verified by an officer of the court; and thenm the gaoler took his prisoners back to Saint Lazare.

Evening came. The prisoners' meal had been served; the duplicate of the death-list had been read in public at the grate; the gell-doors were all locked. From the day of their arrest, Rose and her brother, partly through the influence of a bribe, partly through Lomaque's intercession, had been confined together in one cell; and together they new awaited the dread event of the morrow.

To Rose that event was death – death, to the thought of which, at least, she was now resigned. To Trudaine the fast-nearing future was darkening hour by hour, with the uncertainty which is worse than death; with the faint, fearful, unpartaken suspense, which keeps the mind ever on the rack, and wears away the heart slowly. Through the long unsolaced agony of that dreadful night, but one relief came to him. The tension of every nerve, the crushing weight of the one fatal oppression that clung to every thought, relaxed a little, when Rose's bodily powers began to sink under her mental exhaustion – when her sad dying talk of the happy times that were passed ceased softly, and she laid her head on his shoulder, and let the angel of slumber take her yet for a little while, even though she lay already under the shadow of the angel of death.

The morning came, and the hot summer sunrise. What life was left in the terror-struck city awoke for the day faintly; and still the suspense of the long night remained unlightened. It was drawing near the hour when the tumbrils were to come for the victims doomed on the day before. Trudaine's ear could detect even the faintest sound in the echoing prison-region outside his cell. Soon, listening near the door, he heard voices disputing on the other side of it. Suddenly, the bolts were drawn back, the key turned in the lock, and he found himself standing face to face with the hunchback and one of the subordinate attendants on the prisoners.

'Look!' muttered this last man, sulkily, 'there they are, safe in their cell, just as I said; but I tell you again they are not down in the list. What do you mean by bullying me about not chalking their door, last night, along with the rest? Catch me doing your work for you again, when you're too drunk to do it yourself!'

'Hold your tongue, and let me have another look at the list!' returned the hunchback, turning away from the cell-door, and snatching a slip of paper from the other's hand. 'The devil take me if I can make head or tail of it!' he exclaimed, scratching his head, after a careful examination of the list. 'I could swear that I read over their names at the grate yesterday afternoon, with my own two lips; and yet, look as long as I may, I certainly can't find them written down here. Give us a pinch, friend. Am I awake, or dreaming? – drunk or sober this morning?'

'Sober, I hope,' said a quiet voice at his elbow, 'I have just looked in to see how you are after yesterday.'

'How I am, citizen Lomaque? Petrified with astonishment. You yourself took charge of that man and woman for me, in the waiting-room, yesterday morning; and as for myself, I could swear to having read their names at the grate yesterday afternoon. Yet this morning here are no such things as these said names to be found in the list! What do you think of that?'

'And what do you think,' interrupted the aggrieved subordinate, 'of his having the impudence to bully me for being careless in chalking the doors, when he was too drunk to do it himself? – too drunk to know his right hand from his left! If I wasn't the best-natured man in the world, I should report him to the head-gaoler.'

Quite right of you to excuse him, and quite wrong of him to bully you,' said Lomaque, persuasively. 'Take my advice,' he continued confidentially to the hunchback, 'and don't trust too implicitly to that slippery memory of yours, after our little drinking bout yesterday. You could not really have read their names at the grate, you know, or of course they would be down on the list. As for the waiting-room at the tribunal, a word in your ear: chief-agents of police know strange secrets. The president of the court condemns and pardons in public; but there is somebody else, with the power of ten thousand presidents, who now and then condemns and pardons in private. You can guess who. I say no more, except that I recommend you to keep your head on your shoulders, by troubling it about nothing but the list there in your hand. Stick to that literally, and no body can blame you. Make a fuss about mysteries that don't concern you, and—'

Lomaque stopped, and holding his hand edgewise, let it drop significantly over the hunchback's head. That action, and the hints which preceded it, seemed to bewilder the little man more than ever. He stared perplexedly at Lomaque; uttered a word or two of rough apology to his subordinate, and rolling his mishapen head portentously, walked away with the death-list crumpled up nervously in his hand.

'I should like to have a sight of them, and see if they really are the same man and woman whom I looked after yesterday morning in the waiting-room,' said Lomaque, putting his hand on the cell-door, just as the deputy-gaoler was about to close it again.

'Look in, by all means,' said the man. 'No doubt you will find that drunken booby as wrong in what he told you about them as he is about everything else.'

Lomaque made use of the privilege granted to him immediately. He saw Trudaine sitting with his sister in the corner of the cell farthest from the door, evidently for the purpose of preventing her from overhearing the conversation outside. There was an unsettled look, however, in her eyes, a slowly-heightening colour in her cheeks, which showed her to be at least vaguely aware that something unusual had been taking place in the corridor.

Lomaque beckoned to Trudaine to leave her; and whispered to him – 'The prescription has worked well. You are safe for to-day. Break the news to your sister as gently as you can. Danville' — He stopped and listened till he satisfied himself, by the sound of the deputy-gaoler's footsteps, that the man was lounging towards the farther end of the corridor. 'Danville,' he resumed, 'after having mixed with the people outside the grate, yesterday, and having heard your names read, was arrested in the evening by secret order from Robespierre, and sent to the Temple. What charge will be laid to him, or when he will be brought to trial, it is impossible to say. I only know that he is arrested. Hush! don't talk now; my friend outside is coming back. Keep quiet – hope everything from the chances and changes of public affairs; and comfort yourself with the thought that you are both safe for to-day.'

'And to-morrow?' whispered Trudaine.

'Don't think of to-morrow,' returned Lomaque, turning away hurriedly to the door. 'Let to-morrow take care of itself.'

PART THIRD

CHAPTER I

On a spring morning, in the year seventeen hundred and ninety-eight, the public conveyance then running between Chalons-sur-Marne and Paris set down one of its outside passengers at the first post-station beyond Meaux. The traveller, an old man, after looking about him hesitatingly for a moment or two, betook himself to a little inn opposite the post-house known by the sign of the Piebald Horse, and kept by the Widow Duval, – a woman who enjoyed and deserved the reputation of being the fastest talker and the best maker of *gibelotte* in the whole locality.

Although the traveller was carelessly noticed by the village idlers, and received without ceremony by the Widow Duval, he was by no means so ordinary and uninteresting a stranger as the rustics of the place were pleased to consider him. The time had been when this quiet, elderly, unobtrusive applicant for refreshment at the Piebald Horse was trusted with the darkest secrets of the Reign or Terror, and was admitted at all times and seasons to speak face to face with Maximilien Robespierre himself. The Widow Duval and the hangers-on in front of the post-house would have been all astonished indeed, if any well-informed personage from the metropolis had been present to tell them that the modest old traveller, with the shabby little carpet-bag, was an ex-chief agent of the secret police of Paris!

Between three and four years had elapsed since Lomaque had exercised, for the last time, his official functions under the Reign of Terror. His shoulders had contracted an extra stoop, and his hair had all fallen off, except at the sides and back of his head. In some other respects, however, advancing age seemed to have improved rather than deteriorated him in personal appearance. His complexion looked healthier, his expression cheerfuller, his eyes brighter than they had ever been of late years. He walked, too, with a brisker step than the step of old times in the police-office; and his dress, although it certainly did not look like the costume of a man in affluent circumstance, was cleaner and far more neatly worn than ever it had been in the past days of his political employment at Paris.

He sat down alone in the inn-parlour, and occupied the time, while his hostess had gone to fetch the half-bottle of wine that he ordered, in examining a dirty old card which he extricated from a mass of papers in his pocket-book, and which bore, written on it, these lines:—

"When the troubles are over, do not forget those who remember you with eternal gratitude. Stop at the first post-station beyond Meaux, on the high road to Paris, and ask at the inn for citizen Maurice, whenever you wish to see us or to hear of us again."

'Pray,' inquired Lomaque, putting the card in his pocket when the Widow Duval brought in the wine, 'can you inform me whether a person named Maurice lives anywhere in this neighbourhood?'

'Can I inform you?' repeated the voluble widow. "Of course I can! Citizen Maurice, and the citoyenne, his amiable sister – who is not to be passed over because you don't mention her, my honest man! – live within ten minutes' walk of my house. A charming cottage, in a charming situation, inhabited by two charming people, – so quiet, so retiring, such excellent pay. I supply them with everything, – fowls, eggs, bread, butter, vegetables (not that they eat much of anything), wine (which they don't drink half enough of to do them good); in short, I victual the dear little hermitage, and love the two amiable recluses with all my heart. Ah! they have had their troubles, poor people, the sister especially, though they never talk about them. When they first came to live in our neighbourhood' —

'I beg pardon, citoyenne, but if you would only be so kind as to direct me' —

'Which is three – no, four – no, three years and a half ago – in short, just after the time when that Satan of a man, Robespierre, had his head cut off (and serve him right!), I said

to my husband (who was on his last legs then, poor man!),
"She'll die," – meaning the lady. She didn't though. My
fowls, eggs, bread, butter, vegetables, and wine, carried her
through, – always in combination with the anxious care of
citizen Maurice. Yes, yes! let us be tenderly conscientious in
giving credit where credit is due; let us never forget that the
citizen Maurice contributed something to the cure of the
interesting invalid, as well as the victuals and drink from the
Piebald Horse. There she is now, the prettiest little woman in
the prettiest little cottage'—

'Where? Will you be so obliging as to tell me where?'

'And in excellent health, except that she is subject now and
then to nervous attacks, having evidently, as I believe, been
struck with some dreadful fright, – most likely during that
accursed time of the Terror, for they came from Paris – you
don't drink, honest man! Why don't you drink? – Very, very
pretty in a pale way; figure perhaps too thin – let me pour it
out for you – but an angel of gentleness, and attached in such
a touching way to the citizen Maurice' —

'Citizen hostess! will you, or will you not, tell me where
they live?'

'You droll little man! why did you not ask me that before,
if you wanted to know? Finish your wine and come to the
door. There's your change, and thank you for your custom
though it isn't much. Come to the door, I say, and don't
interrupt me! You're an old man, – can you see forty yards
before you? – Yes, you can! Don't be peevish, – that never did
anybody any good yet. Now look back, along the road where
I am pointing. You see a large heap of stones? Good. On the
other side of the heap of stones, there is a little path, – you
can't see that, but you can remember what I tell you? Good.
You go down the path till you get to a stream; down the
stream till you get to a bridge; down the other bank of the
stream (after crossing the bridge) till you get to an old
water-mill, – a jewel of a water-mill! famous for miles round;
artists from the four quarters of the globe are always coming
to sketch it! Ah! what, you are getting peevish again? You
won't wait? Impatient old man, what a life your wife must
lead, if you have got one! Remember the bridge! Ah! your
poor wife and children, I pity them, your daughters espe-

cially. Pst! pst! Remember the bridge, – peevish old man, remember the bridge!'

Walking as fast as he could out of hearing of the Widow Duval's tongue, Lomaque took the path by the heap of stones which led out of the high-road, crossed the stream, and arrived at the old water-mill. Close by it stood a cottage, – a rough, simple building, with a strip of garden in front. Lomaque's observant eyes marked the graceful arrangement of the flower-beds and the delicate whiteness of the curtains that hung behind the badly-glazed narrow windows. 'This must be the place,' he said to himself as he knocked at the door with his stick. 'I can see the traces of her hand before I cross the threshold.'

The door was opened. 'Pray, does the citizen Maurice?' — Lomaque began, not seeing clearly, for the first moment, in the dark little passage.

Before he could say any more his hand was grasped, his carpet-bag was taken from him, and a well-known voice cried, 'Welcome! a thousand times welcome, at last! Citizen Maurice is not at home; but Louis Trudaine takes his place, and is overjoyed to see once more the best and dearest of his friends!'

'I hardly know you again. How you are altered for the better!' exclaimed Lomaque as they entered the parlour of the cottage.

'Remember that you see me after a long freedom from anxiety. Since I have lived here, I have gone to rest at night, and have not been afraid of the morning,' replied Trudaine. He went out into the passage while he spoke, and called at the foot of the one flight of stairs which the cottage possessed, 'Rose! Rose! come down! The friend whom you most wished to see has arrived at last!'

She answered the summons immediately. The frank friendly warmth of her greeting; her resolute determination, after the first inquiries were over, to help the guest to take off his upper coat with her own hands, so confused and delighted Lomaque, that he hardly knew which way to turn, or what to say.

'This is even more trying, in a pleasant way, to a lonely old fellow like me' – he was about to add, 'than the unexpected civility of the hot cup of coffee years ago;' but remembering what recollections even that trifling circumstance might recall, he checked himself.

'More trying than what?' asked Rose, leading him to a chair.

'Ah! I forget. I am in my dotage already!' he answered, confusedly. 'I have not got used just yet to the pleasure of seeing your kind face again.'

It was indeed a pleasure to look at that face now, after Lomaque's last experience of it. Three years of repose, though they had not restored to Rose those youthful attractions which she had lost for ever in the days of the Terror, had not passed without leaving kindly outward traces of their healing progress. Though the girlish roundness had not returned to her cheeks, or the girlish delicacy of colour to her complexion, her eyes had recovered much of their old softness, and her expression all of its old winning charm. What was left of latent sadness in her face, and of significant quietness in her manner, remained gently and harmlessly – remained rather to show what had been once than what was now.

When they were all seated, there was, however, something like a momentary return to the suspense and anxiety of past days in their faces, as Trudaine, looking earnestly at Lomaque, asked – 'Do you bring any news from Paris?'

'None,' he replied; 'but excellent news, instead, from Rouen. I have heard, accidentally, through the employer whom I have been serving since we parted, that your old house by the river side is to let again.'

Rose started from her chair. 'Oh! Louis, if we could only live there once more! My flower-garden?' she continued, turning to Lomaque.

'Cultivated throughout,' he answered, 'by the late proprietor.'

'And the laboratory?' added her brother.

'Left standing.' said Lomaque. 'Here is a letter with all the particulars. You may depend upon them, for the writer is the person charged with the letting of the house.'

Trudaine looked over the letter eagerly.

'The price is not beyond our means,' he said. 'After our three years' economy here, we can afford to give something for a great pleasure.'

'Oh! what a day of happiness it will be when we go home again!' cried Rose. 'Pray, write to your friend at once,' she added, addressing Lomaque, 'and say we take the house, before any one else is beforehand with us!'

He nodded; and, folding up the letter mechanically in the old official form, made a note on it in the old official manner. Trudaine observed the action, and felt its association with the past times of trouble and terror. His face grew grave again, as he said to Lomaque, 'And is this good news really all the news of importance you have to tell us?'

Lomaque hesitated, and fidgeted in his chair. 'What other news I have will well bear keeping,' he replied. 'There are many questions I should like to ask first, about your sister and yourself. Do you mind allowing me to refer for a moment to the time when we last met?'

He addressed this inquiry to Rose, who answered in the negative; but her voice seemed to alter, even in saying the one word 'No.' She turned her head away when she spoke; and Lomaque noticed that her hands trembled as she took up some work lying on a table near, and hurriedly occupied herself with it.

'We speak as little about that time as possible,' said Trudaine, looking significantly towards his sister; 'but we have some questions to ask you in our turn; so the allusion, for this once, is inevitable. Your sudden disappearance at the very crisis of that terrible time of danger has not yet been fully explained to us. The one short note which you left behind you helped us to guess at what had happened rather than to understand it.'

'I can easily explain it now,' answered Lomaque. 'The sudden overthrow of the Reign of Terror, which was salvation to you, was destruction to me. The new republican reign was a reign of mercy, except for the tail of Robespierre, as the phrase ran then. Every man who had been so wicked or so unfortunate as to be involved, even in the meanest capacity, with the machinery of the government of Terror, was threatened, and justly, with the fate of Robespierre. I, among others, fell under this menace of death. I deserved to die, and should have resigned myself to the guillotine, but for you. From the course taken by public events, I knew you would be

saved; and although your safety was the work of circumstances, still I had a hand in rendering it possible at the outset; and a
yearning came over me to behold you both free again with my
own eyes – a selfish yearning to see, in you, a living, breathing,
real result of the one good impulse of my heart, which I could
look back on with satisfaction. This desire gave me a new
interest in life. I resolved to escape death if it were possible. For
ten days I lay hidden in Paris. After that – thanks to certain
scraps of useful knowledge which my experience in the office
of secret police had given me – I succeeded in getting clear of
Paris, and in making my way safely to Switzerland. The rest of
my story is so short, and so soon told, that I may as well get it
over at once. The one relation I knew of in the world to apply
to, was a cousin of mine (whom I had never seen before),
established as a silk-mercer at Berne. I threw myself on this
man's mercy. He discovered that I was likely, with my
business habits, to be of some use to him, and he took me into
his house. I worked for what he pleased to give me; travelled
about for him in Switzerland; deserved his confidence, and
won it. Till within the last few months I remained with him;
and only left my employment to enter, by my master's own
desire, the house of his brother, established also as a silk-
mercer, at Chalons-sur-Marne. In the counting-house of this
merchant I am corresponding clerk; and am only able to come
and see you now, by offering to undertake a special business-
mission, for my employer, at Paris. It is drudgery, at my time
of life, after all I have gone through – but my hard work is
innocent work. I am not obliged to cringe for every crown-
piece I put in my pocket – not bound to denounce, deceive, and
dog to death other men, before I can earn my bread, and scrape
together money enough to bury me. I am ending a bad, base
life harmlessly at last. It is a poor thing to do, but it is
something done – and even that contents a man at my age. In
short, I am happier than I used to be, or at least less ashamed
when I look people like you in the face.'

'Hush! hush!' interrupted Rose, laying her hand on his arm.
'I cannot allow you to talk of yourself in that way, even in jest.'

'I was speaking in earnest,' answered Lomaque, quietly; 'but
I won't weary you with any more words about myself. My
story is told.'

'All?' asked Trudaine. He looked searchingly, almost suspiciously, at Lomaque, as he put the question. 'All?' he repeated. 'Yours is a short story, indeed, my good friend! Perhaps you have forgotten some of it?'

Again Lomaque fidgeted and hesitated.

'Is it not a little hard on an old man to be always asking questions of him, and never answering one of his inquiries in return?' he said to Rose, very gaily as to manner, but rather uneasily as to look.

'He will not speak out till we two are alone,' thought Trudaine. 'It is best to risk nothing, and to humour him.'

'Come, come,' he said aloud, 'no grumbling. I admit that it is your turn to hear out story now; and I will do my best to gratify you. But before I begin,' he added, turning to his sister, 'let me suggest, Rose, that if you have any household matters to settle up-stairs' —

'I know what you mean,' she interrupted, hurriedly taking up the work which, during the last few minutes, she had allowed to drop into her lap; 'but I am stronger than you think; I can face the worst of our recollections composedly. Go on, Louis; pray go on – I am quite fit to stop and hear you.'

'You know what we suffered in the first days of our suspense, after the success of your stratagem,' said Trudaine, turning to Lomaque. 'I think it was on the evening after we had seen you for the last at St Lazare, that strange confused rumours of an impending convulsion in Paris first penetrated within our prison walls. During the next few days, the faces of our gaolers were enough to show us that those rumours were true, and that the Reign of Terror was actually threatened with overthrow at the hands of the Moderate Party. We had hardly time to hope everything from this blessed change, before the tremendous news of Robespierre's attempted suicide, then of his condemnation and execution, reached us. The confusion produced in the prison was beyond all description. The accused who had been tried and the accused who had not been tried got mingled together. From the day of Robespierre's arrest, no orders came to the authorities, no death-lists reached the prison. The gaolers, terrified by rumours that the lowest accomplices of the tyrant would be held responsible, and be condemned with him, made no attempt to maintain order.

Some of them – that humpbacked man among the rest –
deserted their duties altogether. The disorganization was so
complete, that when the commissioners from the new government came to St Lazare, some of us were actually half-
starving from want of the bare necessities of life. To inquire
separately into our cases was found to be impossible.
Sometimes the necessary papers were lost; sometimes what
documents remained were incomprehensible to the new
commissioners. They were obliged, at last, to make short
work of it by calling us up before them in dozens. Tried or not
tried, we had all been arrested by the tyrant, had all been
accused of conspiracy against him, and were all ready to hail
the new government as the salvation of France. In nine cases
out of ten, our best claim to be discharged was derived from
these circumstances. We were trusted by Tallien and the men
of the Ninth Thermidor, because we had been suspected by
Robespierre, Couthon, and St Just. Arrested informally, we
were now liberated informally. When it came to my sister's
turn and mine, we were not under examination five minutes.
No such thing as a searching question was asked of us; I
believe we might even have given our own names with perfect
impunity. But I had previously instructed Rose that we were
to assume our mother's maiden name – Maurice. As the
citizen and citoyenne Maurice, accordingly, we passed out of
prison – under the same name we have lived ever since in
hiding here. Our past repose has depended, our future happiness will depend, on our escape from death being kept the
profoundest secret among us three. For one all-sufficient
reason, which you can easily guess at, the brother and sister
Maurice must still know nothing of Louis Trudaine and Rose
Danville, except that they were two among the hundreds of
victims guillotined during the Reign of Terror.'

He spoke the last sentence with a faint smile, and with the
air of a man trying, in spite of himself, to treat a grave subject
lightly. His face clouded again, however, in a moment, when
he looked to-wards his sister, as he ceased. Her work had once
more dropped on her lap; her face was turned away so that he
could not see it; but he knew by the trembling of her clasped
hands, as they rested on her knee, and by the slight swelling of
the veins on her neck which she could not hide from him, that

her boasted strength of nerve had deserted her. Three years of
repose had not yet enabled her to hear her marriage name
uttered, or to be present when past times of deathly suffering
and terror were referred to, without betraying the shock in her
face and manner. Trudaine looked saddened, but in no way
surprised by what he saw. Making a sign to Lomaque to say
nothing, he rose and took up his sister's hood, which lay on a
window-seat near him.

'Come, Rose,' he said, 'the sun is shining, the sweet spring
air is inviting us out. Let us have a quiet stroll along the banks
of the stream. Why should we keep our good friend here
cooped up in this narrow little room, when we have miles and
miles of beautiful landscape to show him on the other side of
the threshold? Come! it is high treason to Queen Nature to
remain indoors on such a morning as this.'

Without waiting for her to reply, he put on her hood, drew
her arm through his, and led the way out. Lomaque's face
grew grave as he followed them.

'I am glad I only showed the bright side of my budget of
news in her presence,' thought he. 'She is not well at heart yet.
I might have hurt her, poor thing! I might have hurt her again
sadly, if I had not held my tongue!'

They walked for a little while down the banks of the stream,
talking of indifferent matters; then returned to the cottage. By
that time Rose had recovered her spirits, and could listen with
interest and amusement to Lomaque's drily-humorous description of his life as a clerk at Chalons-sur-Marne. They parted
for a little while at the cottage-door. Rose retired to the
up-stairs room from which she had been summoned by her
brother. Trudaine and Lomaque returned to wander again
along the banks of the stream.

With one accord, and without a word passing between
them, they left the neighbourhood of the cottage hurriedly;
then stopped on a sudden, and attentively looked each other in
the face – looked in silence for an instant. Trudaine spoke first.

'I thank you for having spared her,' he began, abruptly. 'She
is not strong enough yet to bear hearing of a new misfortune,
unless I break the tidings to her first.'

'You suspect me then of bringing bad news?' said Lomaque.
'I know you do. When I saw your first look at her, after we

were all seated in the cottage-parlour, I knew it. Speak!
without fear, without caution, without one useless word of
preface. After three years of repose, if it pleases God to afflict
us again, I can bear the trial calmly; and, if need be, can
strengthen her to bear it calmly too. I say again, Lomaque,
speak at once, and speak out! I know your news is bad, for I
know beforehand that it is news of Danville.'

'You are right, my bad news is news of him.'

'He has discovered the secret of our escape from the
guillotine?' —

'No – he has not a suspicion of it. He believes – as his
mother, as every one does – that you were both executed the
day after the Revolutionary Tribunal sentenced you to death.'

'Lomaque! you speak positively of that belief of his – but
you cannot be certain of it.'

'I can, on the most indisputable, the most startling evidence
– on the authority of Danville's own act. You have asked me
to speak out?' —

'I ask you again – I insist on it! Your news, Lomaque – your
news, without another word of preface!'

'You shall have it without another word of preface.
Danville is on the point of being married.'

As the answer was given they both stopped by the bank of
the stream, and again looked each other in the face. There was
a minute of dead silence between them. During that minute,
the water bubbling by happily over its bed of pebbles, seemed
strangely loud, the singing of birds in a little wood by the
stream side strangely near and shrill, in both their ears. The
light breeze, for all its mid-day warmth, touched their cheeks
coldly; and the spring sunlight pouring on their face, felt as if
it were glimmering on them through winter clouds.

'Let us walk on,' said Trudaine, in a low voice. 'I was
prepared for bad news, yet not for that. Are you certain of
what you have just told me?'

'As certain as that the stream here is flowing by our side.
Here how I made the discovery, and you will doubt no longer.
Before last week, I knew nothing of Danville, except that his
arrest on suspicion by Robespierre's order was, as events
turned out, the saving of his life. He was imprisoned, as I told
you, on the evening after he had heard your names read from

the death-list at the prison-grate. He remained in confinement at the Temple, unnoticed in the political confusion out of doors, just as you remained unnoticed at St Lazare; and he profited precisely in the same manner that you profited by the timely insurrection which overthrew the Reign of Terror. I knew this, and I knew that he walked out of prison in the character of a persecuted victim of Robespierre's – and for better than three years past, I knew no more. Now listen. Last week I happen to be waiting in the shop of my employer, citizen Clairfait, for some papers to take into the counting-house, when an old man enters with a sealed parcel, which he hands to one of the shopmen, saying:

"Give that to citizen Clairfait.'

"Any name?' says the shopman.

"The name is of no consequence,' answers the old man; 'but if you please you can give mine. Say the parcel came from citizen Dubois;' and then he goes out. His name, in connexion with his elderly look, strikes me directly.

"Does that old fellow live at Chalons?' I ask.

"No' says the shopman. 'He is here in attendance on a customer of ours – an old ex-aristocrat named Danville. She is on a visit in our town.'

I leave you to imagine how that reply startles and amazes me. The shopman can answer none of the other questions I put to him; but the next day I am asked to dinner by my employer (who, for his brother's sake, shows me the utmost civility). On entering the room, I find his daughter just putting away a lavender-coloured silk scarf, on which she has been embroidering in silver what looks to me very like a crest and coat of arms.

"I don't mind your seeing what I am about, citizen Loma-que,' says she; 'for I know my father can trust you. That scarf is sent back to us by the purchaser, an ex-emigrant lady of the old aristocratic school, to have her family coat-of-arms embroidered on it.'

'Rather a dangerous commission even in these mercifully democratic times, is it not?' says I.

'The old lady, you must know,' says she, 'is as proud as Lucifer; and having got back safely to France in these days of moderate republicanism, thinks she may now indulge with impunity in all her old-fashioned notions. She has been an excellent customer of ours, so my father thought it best to humour her, without, however, trusting her commission to any of the work-room women to execute. We are not living under the Reign of Terror now, certainly; still there is nothing like being on the safe side.'

'Nothing,' I answer. 'Pray what is this ex-emigrant's name?'

'Danville,' replies the citoyenne Clairfait. 'She is going to appear in that fine scarf at her son's marriage.'

'Marriage,' I exclaim, perfectly thunderstruck.

'Yes,' says she. 'What is there so amazing in that? By all accounts, the son, poor man, deserves to make a lucky marriage this time. His first wife was taken away from him in the Reign of Terror by the guillotine.'

'Who is he going to marry?' I inquire, still breathless.

'The daughter of General Berthelin – an ex-aristrocrat by family, like the old lady, but by principle as good a republican as ever lived – a hard-drinking, loud-swearing, big-whiskered old soldier, who snaps his fingers at his ancestors, and says we are all descended from Adam, the first genuine sansculotte in the world.'

'In this way the citoyenne Clairfait gossips on all dinner-time, but says nothing more of any importance. I, with my old police-office habits, set to the next day, and try to make some discoveries for myself. The sum of what I find out is this: Danville's mother is staying with General Berthelin's sister and daughter at Chalons, and Danville himself is expected to arrive every day to escort them all three to Paris, where the marriage-contract is to be signed at the general's house. Discovering this, and seeing that prompt action is now of the most vital importance, I undertake, as I told you, my employer's commission for Paris; depart with all speed; and stop here on my way. – Wait! I have not done yet. All the haste I can make is not haste enough to give me a good start of the wedding party. On my road here, the diligence by which I travel is passed by a carriage, posting along at full speed. I cannot see inside that carriage; but I look at the box-seat, and recognise on it the old man Dubois. He whirls by in a cloud of dust, but I am certain of him; and I say to myself, what I now say again to you no time is to be lost!'

'No time *shall* be lost,' answered Trudaine firmly. Three years have passed,' he continued, in a lower voice, speaking to himself rather than to Lomaque; 'three years since the day when I led my sister out of the gates of the prison, – three years since I said in my heart, I will be patient, and will not seek to avenge myself. Our wrongs cry from earth to heaven; from man who inflicts to God who redresses. When the day of reckoning comes, let it by the day of His vengeance, not of mine. In my heart I said those words – I have been true to them – I have waited. The day has come, and the duty it demands of me shall be fulfilled.'

There was a moment's silence before Lomaque spoke again. 'Your sister?' he began hesitatingly.

'It is there only that my purpose falters,' said the other earnestly. 'If it were but possible to spare her all knowledge of this last trial, and to leave the accomplishment of the terrible task to me alone?'

'I think it is possible,' interposed Lomaque. 'Listen to what I advise. We must depart for Paris by the diligence to-morrow morning, and we must take your sister with us – to-morrow will be time enough: people don't sign marriage-contracts on the evening after a long day's journey. We must go then, and we must take your sister. Leave the care of her in Paris, and the responsibility of keeping her in ignorance of what you are doing, to me. Go to this General Berthelin's house at a time when you Danville is there (we can get that knowledge through the servants); confront him without a moment's previous warning; confront him as a man risen from the dead; confront him before every soul in the room, though the room should be full of people – and leave the rest to the self-betrayal of a panic-stricken man. Say but three words, and *your* duty will be done; you may return to your sister, and may depart with her in safety to your old retreat at Rouen, or where else you please, on the very day when you have put it out of her infamous husband's power to add another to the list of his crimes.'

'You forget the suddenness of the journey to Paris,' said Trudaine. 'How are we to account for it without the risk of awakening my sister's suspicions?'

'Trust that to me,' answered Lomaque. 'Let us return to the cottage at once. No! not you,' he added suddenly, as they

turned to retrace their steps. 'There is that in your face which
which would betray us. Leave me to go back alone – I will say
that you have gone to give some orders at the inn. Let us
separate immediately. You will recover your self-possession –
you will get to look yourself again sooner, if you are left alone
– I know enough of you to know that. We will not waste
another minute in explanations, even minutes are precious to
us on such a day as this. By the time you are fit to meet your
sister again, I shall have had time to say all I wish to her, and
shall be waiting at the cottage to tell you the result.'

He looked at Trudaine, and his eyes seemed to brighten
again with something of the old energy and sudden decision of
the days when he was a man in office under the Reign of
Terror. 'Leave it to me,' he said; and, waving his hand, turned
away quickly in the direction of the cottage.

Nearly an hour passed before Trudaine ventured to follow
him. When he at length entered the path which led to the
garden-gate, he saw his sister waiting at the cottage-door. Her
face looked unusually animated; and she ran forward a step or
two to meet him.

'Oh, Louis!' she said, 'I have a confession to make, and I
must beg you to hear it patiently to the end. You must know
that our good Lomaque, though he came in tired from his
walk, occupied himself the first thing, at my request, in
writing the letter which is to secure to us our dear old home by
the banks of the Seine. When he had done, he looked at me,
and said, "I should like to be present at your happy return to
the house where I first saw you." "Oh, come, come with us!"
I said directly. "I am not an independent man," he answered;
"I have a margin of time allowed me at Paris, certainly, but it
is not long – if I were only my own master"— and then he
stopped. Louis! I remembered all we owed to him; I remembered that there was no sacrifice we ought not to be too glad to
make for his sake; I felt the kindness of the wish he had
expressed; and, perhaps, I was a little influenced by my own
impatience to see once more my flower-garden and the rooms
where we used to be so happy. So I said to him, "I am sure
Louis will agree with me, that our time is yours, and that we
shall be only too glad to advance our departure so as to make
travelling-leisure enough for you to come with us to Rouen.

We should be worse than ungrateful"— He stopped me. "You have always been good to me," he said, "I must not impose on your kindness now. No! no! you have formalities to settle before you can leave this place." "Not one," I said – for we have not, as you know, Louis? "Why, here is your furniture to begin with," he said. "A few chairs and tables hired from the inn," I answered; "we have only to give the landlady our key, to leave a letter for the owner of the cottage, and then"— He laughed. "Why, to hear you talk, one would think you were as ready to travel as I am!" "So we are," I said, "quite as ready, living in the way we do here." He shook his head; but you will not shake yours, Louis, I am sure, now you have heard all my long story? You can't blame me, can you?'

Before Trudaine could answer, Lomaque looked out of the cottage window.

I have just been telling my brother everything,' said Rose, turning round towards him.

'And what does he say?' asked Lomaque.

'He says what I say,' replied Rose, answering for her brother; 'that our time is your time – the time of our best and dearest friend.'

'Shall it be done, then?' asked Lomaque, with a meaning look at Trudaine.

Rose glanced anxiously at her brother: his face was much graver than she had expected to see it, but his answer relieved her from all suspense.

'You were quite right, love, to speak as you did,' he said, gently. Then, turning to Lomaque, he added in a firmer voice, 'It shall be done!'

CHAPTER II

Two days after the travelling carriage described by Lomaque had passed the diligence on the road to Paris, Madame Danville sat in the drawing-room of an apartment in the Rue de Grenelle, handsomely dressed for driving out. After consulting a large gold watch that hung at her side, and finding that it wanted a quarter of an hour only to two o'clock, she rang her hand-bell, and said to the maid-servant who answered the summons: 'I have five minutes to spare. Send Dubois here with my chocolate.'

The old man made his appearance with great alacrity. After handing the cup of chocolate to his mistress, he ventured to use the privilege of talking, to which his long and faithful services entitled him, and paid the old lady a compliment. 'I am rejoiced to see madame looking so young and in such good spirits this morning,' he said, with a low bow and a mild deferential smile.

'I think I have some reason for being in good spirits on the day when my son's marriage-contract is to be signed,' said Madame Danville, with a gracious nod of the head. 'Ha, Dubois, I shall live yet to see him with a patent of nobility in his hand. The mob has done its worst; the end of this infamous revolution is not far off; our order will have its turn again soon, and then who will have such a chance at court as my son? He is noble already through his mother; he will then be noble also through his wife. Yes, yes, let that coarse-mannered, passionate, old soldier-father of hers be as unnaturally republican as he pleases, he has inherited a name which will help my son to a peerage! The Vicomte D'Anville (D with an apostrophe, Dubois, you understand)? The Vicomte D'Anville – how prettily it sounds!'

'Charmingly, madame – charmingly. Ah! this second marriage of my young master's begins under much better auspices than the first.'

The remark was an unfortunate one. Madame Danville frowned portentously, and rose in a great hurry from her chair.

'Are your wits failing you, you old fool?' she exclaimed, indignantly; 'what do you mean by referring to such a subject as that, on this day of all others? You are always harping on those two wretched people who were guillotined, as if you thought I could have saved their lives. Were you not present when my son and I met, after the time of the Terror? Did you not hear my first words to him, when he told me of the catastrophe? Were they not: – 'Charles, I love you; but if I thought you had let those two unfortunates, who risked themselves to save me, die without risking you life in return to save them, I would break my heart rather than ever look at you or speak to you again' – Did I not say that? And did he not answer: – 'Mother, my life was risked for them. I proved my devotion by exposing myself to arrest – I was imprisoned for my exertions, – and then I could do no more!' Did you not stand by and hear him give that answer, overwhelmed while he spoke by generous emotion? Do you not know that he really was imprisoned in the Temple? Do you dare to think that we are to blame after that? I owe you much, Dubois, but if you are to take liberties with me —'

'Oh, madame! I beg pardon a thousand times. I was thoughtless – only thoughtless—'

'Silence! Is my coach at the door? – Very well. Get ready to accompany me. Your master will not have time to return here. He will meet me, for the signing of the contract, at General Berthelin' house at two precisely. – Stop! Are there many people in the street? I can't be stared at by the mob, as I go to my carriage.'

Dubois hobbled penitently to the window and looked out, while his mistress walked to the door.

'The street is almost empty, madame,' he said. 'Only a man, with a woman on his arm, stopping and admiring your carriage. They seem like decent people, as well as I can tell without my spectacles. Not mob, I should say, madame, certainly not a mob!'

'Very well. Attend me down stairs; and bring some loose silver with you, in case those two decent people should be fit

objects for charity. No orders for the coachman, except that
he is to go straight to the general's house.'

The party assembled at General Berthelin's to witness the
signature of the marriage-contract, comprised, besides the
persons immediately interested in the ceremony of the day,
some young ladies, friends of the bride, and a few officers,
who had been comrades of her father's in past years. The
guests were distributed, rather unequally, in two handsome
apartments opening into each other, – one called in the house
the drawing-room, and the other the library. In the drawing-
room were assembled the notary, with the contract ready, the
bride, the young ladies, and the majority of General Berthelin's friends. In the library, the remainder of the military
guests were amusing themselves at a billiard-table until the
signing of the contract should take place; while Danville and
his future father-in-law walked up and down the room
together; the first listening absently, the last talking with all
his accustomed energy, and with more than his accustomed
allowance of barrack-room expletives. The general had taken
it into his head to explain some of the clauses in the
marriage-contract to the bridegroom, who, though far better
acquainted with their full scope and meaning than his father-
in-law, was obliged to listen for civility's sake. While the old
soldier was still in the midst of his long and confused
harangue, a clock struck on the library mantelpiece.

'Two o'clock!' exclaimed Danville, glad of any pretext for
interrupting the talk about the contract. 'Two o'clock; and
my mother not here yet! What can be delaying her?'

'Nothing,' cried the general. 'When did you ever know a
woman punctual, my lad? If we wait for your mother – and
she's such a rabid aristocrat that she would never forgive us
for not waiting – we shan't sign the contract yet this
half-hour. Never mind! let's go on with what we were talking
about. Where the devil was I when that cursed clock struck
and interrupted us? Now then, Black Eyes, what's the
matter?'

This last question was addressed to Mademoiselle Berthelin, who at that moment hastily entered the library from the
drawing-room. She was a tall and rather masculine-looking
girl, with superb black eyes, dark hair growing low on her

forehead, and something of her father's decision and bluntness in her manner of speaking.

'A stranger in the other room, papa, who wants to see you. I suppose the servants showed him upstairs, thinking he was one of the guests. Ought I to have had him shown down again?'

'A nice question! How should I know? Wait till I have seen him, miss, and then I'll tell you.' With these words the general turned on his heel, and went into the drawing-room.

His daughter would have followed him, but Danville caught her by the hand.

'Can you be hard-hearted enough to leave me here alone?' he asked.

'What is to become of all my bosom friends in the next room, you selfish man, if I stop here with you?' retorted mademoiselle, struggling to free herself.

'Call them in here,' said Danville, gaily, making himself master of her other hand.

She laughed, and drew him away towards the drawing-room.

'Come!' she cried, 'and let all the ladies see what a tyrant I am going to marry. Come and show them what an obstinate, unreasonable, wearisome'—

Her voice suddenly failed her; she shuddered, and turned faint. Danville's hand had in one instant grown cold as death in hers: the momentary touch of his fingers, as she felt their grasp loosen, struck some mysterious chill through her from head to foot. She glanced round at him affrightedly; and saw his eyes looking straight into the drawing-room. They were fixed in a strange, unwavering, awful stare; while, from the rest of his face, all expression, all character, all recognisable play and movement of features had utterly gone. It was a breathless, lifeless mask – a white blank. With a cry of terror, she looked where he seemed to be looking; and could see nothing but the stranger standing in the middle of the drawing-room. Before she could ask a question, before she could speak even a single word, her father came to her, caught Danville by the arm, and pushed her roughly back into the library.

'Go there, and take the women with you,' he said in a quick fierce whisper. Into the library!' he continued, turning to the

ladies, and raising his voice. 'Into the library, all of you, along
with my daughter.'

The women, terrified by his manner, obeyed him in the
greatest confusion. As they hurried past hfim into the library,
he signed to the notary to follow; and then closed the door of
communication between the two rooms.

'Stop where you are!' he cried, addressing the old officers,
who had risen from their chairs. 'Stay, I insist on it! Whatever
happens, Jacques Berthelin has done nothing to be ashamed of
in the presence of his old friends and companions. You have
seen the beginning, now stay and see the end.'

While he spoke, he walked into the middle of the room. He
had never quitted his hold of Danville's arm – step by step, they
advanced together to the place where Trudaine was standing.

'You have come into my house, and asked me for my
daughter in marriage – and I have given her to you.' said the
general, addressing Danville quietly. 'You told me that your
first wife and her brother were guillotined three years ago in
the time of the Terror – and I believed you. Now, look at that
man – look him straight in the face. He has announced himself
to me as the brother of your wife, and he asserts that his sister is
alive at this moment. One of you two has deceived me. Which
is it?'

Danville tried to speak; but no sound passed his lips; tried to
wrench his arm from the grasp that was on it, but could not stir
the old soldier's steady hand.

'Are you afraid? are you a coward? Can't you look him in the
face?' asked the general, tightening his hold sternly.

'Stop! stop!' interposed one of the old officers, coming
forward. 'Give him time. This may be a case of strange
accidental resemblance; which would be enough, under the
circumstance, to discompose any man. You will excuse me,
citizen,' he continued, turning to Trudaine. 'But you are a
stranger; you have given us no proof of your identity.'

'There is the proof,' said Trudaine, pointing to Danville's
face.

'Yes, yes,' pursued the other; 'he looks pale and startled
enough, certainly. But I say again – let us not be too hasty:
there are strange cases on the record of accidental resemblances,
and this may be one of them!'

As he repeated those words, Danville looked at him with a faint, cringing gratitude stealing slowly over the blank terror of his face. He bowed his head, murmured something, and gesticulated confusedly with the hand that he was free to use.

'Look!' cried the old officer; 'look, Berthelin, he denies the man's identity.'

'Do you hear that?' said the general, appealing to Trudaine. 'Have you proofs to confute him? If you have, produce them instantly.'

Before the answer could be given, the door leading into the drawing-room from the staircase was violently flung open, and Madame Danville – her hair in disorder, her face in its colourless terror looking like the very counterpart of her son's – appeared on the threshold, with the old man Dubois and a group of amazed and startled servants behind her.

'For God's sake don't sign! for God's sake come away!' she cried. 'I have seen your wife – in spirit, or in the flesh, I know not which – but I have seen her. Charles! Charles! as true as Heaven is above us, I have seen your wife!'

'You have seen her in the flesh, living and breathing as you see her brother yonder,' said a firm quiet voice from among the servants on the landing outside.

'Let that man enter, whoever he is!' cried the general.

Lomaque passed Madame Danville on the threshold. She trembled as he brushed by her; then, supporting herself by the wall, followed him a few paces into the room. She looked first at her son – after that, at Trudaine – after that, back again at her son. Something in her presence silenced everyone. There fell a sudden stillness over all the assembly – a stillness so deep, that the eager, frightened whispering, and sharp rustling of dresses among the women in the library became audible from the other side of the closed door.

'Charles! she said, slowly advancing; why do you look?' – She stopped, and fixed her eyes again on her son more earnestly than before; then turned them suddenly on Trudaine. 'You are looking at my son, sir' she said, 'and I see contempt in your face. By what right do you insult a man whose grateful sense of his mother's obligations to you, made him risk his life for the saving of yours and your sister's? By what right have you kept the escape of my son's wife from

death by the guillotine – an escape which, for all I know to the
contrary, his generous exertions were instrumental in effecting – a secret from my son? By what right, I demand to
know, has your treacherous secrecy placed us in such a
position as we now stand in before the master of this house?'

An expression of sorrow and pity passed over Trudaine's
face while she spoke. He retired a few steps, and gave her no
answer. The general looked at him with eager curiosity; and,
dropping his hold of Danville's arm, seemed about to speak;
but Lomaque stepped forward at the same time, and held up
his hand to claim attention.

'I think I shall express the wishes of citizen Trudaine,' he
said, addressing Madame Danville, 'if I recommend this lady
not to press for too public an answer to her questions.'

'Pray who are you, sir, who take it on yourself to advise
me?' she retorted haughtily. 'I have nothing to say to you,
except that I repeat those questions, and that I insist on their
being answered.'

'Who is this man?' asked the general, addressing Trudaine,
and pointing to Lomaque.

'A man unworthy of credit,' cried Danville, speaking
audibly for the first time, and darting a look of deadly hatred
at Lomaque. 'An agent of police under Robespierre.'

'And in that capacity capable of answering questions which
refer to the transactions of Robespierre's tribunals,' remarked
the ex-chief agent with his old official self-possession.

'True!' exclaimed the general; 'the man is right – let him be
heard.'

'There is no help for it,' said Lomaque, looking at Trudaine;
'leave it to me – it is fittest that I should speak. I was present,'
he continued in a louder voice, 'at the trial of citizen Trudaine
and his sister. They were brought to the bar through the
denunciation of citizen Danville. Till the confession of the
male prisoner exposed the fact, I can answer for Danville's not
being aware of the real nature of the offences charged against
Trudaine and his sister. When it became known that they had
been secretly helping this lady to escape from France, and
when Danville's own head was consequently in danger, I
myself heard him save it by a false assertion that he had been
aware of Trudaine's conspiracy from the first' —

'Do you mean to say,' interrupted the general, 'that he proclaimed himself in open court, as having knowingly denounced the man who was on trial for saving his mother?'

'I do,' answered Lomaque. (A murmur of horror and indignation rose from all the strangers present, at that reply). 'The reports of the Tribunal are existing to prove the truth of what I say,' he went on. 'As to the escape of citizen Trudaine and the wife of Danville from the guillotine, it was the work of political circumstances, which there are persons living to speak to if necessary; and of a little stratagem of mine, which need not be referred to now. And, last, with reference to the concealment which followed the escape, I beg to inform you that it was abandoned the moment we knew of what was going on here; and that it was only persevered in up to this time, as a natural measure of precaution on the part of citizen Trudaine. From a similar motive we now abstain from exposing his sister to the shock and the peril of being present here. What man with an atom of feeling would risk letting her even look again on such a husband as that?'

He glanced round him, and pointed to Danville, as he put the question. Before a word could be spoken by any one else in the room, a low wailing cry of 'My mistress! my dear, dear mistress!' directed all eyes first on the old man Dubois, then on Madame Danville.

She had been leaning against the wall, before Lomaque began to speak; but she stood perfectly upright now. She neither spoke nor moved. Not one of the light gaudy ribands, flaunting on her disordered head-dress, so much as trembled. The old servant Dubois was crouched on his knees at her side, kissing her cold right hand, chafing it in his, reiterating his faint mournful cry, 'Oh! my mistress! my dear, dear mistress!' but she did not appear to know that he was near her. It was only when her son advanced a step or two towards her that she seemed to awaken suddenly from that death-trance of mental pain. Then she slowly raised the hand that was free, and waved him back from her. He stopped in obedience to the gesture, and endeavoured to speak. She waved her hand again, and the deathly stillness of her face began to grow troubled. Her lips moved a little – she spoke.

'Oblige me, sir, for the last time, by keeping silence. You and I have henceforth nothing to say to each other. I am the daughter of a race of nobles, and the widow of a man of honour. You are a traitor and a false witness; a thing from which all true men and true women turn with contempt. I renounce you! Publicly, in the presence of these gentlemen, I say it – I have no son.'

She turned her back on him; and, bowing to the other persons in the room with the old formal courtesy of bygone times, walked slowly and steadily to the door. Stopping there, she looked back; and then the artificial courage of the moment failed her. With a faint suppressed cry she clutched at the hand of the old servant, who still kept faithfully at her side; he caught her in his arms, and her head sank on his shoulder.

'Help him!' cried the general to the servants near the door. 'Help him to take her into the next room!'

The old man looked up suspiciously from his mistress to the persons who were assisting him to support her. With a strange sudden jealousy he shook his hand at them. 'Home,' he cried, 'she shall go home, and I will take care of her. Away! you there – nobody holds her head but Dubois. Down-stairs! down-stairs to her carriage! She has nobody but me now, and I say that she shall be taken home.'

As the door closed, General Berthelin approached Trudaine, who had stood silent and apart, from the time when Lomaque first appeared in the drawing-room.

'I wish to ask your pardon,' said the old soldier, 'because I have wronged you by a moment of unjust suspicion. For my daughter's sake, I bitterly regret that we did not see each other long ago; but I thank you, nevertheless, for coming here, even at the eleventh hour.'

While he was speaking, one of his friends came up, and touching him on the shoulder, said:

'Berthelin, is that scoundrel to be allowed to go?'

The general turned on his heel directly, and beckoned contemptuously to Danville to follow him to the door. When they were well out of earshot, he spoke these words:

'You have been exposed as a villain by your brother-in-law, and renounced as a liar by your mother. They have done their duty by you, and now it only remains for me to do mine.

When a man enters the house of another under false pretences, and compromises the reputation of his daughter, we old army men have a very expeditious way of making him answer for it. It is just three o'clock now; at five you will find me and one of my friends' —

He stopped, and looked round cautiously – then whispered the rest in Danville's ear – threw open the door, and pointed down stairs.

'Our work here is done,: said Lomaque, laying his hand on Trudaine's arm. 'Let us give Danville time to get clear of the house, and then leave it too.'

'My sister! where is she?' asked Trudaine, eagerly.

'Make your mind easy about her. I will tell you more when we get out.'

'You will excuse me, I know,' said General Berthelin, speaking to all the persons present, with his hand on the library door, 'if I leave you. I have bad news to break to my daughter, and private business after that to settle with a friend.'

He saluted the company, with his usual bluff nod of the head, and entered the library. A few minutes afterwards, Trudaine and Lomaque left the house.

'You will find your sister waiting for you in our apartment at the hotel,' said the latter. 'She knows nothing, absolutely nothing, of what has passed.'

'But the recognition?' asked Trudaine, amazedly. 'His mother saw her. Surely she?' —

'I managed it so that she should be seen and should not see. Our former experience of Danville suggested to me the propriety of making the experiment, and my old police-office practice came in useful in carrying it out. I saw the carriage standing at the door, and waited till the old lady came down. I walked your sister away as she got in, and walked her back again past the window as the carriage drove off. A moment did it, and it turned out as useful as I thought it would. Enough of that! Go back now to your sister. Keep indoors till the night-mail starts for Rouen. I have had two places taken for you on speculation. Go! resume possession of your old house, and leave me here to transact the business which my employer has intrusted to me, and to see how matters end with Danville and his mother. I will make time somehow to come and bid you goodbye at Rouen, though it should only be for a single day. Bah! no thanks. I was ashamed to take it eight years ago – I can give it a hearty shake now! There is your way; here is mine. Leave me to my business in silks and satins, and go you back to your sister, and help her to pack up for the night-mail.'

CHAPTER III

Three more days have passed. It is evening. Rose, Trudaine, and Lomaque are seated together on the bench that overlooks the windings of the Seine. The old familiar scene spreads before them, beautiful as ever – unchanged, as if it was but yesterday since they had all looked on it for the last time.

They talked together seriously and in low voices. The same recollections fill their hearts – recollections which they refrain from acknowledging, but the influence of which each knows by instinct that the other partakes. Sometimes one leads the conversation, sometimes another; but whoever speaks, the topic chosen is always, as if by common consent, a topic connected with the future.

The evening darkens in, and Rose is the first to rise from the bench. A secret look of intelligence passes between her and her brother; and then she speaks to Lomaque.

'Will you follow me into the house,' she asks, 'with as little delay as possible? I have something that I very much wish to show you.'

Her brother waits till she is out of hearing; then inquires anxiously what has happened at Paris since the night when he and Rose left it.

'Your sister is free,' Lomaque answers.

'The duel took place, then?'

'The same day. They were both to fire together. The second of his adversary asserts that he was paralyzed with terror: his own second declares that he was resolved, however he might have lived, to confront death courageously by offering his life at the first fire to the man whom he had injured. Which account is true, I know not. It is only certain that he did not discharge his pistol; that he fell by his antagonist's first bullet; and that he never spoke afterwards.'

'And his mother?'

'It is hard to gain information. Her doors are closed; the old

219

servant guards her with jealous care. A medical man is in constant attendance, and there are reports in the house that the illness from which she is suffering affects her mind more than her body. I could ascertain no more.'

After that answer they both remain silent for a little while – then rise from the bench and walk towards the house.

'Have you thought yet about preparing your sister to hear of all that has happened?' Lomaque asks, as he sees the lamplight glimmering in the parlour window.

'I shall wait to prepare her till we are settled again here – till the first holiday pleasure of our return has worn off, and the quiet realities of our every-day life of old have resumed their way,' answers Trudaine.

They enter the house. Rose beckons to Lomaque to sit down near her, and places pen and ink and an open letter before him.

'I have a last favour to ask of you,' she says smiling.

'I hope it will not take long to grant,' he rejoins; 'for I have only to-night to be with you. To-morrow morning, before you are up, I must be on my way back to Chalons.'

'Will you sign that letter?' she continues, still smiling, 'and then give it to me to send to the post? It was dictated by Louis, and written by me, and it will be quite complete if you will put your name at the end of it.'

'I suppose I may read it?'

She nods, and Lomaque reads these lines:–

'CITIZEN, – I beg respectfully to apprize you, that the commission you intrusted to me at Paris has been performed.

'I have also to beg that you will accept my resignation of the place I hold in your counting-house. The kindness shown me by you and your brother before you, emboldens me to hope that you will learn with pleasure the motive of my withdrawal. Two friends of mine, who consider that they are under some obligations to me, are anxious that I should pass the rest of my days in the quiet and protection of their home. Troubles of former years have knit us together as closely as if we were all three members of one family. I need the repose of a happy fireside as much as any man, after the life I have led; and my friends assure me so earnestly that their whole hearts are set on establishing the old man's easy chair by their hearth, that I cannot summon resolution enough to turn my back on them and their offer.

'Accept then, I beg of you, the resignation which this letter contains, and with it the assurance of my sincere gratitude and respect.

'To Citizen Clairfait, silk-mercer,
Chalons-sur-Marne.'

After reading these lines, Lomaque turned round to Trudaine and attempted to speak; but the words would not come at command. He looked up at Rose, and tried to smile; but his lip only trembled. She dipped the pen in the ink, and placed it in his hand. He bent his head down quickly over the paper, so that she could not see his face; but still he did not write his name. She put her hand caressingly on his shoulder, and whispered to him:—

'Come, come, humour "Sister Rose." She must have her own way now she is back again at home.'

He did not answer – his head sunk lower – he hesitated for an instant – then signed his name in faint, trembling characters at the end of the letter.

She drew it away from him gently. A few teardrops lay on the paper. As she dried them with her handkerchief she looked at her brother.

'They are the last he shall ever shed, Louis: you and I will take care of that!'

EPILOGUE

I have now related all that is eventful in the history of SISTER ROSE. To the last the three friends dwelt together happily in the cottage on the river bank. Mademoiselle Clairfait was fortunate enough to know them, before Death entered the little household and took away, in the fulness of time, the eldest of its members. She describes Lomaque, in her quaint foreign English, as 'a brave, big heart;' generous, affectionate, and admirably free from the small obstinacies and prejudices of old age, except on one point: – he could never be induced to take his coffee, of an evening, from any other hand than the hand of Sister Rose.

I linger over these final particulars with a strange unwillingness to separate myself from them, and give my mind to other thoughts. Perhaps the persons and events that have occupied my attention for so many nights past, have some peculiar interest for me that I cannot analyze. Perhaps the labour and time which this story has cost me, have specially endeared it to my sympathies now that I have succeeded in completing it.

THE LAWYER'S STORY OF A STOLEN LETTER

PROLOGUE

The beginning of an excellent connexion which I succceded in establishing in and around that respectable watering-place, Tidbury-on-the-Marsh, was an order for a life-size oil-portrait of a great local celebrity – one Mr Boxsious, a Solicitor, who was understood to do the most thriving business of any lawyer in the town.

The portrait was intended as a testimonial 'expressive (to use the language of the circular forwarded to me at the time) of the eminent services of Mr Boxsious in promoting and securing the prosperity of the town.' It had been subscribed for by the 'Municipal Authorities and resident Inhabitants' of Tidbury-on-the-Marsh; and it was to be presented, when done, to Mrs Bouxsious, 'as a slight but sincere token' and so forth. A timely recommendation from one of my kindest friends and patrons placed the commission for painting the likeness in my lucky hands; and I was instructed to attend on a certain day at Mr Boxsious's private residence with all my materials ready for taking a first sitting.

On arriving at the house, I was shown into a very prettily furnished morning-room. The bow-window looked out on a large enclosed meadow which represented the principal square in Tidbury. On the opposite side of the meadow I could see the new hotel (with a wing lately added), and, close by, the old hotel obstinately unchanged since it had first been built. Then, further down the street, the doctor's house, with a coloured lamp and a small doorplate, and the banker's office, with a plain lamp and a big doorplate – then some dreary private lodging-houses – then, at right angles to these, a street of shops; the cheesemonger's very small, the chemist's very smart, the pastrycook's very dowdy, and the greengrocer's very dark. I was still looking out at the view thus presented, when I was suddenly apostrophized by a glib disputatious voice behind me.

'Now, then, Mr Artist!' cried the voice, 'do you call that getting ready for work? Where are your paints and brushes, and all the rest of it? My name's Boxsious, and I'm here to sit for my picture.'

I turned round and confronted a little man with his legs astraddle and his hands in his pockets. He had light-grey eyes, red all round the lids, bristling pepper-coloured hair, an unnaturally rosy complexion, and an eager, impudent, clever look. I made two discoveries in one glance at him: – First, that he was a wretched subject for a portrait; secondly, that, whatever he might do or say, it would not be of the least use for me to stand on my dignity with him.

'I shall be ready directly, sir,' said I.

'Ready directly?' repeated my new sitter. 'What do you mean, Mr Artist, by ready directly? I'm ready *now*. What was your contract with the Town Council who have subscribed for this picture? To paint the portrait! And what was my contract? To sit for it! Here am I ready to sit, and there are you not ready to paint me. According to all the rules of law and logic, you are committing a breach of contract already. — Stop! let's have a look at your paints. Are they the best quality? If not, I warn you, sir, there's a second breach of contract! – Brushes too? Why, they're old brushes, by the Lord Harry! The Town Council pay you well, Mr Artist; why don't you work for them with new brushes? – What? you work best with old? I contend, sir, that you can't. Does my housemaid clean best with an old broom? Do my clerks write best with old pens? Don't colour up, and don't look as if you were going to quarrel with me! You can't quarrel with me. If you were fifty times as irritable a man as you look you couldn't quarrel with me. I'm not young, and I'm not touchy – I'm Boxsious, the lawyer; the only man in the world who can't be insulted, try it how you like!'

He chuckled as he said this, and walked away to the window. It was quite useless to take anything he said seriously, so I finished preparing my palette for the morning's work with the utmost serenity of look and manner that I could possibly assume.

'There!' he went on, looking out of the window, 'do you see that fat man slouching along the Parade, with a snuffy nose? That's my favourite enemy, Dunball. He tried to quarrel with me ten years ago, and he has done nothing but bring out the hidden benevolence of my character ever since. Look at him! look how he frowns as he turns this way. – And now look at me! I can smile and nod to him. I make a point of always smiling and nodding to him – it keeps my hand in for other enemies. – Good morning! (I've cast him twice in heavy damages) good morning, Mr Dunball! He bears malice, you see; he won't speak; he's short in the neck, passionate, and four times as fat as he ought to be; he has fought against my amiability for ten mortal years; when he can't fight any longer, he'll die suddenly, and I shall be the innocent cause of it.'

Mr Boxsious uttered this fatal prophecy with extraordinary complacency, nodding and smiling out of the window all the time at the unfortunate man who had rashly tried to provoke him. When his favourite enemy was out of slight, he turned away and indulged himself in a brisk turn or two up and down the room. Meanwhile I lifted my canvass on the easel, and was on the point of asking him to sit down, when he assailed me again.

'Now, Mr Artist!' he cried, quickening his walk impatiently, 'in the interests of the Town Council, your employers, allow me to ask you for the last time when you are going to begin?'

'And allow me, Mr Boxsious, in the interest of the Town Council also,' said I, 'to ask you if your notion of the proper way of sitting for your portrait is to walk about the room?'

'Aha! well put – devilish well put!' returned Mr Boxsious; 'that's the only sensible thing you have said since you entered my house; I begin to like you already.' With these words he nodded at me approvingly, and jumped into the high chair that I had placed for him with the alacrity of a young man.

'I say, Mr Artist,' he went on, when I had put him into the right position (he insisted on the front view of his face being taken, because the Town Council would get the most for their money in that way), 'you don't have many such good jobs as this, do you?'

'Not many,' I said. 'I should not be a poor man if commissions for life-size portraits often fell in my way.'

'You poor!' exclaimed Mr Boxsious, contemptuously. 'I dispute that point with you at the outset. Why, you've got a good cloth coat, a clean shirt, and a smooth-shaved chin! You've got the sleek look of a man who has slept between sheets and had his breakfast. You can't humbug me about poverty, for I know what it is. Poverty means looking like a scarecrow, feeling like a scarecrow, and getting treated like a scarecrow. That was my luck, let me tell you, when I first thought of trying the law. – Poverty indeed! Do you shake in your shoes, Mr Artist, when you think what you were at twenty? I do, I can promise you!'

He began to shift about so irritably in his chair, that, in the interests of my work, I was obliged to make an effort to calm him.

'It must be a pleasant occupation for you in your present prosperity,' said I, 'to look back sometimes at the gradual processes by which you passed from poverty to competence, and from that to the wealth you now enjoy.'

'Gradual, did you say?' cried Mr Boxsious; 'it wasn't gradual at all. I was sharp, damned sharp, and I jumped at my first start in business slap into five hundred pounds in one day.'

'That was an extraordinary step in advance,' I rejoined. 'I suppose you contrived to make some profitable investment—?'

'Not a bit of it! I hadn't a spare sixpence to invest with. I won the money by my brains, my hands, and my pluck; and, what's more, I'm proud of having done it! That was rather a curious case, Mr Artist. Some men might be shy of mentioning it: I never was shy in my life, and I mention it right and left everywhere – the whole case, just as it happened, except the names. Catch me ever committing myself to mentioning names! Mum's the word, sir, with yours to command, Thomas Boxsious.'

'As you mention 'the case' everywhere,' said I, 'perhaps you would not be offended with me if I told you I should like to hear it.'

'Man alive! haven't I told you already that I can't be offended? And didn't I say a moment ago that I was proud of the case? I'll tell you, Mr Artist – but, stop! I've got the interests of the Town Council to look after in this business.

Can you paint as well when I'm talking as when I'm not? Don't sneer, sir; you're not wanted to sneer – you're wanted to give an answer – yes or no?'

'Yes, then,' I replied, in his own sharp way. 'I can always paint the better when I am hearing an interesting story.'

'What do you mean by talking about a story. I'm not going to tell you a story: I'm going to make a statement. A statement is a matter of fact, therefore the exact opposite of a story, which is a matter of fiction. What I am now going to tell you really happened to me.'

I was glad to see that he settled himself quietly in his chair before he began. His odd manners and language made such an impression on me at the time, that I think I can repeat his "statement" now almost word for word as he addressed it to me.

THE LAWYER'S STORY OF A STOLEN LETTER

I served my time – never mind in whose office – and I started in business for myself in one of our English country towns – I decline stating which. I hadn't a farthing of capital, and my friends in the neighbourhood were poor and useless enough, with one exception. That exception was Mr Frank Gatliffe, son of Mr Gatliffe, member for the county, the richest man and the proudest for many a mile round about our parts. – Stop a bit, Mr Artist! you needn't perk up and look knowing. You won't trace any particulars by the name of Gatliffe. I'm not bound to commit myself or anybody else by mentioning names. I have given you the first that came into my head.

Well, Mr Frank was a staunch friend of mine, and ready to recommend me whenever he got the chance. I had contrived to get him a little timely help – for a consideration, of course – in borrowing money at a fair rate of interest: in fact, I had saved him from the Jews. The money was borrowed while Mr Frank was at college. He came back from college, and stopped at home a little while, and then there got spread about all our neighbourhood a report that he had fallen in love, as the saying is, with his young sister's governess, and that his mind was made up to marry her. – What! you're at is again, Mr Artist! You want to know her name, don't you? What do you think of Smith?

Speaking as a lawyer, I consider Report, in a general way, to be a fool and a liar. But in this case report turned out to be something very different. Mr Frank told me he was really in love, and said upon his honour (an absurd expression which young chaps of his age are always using) he was determined to marry Smith the governess – the sweet darling girl, as *he* called her; but I'm not sentimental, and *I* call her Smith the governess. Well, Mr Frank's father, being as proud as Lucifer, said "No" as to marrying the governess, when Mr Frank wanted him to say "Yes." He was a man of business, was old

230

Gatliffe, and he took the proper business course. He sent the governess away with a first-rate character and a spanking present, and then he looked about him to get something for Mr Frank to do. While he was looking about, Mr Frank bolted to London after the governess, who had nobody alive belonging to her to go to but an aunt – her father's sister. The aunt refuses to let Mr Frank in without the squire's permission. Mr Frank writes to his father, and says he will marry the girl as soon as he is of age, or shoot himself. Up to town comes the squire and his wife and his daughter, and a lot of sentimentality, not in the slightest degree material to the present statement, takes place among them; and the upshot, of it is that old Gatliffe is forced into withdrawing the word No, and substituting the word Yes.

I don't believe he would ever have done it, though, but for one lucky peculiarity in the case. The governess's father was a man of good family – pretty nigh as good as Gatliffe's own. He had been in the army: had sold out: set up as a wine-merchant – failed – died: ditto his wife, as to the dying part of it. No relation, in fact, left for the squire to make inquiries about but the father's sister – who had behaved, as old Gatliffe said, like a thorough-bred gentlewoman in shutting the door against Mr Frank in the first instance. So, to cut the matter short, things were at last made up pleasant enough. The time was fixed for the wedding, and an announcement about it – Marriage in High Life and all that – put into the county paper. There was a regular biography, besides, of the governess's father, so as to stop people from talking – a great flourish about his pedigree, and a long account of his services in the army; but not a word, mind ye, of his having turned wine-merchant afterwards. Oh, no – not a word about that!

I knew it, though, for Mr Frank told me. He hadn't a bit of pride about him. He introduced me to his future wife one day when I met them out walking, and asked me if I did not think he was a lucky fellow. I don't mind admitting that I did, and that I told him so. Ah! but she was one of my sort, was that governess. Stood, to the best of my recollection, five foot four. Good lissome figure, that looked as if it had never been boxed up in a pair of stays. Eyes that made me feel as if I was under a pretty stiff cross-examination the moment she looked at me. Fine red, fresh, kiss-and-come again sort of lips. Cheeks and complexion — No, Mr Artist, you wouldn't identify her by her cheeks and complexion, if I drew you a picture of them this very moment. She has had a family of children since the time I'm talking of; and her cheeks are a trifle fatter and her complexion is a shade or two redder now than when I first met her out walking with Mr Frank.

The marriage was to take place on a Wednesday. I decline mentioning the year or the month. I had started as an attorney on my own account – say six weeks, more or less, and was sitting alone in my office on the Monday morning before the wedding-day, trying to see my way clear before me and not succeeding particularly well, when Mr Frank suddenly bursts in, as white as any ghost that ever was painted, and says he's got the most dreadful case for me to advise on, and not an hour to lose in acting on my advice.

'Is this in the way of business, Mr Frank?' says I, stopping him just as he was beginning to get sentimental. 'Yes or no, Mr Frank?' rapping my new office paper-knife on the table to pull him up short all the sooner.

'My dear fellow' – he was always familiar with me – 'it's in the way of business, certainly; but friendship' —

I was obliged to pull him up short again and regularly examine him as if he had been in the witness-box, or he would have kept me talking to no purpose half the day.

'Now, Mr Frank,' says I, 'I can't have any sentimentality mixed up with business matters. You please to stop talking, and let me ask questions. Answer in the fewest words you can use. Nod when nodding will do instead of words.'

I fixed him with my eye for about three seconds, as he sat groaning and wriggling in his chair. When I'd done fixing him, I gave another rap with my paper-knife on the table to startle him up a bit. Then I went on.

'From what you have been stating up to the present time,' says I, 'I gather that you are in a scrape which is likely to interfere seriously with your marriage on Wednesday?'

(He nodded, and I cut in again before he could say a word):-

'The scrape affects your young lady, and goes back to the period of a transaction in which her late father was engaged, don't it?'

(He nods, and I cut in once more):-

'There is a party who turned up after seeing the announcement of your marriage in the paper, who is cognizant of what he oughtn't to know, and who is prepared to use his knowledge of the same to the prejudice of the young lady and of your marriage, unless he receives a sum of money to quiet him? Very well. Now, first of all, Mr Frank, state what you have been told by the young lady herself about the transaction of her late father. How did you first come to have any knowledge of it?'

'She was talking to me about her father one day so tenderly and prettily, that she quite excited my interest about him,' begins Mr Frank; 'and I asked her, among other things, what had occasioned his death. She said she believed it was distress of mind in the first instance; and added that this distress was connected with a shocking secret, which she and her mother had kept from everybody, but which she could not keep from me, because she was determined to begin her married life by having no secrets from her husband.' Here Mr Frank began to get sentimental again, and I pulled him up short once more with the paper-knife.

'She told me,' Mr Frank went on, 'that the great mistake of her father's life was his selling out of the army and taking to the wine trade. He had no talent for the business; things went wrong with him from the first. His clerk, it was strongly suspected, cheated him'—

'Stop a bit,' says I. 'What was that suspected clerk's name?'

'Davager, says he.

'Davager,' says I, making a note of it. 'Go on, Mr Frank.'

'His affairs got more and more entangled,' says Mr Frank; 'he was pressed for money in all directions; bankruptcy, and consequent dishonour (as he considered it), stared him in the face. His mind was so affected by his troubles that both his wife and daughter, towards the last, considered him to be hardly responsible for his own acts. In this state of desperation and misery, he' — Here Mr Frank began to hesitate.

We have two ways in the law of drawing evidence off nice and clear from an unwilling client or witness. We give him a fright or we treat him to a joke. I treated Mr Frank to a joke.

'Ah!' says I, 'I know what he did. He had a signature to write; and, by the most natural mistake in the world, he wrote another gentleman's name instead of his own – eh?'

'It was to a bill,' says Mr Frank, looking very crest-fallen, instead of taking the joke. 'His principal creditor wouldn't wait till he could raise the money, or the greater part of it. But he was resolved, if he sold off everything, to get the amount and repay'—

'Of course!' says I, 'drop that. The forgery was discovered. When?'

'Before even the first attempt was made to negotiate the bill. He had done the whole thing in the most absurdly and innocently wrong way. The person whose name he had used was a staunch friend of his, and a relation of his wife's: a good man as well as a rich one. He had influence with the chief creditor, and he used it nobly. He had a real affection for the unfortunate man's wife, and he proved it generously.'

'Come to the point,' says I. 'What did he do? In a business way what did he do?'

'He put the false bill into the fire, drew a bill of his own to replace it, and then – only then – told my dear girl and her mother all that had happened. Can you imagine anything nobler?' asks Mr Frank.

'Speaking in my professional capacity, I can't imagine anything greener?' says I. 'Where was the father? Off, I suppose?'

'Ill in bed,' says Mr Frank, colouring. But, he mustered strength enough to write a contrite and grateful letter the same day, promising to prove himself worthy of the noble moderation and forgiveness extended to him, by selling off everything he possessed to repay his money-debt. He did sell off everything, down to the some old family pictures that were heirlooms; down to the little plate he had; down to the very tables and chairs that furnished his drawing-room. Every farthing of the debt was paid; and he was left to begin the world again, with the kindest promises of help from the generous man who had forgiven him. It was too late. His crime of one rash moment – atoned for though it had been – preyed upon his mind. He became possessed with the idea that he had lowered himself for ever in the estimation of his wife and daughter, and' —

'He died,' I cut in. 'Yes, yes, we know that. Let's go back for a minute to the contrite and grateful letter that he wrote. My experience in the law, Mr Frank, has convinced me that if everybody burnt everybody else's letters, half the Courts of Justice in this country might shut up shop. Do you happen to know whether the letter we are now speaking of contained anything like an avowal or confession of the forgery?'

'Of course it did,' says he. 'Could the writer express his contrition properly without making some such confession?'

'Quite easy, if he had been a lawyer,' says I. 'But never mind that; I'm going to make a guess, – a desperate guess, mind. Should I be altogether in error, if I thought that this letter had been stolen; and that the fingers of Mr Davager, of suspicious commercial celebrity, might possibly be the fingers which took it?'

'That is exactly what I wanted to make you understand,' cries Mr Frank.

'How did he communicate the interesting fact of the theft to you?'

'He has not ventured into my presence. The scoundrel actually had the audacity' —

'Aha!' says I. 'The young lady herself! Sharp practitioner, Mr Davager.'

'Early this morning when she was walking alone in the shrubbery,' Mr Frank goes on, 'he had the assurance to approach her, and to say that he had been watching his opportunity of getting a private interview for the days past. He then showed her – actually showed her – unfortunate father's letter; put into her hands another letter directed to me; bowed, and walked off; leaving her half-dead with astonishment and terror. If I had only happened to be there at the time —!' says Mr Frank, shaking his fist murderously in the air by way of a finish.

'It's the greatest luck in the world that you were not,' says I. 'Have you got that other letter?'

He handed it to me. It was so remarkably humorous and short, that I remember every word of it at this distance of time. It began in this way:

'To Francis Gatliffe, Esq., jun. – Sir, – I have an extremely curious autograph letter to sell. The price is a Five hundred pound note. The young lady to whom you are to be married on Wednesday will inform you of the nature of the letter, and the genuineness of the autograph. If you refuse to deal, I shall send a copy to the local paper, and shall wait on your highly respected father with the original curiosity, on the afternoon of Tuesday next. Having come down here on family business, I have put up at the family hotel – being to be heard of at the Gatliffe Arms. Your very obedient servant,

'ALFRED DAVAGER.'

'A clever fellow that,' says I, putting the letter into my private drawer.

'Clever!' cries Mr Frank, 'he ought to be horeswhipped within an inch of his life. I would have done it myself; but she made me promise, before she told me a word of the matter, to come straight to you.'

'That was one of the wisest promises you ever made,' says I. 'We can't afford to bully this fellow, whatever else we may do with him. Do you think I am saying anything libellous against your excellent father's character when I assert that if he saw the letter he would certainly insist on your marriage being put off, at the very least?'

'Feeling as my father does about my marriage, he would insist on its being dropped altogether, if he saw this letter,' says Mr Frank, with a groan. 'But even that is not the worst of it. The generous, noble girl herself says, that if the letter appears in the paper, with all the unanswerable comments this scoundrel would be sure to add to it, she would rather die than hold me to my engagement – even if my father would let me keep it.'

As he said this his eyes began to water. He was a weak young fellow, and ridiculously fond of her. I brought him back to business with another rap of the paper-knife.

'Hold up, Mr Frank,' says I. 'I have a question or two more. Did you think of asking the young lady, whether, to the best of her knowledge, this infernal letter was the only written evidence of the forgery now in existence?'

'Yes, I did think directly of asking her that,' says he; 'and she told me she was quite certain that there was no written evidence of the forgery except that one letter.'

'Will you give Mr Davager his price for it?' says I.

'Yes,' says Mr Frank, quite peevish with me for asking him such a question. He was an easy young chap in money-matters, and talked of hundreds as most men talk of sixpences.

'Mr Frank,' says I, 'you came here to get my help and advice in this extremely ticklish business, and you are ready, as I know without asking, to remunerate me for all and any of my services at the usual professional rate. Now, I've made up my mind to act boldly – desperately if you like – on the hit or miss – win-all-or-lose-all principle – in dealing with this matter. Here is my proposal. I'm going to try if I can't do Mr Davager out of his letter. If I don't succeed before to-morrow after-noon, you hand him the money and I charge you nothing for professional services. If I do succeed, I hand you the letter instead of Mr Davager; and you give me the money instead of giving it to him. It's a precious risk for me, but I'm ready to run it. You must pay your five hundred any way. What do you say to my plan? Is it Yes, Mr Frank – or No?'

'Hang your questions!' cries Mr Frank jumping up; 'you know it's Yes ten thousand times over. Only you earn the money and'—

'And you will be too glad to give it to me. Very good. Now go home. Comfort the young lady – don't let Mr Davager so much as set eyes on you – keep quiet – leave everything to me – and feel as certain as you please that all the letters in the world can't stop your being married on Wednesday,' With these words I hustled him off out of the office; for I wanted to be left alone to make my mind up about what I should do.

The first thing, of course, was to have a look at the enemy. I wrote to Mr Davager, telling him that I was privately appointed to arrange the little business-matter between himself and "another party" (no names!) on friendly terms; and begging him to call on me at his earliest convenience. At the very beginning of the case, Mr Davager bothered me. His answer was, that it would not be convenient to him to call till between six and seven in the evening. In this way, you see, he contrived to make me lose several precious hours, at a time when minutes almost were of importance. I had nothing for it but to be patient, and to give certain instructions, before Mr Davager came, to my boy Tom.

There never was such a sharp boy of fourteen before, and there never will be again, as my boy Tom. A spy to look after Mr Davager was, of course, the first requisite in a case of this kind; and Tom was the smallest, quickest, quietest, sharpest, stealthiest little snake of a chap that ever dogged a gentleman's steps and kept cleverly out of range of a gentleman's eyes. I settled it with the boy that he was not to show at all, when Mr Davager came; and that he was to wait to hear me ring the bell when Mr Davager left. If I rang twice he was to show the gentleman out. If I rang once, he was to keep out of the way and follow the gentleman wherever he went till he got back to the inn. Those were the only preparations I could make to begin with; being obliged to wait, and let myself be guided by what turned up.

About a quarter to seven my gentleman came.

In the profession of the law we get somehow quite remarkably mixed up with ugly people, blackguard people, a dirty people. But far away the ugliest and dirtiest blackguard I ever say in my life was Mr Alfred Davager. He had greasy white hair and a mottled face. He was low in the forehead, fat in the stomach, hoarse in the voice, and weak in the legs. Both his eyes were bloodshot, and one was fixed in his head. He smelt of spirits, and carried a toothpick in his mouth. 'How are you? I've just done dinner,' says he – and he lights a cigar, sits down with his legs crossed, and winks at me.

I tried at first to take the measure of him in a wheedling confidential way; but it was no good. I asked him in a facetious smiling manner, how he had got hold of the letter. He only told me in answer that he had been in the confidential employment of the writer of it, and that he had always been famous since infancy for a sharp eye to his own interests. I paid him some compliments; but he was not to be flattered. I tried to make him lose his temper; but he kept it in spite of me. It ended in his driving me to my last resource – I made an attempt to frighten him.

'Before we say a word about the money,' I began, 'let me put a case, Mr Davager. The pull you have on Mr Francis Gatliffe is, that you can hinder his marriage on Wednesday. Now, suppose I have got a magistrate's warrant to apprehend you in my pocket? Suppose I have a constable to execute it in the next room? Suppose I bring you up to-morrow – the day before the marriage – charge you only generally with an attempt to extort money, and apply for a day's remand to complete the case? Suppose, as a suspicious stranger, you can't get bail in this town? Suppose'—

'Stop a bit,' says Mr Davager: 'suppose I should not be the greenest fool that ever stood in shoes? Suppose I should not carry the letter about me? Suppose I should have given a certain envelope to a certain friend of mine in a certain place in this town? Suppose the letter should be inside that envelope, directed to old Gatliffe, side by side with a copy of the letter directed to the editor of the local paper? Suppose my friend should be instructed to open the envelope, and take the letters to their right address, if I don't appear to claim them from him this evening? In short, my dear sir, suppose you were born yesterday, and suppose I wasn't?' says Mr Davager, and winks at me again.

He didn't take me by surprise, for I never expected that he had the letter about him. I made a pretence of being very much taken aback, and of being quite ready to give in. We settled our business about delivering the letter and handing over the money in no time. I was to draw out a document which he was to sign. He knew the document was stuff and nonsense just as well as I did, and told me I was only proposing it to swell my client's bill. Sharp as he was, he was wrong there. The document was not to be drawn out to gain money from Mr Frank, but to gain time from Mr Davager. It served me as an excuse to put off the payment of the five hundred pounds till three o'clock on the Tuesday afternoon. The Tuesday morning Mr Davager said he should devote to his amusement, and asked me what sights were to be seen in the neighbourhood of the town. When I told him, he pitched his toothpick into my grate, yawned, and went out.

I rang the bell once – waited till he had passed the window – and then looked after Tom. There was my jewel of a boy on the opposite side of the street, just setting his top going in the most playful manner possible! Mr Davager walked away up the street, towards the market-place. Tom whipped his top up the street towards the market-place too.

In a quarter-of-an-hour he came back, with all his evidence

collected in a beautifully clear and compact state. Mr Davager
had walked to a public-house just outside the town, in a lane
leading to the high road. On a bench outside the public-house
there sat a man smoking. He said 'All right?' and gave a letter
to Mr Davager, who answered 'All right,' and walked back to
the inn. In the hall he ordered hot rum and water, cigars,
slippers, and a fire to be lit in his room. After that he went up
stairs, and Tom came away.

I now saw my road clear before me – not very far on, but
still clear. I had housed the letter, in all probability for that
night, at the Gatliffe Arms. After tipping Tom, I gave him
directions to play about the door of the inn, and refresh
himself when he was tired at the tart-shop opposite, eating as
much as he pleased, on the understanding that he crammed all
the time with his eye on the window. If Mr Davager went out,
or Mr Davager's friend called on him, Tom was to let me
know. He was also to take a little note from me to the head
chambermaid – an old friend of mine – asking her to step over
to my office, on a private matter of business, as soon as her
work was done for the night. After settling these little matters,
having half-an-hour to spare, I turned to and did myself a
bloater at the office-fire, and had a drop of gin and water hot,
and felt comparatively happy.

When the head chambermaid came, it turned out, as good
luck would have it, that Mr Davager had drawn her attention
rather too closely to his ugliness, by offering her a testimony
of his regard in the shape of a kiss. I no sooner mentioned him
than she flew into a passion; and when I added, by way of
clinching the matter, that I was retained to defend the interests
of a very beautiful and deserving young lady (name not
referred to, of course) against the most cruel underhand
treachery on the part of Mr Davager, the head chambermaid
was ready to go any lengths that she could safely to serve my
cause. In few words I discovered that Boots was to call Mr
Davager at eight the next morning, and was to take his clothes
down stairs to brush as usual. If Mr D. had not emptied his
own pockets overnight, we arranged that Boots was to forget
to empty them for him, and was to bring the clothes down
stairs just as he found them. If Mr D.'s pockets were emptied,
then, of course, it would be necessary to transfer the searching

process to Mr D.'s room. Under any circumstances, I was certain of the head chambermaid; and under any circumstances also, the head chambermaid was certain of Boots.

'I waited till Tom came home, looking very puffy and bilious about the face; but as to his intellects, if anything rather sharper than ever. His repost was uncommonly short and pleasant. The inn was shutting up; Mr Davager was going to bed in rather a drunken condition; Mr Davager's friend had never appeared. I sent Tom (properly instructed about keeping our man in view all the next morning) to his shake-down behind the office-desk, where I heard him hicupping half the night, as even the best boys will, when over-excited and too full of tarts.

At half-past seven next morning, I slipped quietly into Boot's pantry.

Down came the clothes. No pockets in trousers. Waistcoat pockets empty. Coat pockets with something in them. First, handkerchief; secondly, bunch of keys; thirdly, cigar-case; fourthly, pocket-book. Of course I wasn't such a fool as to expect to find the letter there, but I opened the pocket-book with a certain curiosity, notwithstanding.

Nothing in the two pockets of the book but some old advertisements cut out of newspapers, a lock of hair tied round with a dirty bit of ribbon, a circular letter about a loan society, and some copies of verses not likely to suit any company that was not of an extremely free-and-easy description. On the leaves of the pocket-book, people's addresses scrawled in pencil, and bets jotted down in red ink. On one leaf, by itself, this queer inscription:

"MEM. 5 ALONG. 4 ACROSS."

I understood everything but those words and figures, so of course I copied them out into my own book. Then I waited in the pantry till Boots had brushed the clothes and had taken them up stairs. His report when he came down was, that Mr D. had asked if it was a fine morning. Being told that it was, he had ordered breakfast at nine, and a saddle horse to be at the door at ten, to take him to Grimwith Abbey – one of the sights in our neighbourhood which I had told him of the evening before.

'I'll be here, coming in by the back way, at half-past ten,' says I to the head chambermaid.

'What for?' says she.

'To take the responsibility of making Mr Davager's bed off your hands for this morning only,' says I.

'Any more orders?' says she.

'One more,' says I. 'I want to hire Sam for the morning. Put it down in the order-book that he's to be brought round to my office at ten.'

In case you should think Sam was a man, I'd better perhaps tell you he was a pony. I'd made up my mind that it would be beneficial to Tom's health, after the tarts, if he took a constitutional airing on a nice hard saddle in the direction of Grimwith Abbey.

'Anything else?' says the head chambermaid.

'Only one more favour,' says I. 'Would my boy Tom be very much in the way if he came, from now till ten, to help with the boots and shoes, and stood at his work close by this window which looks out on the staircase?'

'Not a bit,' says the head chambermaid.

'Thank you,' says I; and stepped back to my office directly.

When I had sent Tom off to help with the boots and shoes, I reviewed the whole case exactly as it stood at that time.

There were three things Mr Davager might do with the letter. He might give it to his friend again before ten – in which case, Tom would most likely see the said friend on the stairs. He might take it to his friend, or to some other friend, after ten – in which case Tom was ready to follow him on Sam the pony. And, lastly, he might leave it hidden somewhere in his room at the inn – in which case, I was all ready for him with a search-warrant of my own granting, under favour always of my friend the head chambermaid. So far I had my business arrangements all gathered up nice and compact in my own hands. Only two things bothered me; the terrible shortness of the time at my disposal, in case I failed in my first experiments for getting hold of the letter, and that queer inscription which I had copied out of the pocket-book.

"MEM. 5 ALONG. 4 ACROSS."

It was the measurement most likely of something, and he was afraid of forgetting it; therefore, it was something important. Query – something about himself? Say "5" (inches) "along" – he doesn't wear a wig. Say "5" (feet) "along" – it can't be a coat, waistcoat, trousers, or undercloth-ing. Say "5" (yards) "along" – it can't be anything about himself, unless he wears round his body the rope that he's sure to be hanged with one of these days. Then it is *not* something about himself. What do I know of that is important to him besides? I know of nothing but the Letter. Can the memoran-dum be connected with that? Say, yes. What do "5 along" and "4 across" mean then? The measurement of something he carries about with him? – or the measurement of something in his room? I could get pretty satisfactorily to myself as far as that; but I could get no further.

Tom came back to the office, and reported him mounted for his ride. His friend had never appeared. I sent the boy off, with his proper instructions, on Sam's back – wrote an encouraging letter to Mr Frank to keep him quiet – then slipped into the inn by the back way a little before half-past ten. The head chambermaid gave me a signal when the landing was clear. I got into his room without a soul but her seeing me, and locked the door immediately.

The case was, to a certain extent, simplified now. Either Mr Davager had ridden out with the letter about him, or he had left it in some safe hiding-place in his room. I suspected it to be in his room, for a reason that will a little astonish you – his truck, his dressing-case, and all the drawers and cupboards were left open. I knew my customer, and I thought this extraordinary carelessness on his part rather suspicious.

Mr Davager had taken one of the best bedrooms at the Gatliffe Arms. Floor carpeted all over, walls beautifully papered, four-poster, and general furniture first-rate. I searched, to begin with, on the usual plain, examining everything in every possible way, and taking more than an hour about it. No discovery. Then I pulled out a carpenter's rule which I had brought with me. Was there anything in the room which – either in inches, feet, or yards – answered to "5 along" and "4 across?" Nothing. I put the rule back in my pocket – measurement was no good, evidently. Was there anything in the room that would count up to 5 one way and 4 another, seeing that nothing would measure up to it? I had got obstinately persuaded by this time that the letter must be in the room – principally because of the trouble I had had in looking after it. And persuading myself that, I took it into my head next, just as obstinately, that "5 along" and "4 across" must be the right clue to find the letter by – principally because I hadn't left myself, after all my searching and thinking, even so much as the ghost of another guide to go by. "5 along" – where could I count five along the room, in any part of it?

Not on the paper. The pattern there was pillars of trellis-work and flowers, enclosing a plain green ground – only four pillars along the wall and only two across. The furniture? There were not five chairs or five separate pieces of any furniture in the room altogether. The fringes that hung from the cornice of the bed? Plenty of them, at any rate! Up I jumped on the counterpane, with my penknife in my hand. Every way that "5 along" and "4 across" could be reckoned on those unlucky fringes I reckoned on them – probed with my penknife – scratched with my nails – crunched with my fingers. No use; not a sign of a letter; and the time was getting on – oh, Lord! how the time did get on in Mr Davager's room that morning.

I jumped down from the bed, so desperate at my ill-luck that I hardly cared whether anybody heard me or not. Quite a little cloud of dust rose at my feet as they thumped on the carpet. 'Hullo!' thought I, 'my friend the head chambermaid takes it easy here. Nice state for a carpet to be in, in one of the best bedrooms at the Gatliffe Arms.' Carpet! I had been jumping up on the bed, and staring up at the walls, but I had never so much as given a glance down at the carpet. Think of me pretending to be a lawyer, and not knowing how to look low enough!

The carpet! It had been a stout article in its time; had evidently begun in the drawing-room; then descended to a coffee-room; then gone upstairs altogether to a bedroom. The ground was brown, and the pattern was bunches of leaves and roses speckled over the ground at regular distances. I reckoned up the bunches. Ten along the room – eight across it. When I had stepped out five one way and four the other, and was down on my knees on the centre bunch, as true as I sit on this chair I could hear my own heat beating so loud that it quite frightened me.

I looked narrowly all over the bunch, and I felt all over it with the ends of my fingers, and nothing came of that, Then I scraped it over slowly and gently with my nails. My second finger-nail stuck a little at one place. I parted the pile of the carpet over that place, and saw a thin slit which had been hidden by the pile being smoothed over it – a slit about half an inch long, with a little end of brown thread, exactly the colour of the carpet-ground, sticking out about a quarter of an inch from the middle of it. Just as I laid hold of the thread gently, I heard a footstep outside the door.

It was only the head chambermaid. 'Haven't you done yet?' she whispers.

'Give me two minutes,' says I, 'and don't let anybody come near the door – whatever you do, don't let anybody startle me again by coming near the door.'

I took a little pull at the thread, and heard something rustle. I took a longer pull, and out came a piece of paper, rolled up tight like those candle-lighters that the ladies make. I unrolled it – and, by George! there was the letter!

'The original letter! – I knew it by the colour of the ink. The letter that was worth five hundred pound to me! It was all I could do to keep myself at first from throwing my hat into the air, and hooraying like mad. I had to take a chair and sit quiet in it for a minute or two, before I could cool myself down to my proper business level. I knew that I was safely down again when I found myself pondering how to let Mr Davager know that he had been done by the innocent country attorney after all.

It was not long before a nice little irritating plan occurred to me. I tore a blank leaf out of my pocket-book, wrote on it with my pencil 'Change for a five hundred pound note,' folded up the paper, tied the thread to it, poked it back into the hiding-place, smoothed over the pile of the carpet, and then bolted off to Mr Frank. He in his turn bolted off to show the letter to the young lady, who first certified to its genuineness, then dropped it into the fire, and then took the initiative for the first time since her marriage engagement, by flinging her arms round his neck, kissing him with all her might, and going into hysterics in his arms. So at least Mr Frank told me, but that's not evidence. It is evidence, however, that I saw them married with my own eyes on the Wednesday; and that while they went off in a carriage and four to spend the honeymoon, I went off on my own legs to open a credit at the Town and County Bank with a five hundred pound note in my pocket.

As to Mr Davager, I can tell you nothing more about him, except what is derived from hearsay evidence, which is always unsatisfactory evidence, even in a lawyer's mouth.

My inestimable boy, Tom, although twice kicked off by Sam the pony, never lost hold of the bridle, and kept his man in sight from first to last. He had nothing particular to report, except that on the way out to the Abbey Mr Davager had stopped at the public-house, had spoken a word or two to his friend of the night before, and had handed him what looked like a bit of paper. This was no doubt a clue to the thread that held the letter, to be used in case of accidents. In every other respect Mr D. had ridden out and ridden in like an ordinary sightseer. Tom reported him to me as having dismounted at the hotel about two. At half-past, I locked my office door, nailed a card under the knocker with 'not at home till to-morrow' written on it, and retired to a friend's house a mile or so out of the town for the rest of the day.

Mr Davager, I have been since given to understand, left the Gatliffe Arms that same night with his best clothes on his back, and with all the valuable contents of his dressing-case in his pockets. I am not in a condition to state whether he ever went through the form of asking for his bill or not; but I can positively testify that he never paid for it, and that the effects left in his bedroom did not pay it either. When I add to these fragments of evidence that he and I have never met (luckily for me, you will say) since I jockeyed him out of his bank-note, I have about fulfilled my implied contract as maker of a statement with you, sir, as hearer of a statement. Observe the expression, will you? I said it was a Statement before I began; and I say it's a Statement now I've done. I defy you to prove it's a Story! – How are you getting on with my portrait? I like you very well, Mr Artist; but if you have been taking advantage of my talking to shirk your work, as sure as you're alive I'll split upon you to the Town Council!'

I attended a great many times as my queer sitter's house before his likeness was completed. To the last he was dissatisfied with the progress I made. Fortunately for me, the Town Council approved of the portrait when it was done. Mr Boxsious, however, objected to them as being much too easy to please. He did not dispute the fidelity of the likeness, but he asserted that I had not covered the canvass with half paint enough for my money. To this day (for he is still alive), he describes me to all inquiring friends as "The Painter-Man who jockeyed the Town Council."